WRATH
OF THE
LAMB

WRATH
OF THE
LAMB

THE WORLD TAKES SIDES

BOOK THREE IN THE *RAPTURE SERIES*

JOCOLBY PHILLIPS

CHRISTIAN

Published in Odessa, Florida, by Christian Warrior Fiction Publishing LLC.

Publisher's Note: This novel is a work of fiction. Names, characters, places, and incidents are either products of the author's imagination or used fictitiously. All characters are fictional, and any similarity to people living or dead is purely coincidental.

Library of Congress Cataloging-in-Publication Data: 2022900032

ISBN: 978-1-7360017-3-8 (Paperback)

978-1-7360017-4-5 (Ebook)

To my wife Kalley, daughter Xona, son Jayven, and daughter Aryana. I LOVE YOU and remain eternally grateful for your support of my writing, encouragement, and prayers.

REVIEWS OF PREVIOUS BOOKS:

Rapture: Advent of The Last Days

Amazon reviewer, Jo: "The author has done a fantastic job of weaving a Biblical account of the end times around the stories of a handful of soldiers and politicians that were left behind. He takes scripture by scripture, verse by verse, and prophecy by prophecy to tell the story of Earth after the Church has been raptured. Every page is an invitation to believe now before it's too late and an outline of the way to salvation available even during those awful days. Every Christian should have a copy of this book in their home for loved ones to find during the actual events that the book portrays!"

Amazon reviewer, AC: "A great book that really gives a picture of the end times as described in Scripture. Extremely well written with interweaving character point of views that put you right in the action and grip the reader from beginning to end. This novel brilliantly shows the juxtaposition of the just judgement of God and the loving mercies he shows. Can't wait for more!"

Amazon reviewer, Michele: "I gotta be honest… I'm such a terrible lector. I rarely get to finish the books I start. But this one… it's a MUST. So much vulnerability, truth and wisdom.

Sometimes books picture the gospel as something mystic or full of fairytales, but this book represents it like truly is. It reminded me how we can encounter God between our struggles, that we don't need to be perfect to become close to him and how our actions could have a positive/negative not only in ourselves but the people around us".

Rise of The Beast: The Tribulation Begins

Amazon reviewer, Ramona: "I enjoyed the first book in this series and this 2nd book certainly did not disappoint. I found myself wanting to know what happens to the main characters, while not wanting the book to end. I highly recommend this book to anyone who enjoys action-packed stories. The author makes the story relatable and interesting to a wide audience. I am excited already to read the next book in the series!"

Writer's Digest Competitions: This is a fantastic story that made me want to find the first book of the series! Phillips is a talented writer with a gift for action. The dialogue and motivations of the characters feel authentic, a bonus that potentially comes from Phillips' real-life experiences. Readers will appreciate the action of the story with a consistent background of hope, courage, and self-sacrifice. Well done! I will pick up the rest of the series!

The Rapture Series

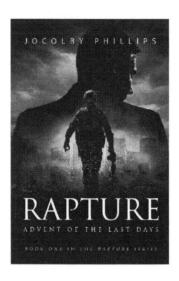

Book 1, Rapture: Advent of The Last Days

In *Rapture,* Christopher Barrett, an elite special operations soldier, has spent his entire life believing that the only person he can trust is himself, and especially not God. With his career, marriage, and life tittering on destruction, Christopher's belief in himself over God faces a test in one cataclysmic moment where millions around the world have disappeared.

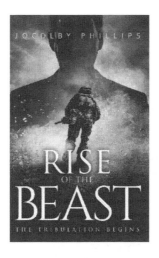

Book 2, Rise of The Beast: The Tribulation Begins

In *Rise of The Beast,* the action-packed sequel to Rapture Advent of The Last Days, the seven-year tribulation has begun with Christopher Barrett and Jackson Williams fighting for survival. At the same, Gabriella Costa finds herself working for the most powerful political leader in history. Who will pay the ultimate price for their beliefs? Who will survive the second year after the Rapture? Whether you're a fan of the first book or new to the series, the Rise of The Beast is a globe-trotting thrill ride full of surprising revelations and provoking questions on the future of humanity.

DOSSIER

30 Months into the Tribulation.

Kingdom of God

The Two Witnesses, Reuel, Eliyahu: age unknown, God's Ambassadors to the Earth. The two men daily proclaim God's message and challenge the rule of the Beast, aka. Draven Cross. Proclaim they will minister to Israel, the world, and the Beast for 1260 days (12 months remaining). **Status, active. Present location Unified Arabian Region, Wailing Wall, Jerusalem, Israel.**

Christopher Barrett, late thirties; former leader of the elite U.S. Special Operations Unit, Omega. There are no known living relatives for Christopher. Remains the leader of the rebranded Christian resistance element, known as Omega. Christopher's wife, Erin, departed in the Rapture; international fugitive from the U.E. **Status, active. Present location Unified British Commonwealth Region, near Uluru, Australia.**

Jackson Williams, mid-forties; former team sergeant of the elite U.S. Special Operations Unit, Omega. Jackson lost his wife Sarah, daughters Sadie and Katie in a plane crash during the Rapture; international fugitive from the U.E. **Status, active. Present location Unified British Commonwealth Region, near Uluru, Australia.**

Dr. Gabriella Costa, mid-thirties; former director in CIA, former Intelligence Chief for Omega. There are no known living relatives for Gabriella. Gabriella served as the former U.E. Intelligence Director, fighting against U.E. Secretary-General Draven Cross by supplying Christopher Barrett information. Gabriella's deception was discovered, leading to her being imprisoned. **Status, unknown. Present location unknown.**

Gilana Edri, mid-thirties; former Israeli Mossad agent. There are no known living relatives for Gilana, after losing her significant other to U.E. forces outside of Babylon, Iraq, two and half years ago. **Status, active, Present location Unified British Commonwealth Region, near Uluru, Australia.**

Abdulkerim (Kerim) Hoshur, early thirties; Uyghur-national, born in Xinjiang Province and conscripted in the former Chinese PLA. Served as a PLA Special Forces Operative, former leader of the Jiātíng Jiàohuì (house church), U.E. resistance group in China. Kerim's parents were killed by the PLA shortly before the Rapture because of their Christian beliefs. International fugitive from the U.E. **Status, active. Present location Unified British Commonwealth Region, near Uluru, Australia.**

Gemma Sutherland, mid-thirties; executive secretary to the U.E. Secretary-General, Draven Cross. Supports Christopher Barrett and his team through her unique placement and access to Draven. The U.E. questioned her support to Gabriella, leading to detainment. **Status unknown. Present location U.E. Headquarters, Rome, Italy.**

Benjamin Havid, early sixties; former Minister of Defense, Israel, former Israeli General and Sayeret Matkal commander; Omega team senior member. Provides support to Omega team through placement and access as Israeli Defense Minister. **Status unknown. Present location unknown.**

Charlie Smith, late fifties; former U.S. Air Force Fighter Pilot, CIA Covert Pilot, and Omega member. **Status deceased. Killed in service to the Kingdom of God, Unified British Commonwealth Region, near Uluru, Australia.**

Jim (Jimbo) Petty, mid-thirties; former U.S. Air Force Pararescue (PJ), Omega member. **Status deceased. Killed in service to the Kingdom of God, Unified Asian Nations Region, Jakarta, Indonesia.**

Kingdom of Satan

Draven Cross, mid-forties; called the Beast, by primary enemies the Two Witnesses. Current U.E. Secretary-General and first political leader to lead a unified world government. Currently attempting to consolidate his power amidst challenges from the Two Witnesses and the fallout from God's judgments. **Status, active. Present location U.E. Headquarters, Rome, Italy.**

Evan Mallory, late-fifties; Deputy U.E. Secretary-General; founder of the Interfaith religion. Called the False Prophet by the Two Witnesses. Propagandist and image bearer for Draven. **Status, active. Present location U.E. Headquarters, Rome, Italy.**

John Barnes, late-thirties; Commander of the U.E. Special Activities Group; hitman for Draven. Tasked by Draven to hunt down and eliminate the Omega Group. Status, unknown. **Present location Unified British Commonwealth Region, near Uluru, Australia.**

Pontiff Conti, mid-fifties; leader of the Interfaith World Religion. Promotes unity and peace narratives of Draven and Evan. **Status, active. Present location U.E. Headquarters, Apostolic Palace, Rome, Italy.**

CHAPTER 1

IF MAN COULD *have one wish from God, it would be the ability to control time.* This thought flooded Christopher's mind as he rode through the Simpson Desert toward the Alice Springs airport. He glanced at the night sky. His view was full of fiery red meteors, an ominous signal of God's judgment. Christopher was tired of fighting against the cruel hands of time. He didn't want to know the details of why the sky was ablaze. Surviving the past two years as a newfound believer in Jesus took every ounce of energy; he had to maintain trust. There was no time to wonder why things happened anymore. Christopher's instincts told him going forward, the worst was always waiting. Christopher's harrowing experience at the Ayer's Rock IEC hours ago drilled this thought into his soul. Surviving the past two-plus years in the God orchestrated saga, named the Tribulation, took several miracles. Living to see Jesus's Glorious Appearance was hard for Christopher to fathom.

The recent firefight against the UE that cost him another friend, Charlie, lingered in his thoughts. God's judgment of a rebellious world and the chaos that followed was the environment for all that lived through the initial terrifying seconds of the Rapture. If Christopher could go back in time, he would find more advantages over the United Earth, or easier said UE forces. He would warn General Havid of the danger he faced before being kidnapped, if time were at his command. He'd force Gabriella away from the UE headquarters sooner. Christopher would beg Jimbo to stay behind cover for a second longer. Above all things, he'd accept Jesus Christ as his Lord and Savior before the Rapture.

A crackle of the UE vehicle's radio brought Christopher's attention to emerging problems instead of past challenges.

"Attention all UE personnel at Alice Springs. Omega terrorists destroyed the Ayers Rock IEC; be on the lookout for three UE vehicles. I'm requesting immediate MEDEVAC at the Ayers Rock location. Commander Barnes out."

Christopher glanced at Jackson behind the wheel and Gilana in the vehicle's backseat. "I've got half a mind to turn around and shoot Barnes myself. It's too bad he survived, but it sounds like he's in terrible shape."

"I hope the MEDEVAC is late; suffering is what John Barnes deserves," Jackson said.

The Omega team's lone cell phone rang.

Christopher fumbled to retrieve the phone from his tactical vest.

"Hello, Kerim. So, I am sure the UE knows we're alive and are looking for us. We have twenty miles before we reach Alice Springs airport. I say we ditch the vehicles before the airport exit and walk across the desert to the airport if we can get there and stay off the radio."

Kerim responded, "That sounds good to me."

When Christopher ended the call, the glowing orbs that filled the sky captured his attention as they raced toward unknown destinations. A few had landed in the sparse alien landscape of the Northern Territory, Australia. The impacts, while sparse, created thunderous booms. It took a moment to understand the red streak piercing the black horizon ahead of the truck was different. The signature of an inbound vehicle-launched rocket proved the UE had found them.

"Jackson, incoming!" Christopher yelled.

The up-armored vehicle swerved violently to the right to avoid the inevitable death racing toward them.

There was a bright flash of light and a concussive boom. The tearing of metal drowned out the vehicle's occupants' screams as it rolled down the Stuart Highway embankment.

A warm trickle streamed down Christopher's face. The distinctive salty and tart flavor of blood coated his lips as the pain of the gash throbbed.

He looked around the overturned dark vehicle, straining to find signs of life in his team. *"God, please don't take anybody else from me. I'm trying to trust in you, please."*

Beads of sweat rose on Christopher's forehead. "Jackson, Gilana, are you okay?"

The tactical flashlight he pulled from his vest found the bloodied face of Jackson, who moaned. As the light illuminated Gilana, she looked to be in better condition than Jackson, or how he imagined himself.

The vehicle came to rest on the driver's side in a dry ravine. Christopher released his five-point harness, careful not to fall on top of Jackson by bracing himself against the windshield and his seat.

Christopher heard the wail of Gilana, as she didn't assess the situation and careened from her passenger-side seat, slamming into the driver's side of the vehicle.

"We need to get out of here!"

"Good call, Captain Obvious," Jackson said. "Now get out of the way so I can climb out behind you."

Christopher knew Jackson's smarting off meant he was okay. He took a long glance back up the ravine where Kerim's vehicle sat silhouetted by the flames of Mujahit's truck, hearing the screech of tires and slamming of doors.

Kerim and two of his operatives eased Christopher's fears by joining Gilana and Jackson near his vehicle.

Christopher listened to Kerim shout over his exploding truck at the top of the ravine. "Go! Mujahit and my other two men died!"

3

The group wasted no time moving toward the Alice Springs airport as UE soldiers' voices at the top of the ravine signaled an intent to finish the job they started.

❧

The destruction of Christopher's vehicle left no doubt of the UE's intentions. He led the beleaguered special operations soldiers through a shallow ravine that cut across the desert. The celestial light show produced by Heaven was fading, along with the rockets from the UE. The returning calm to the night, left a star-filled sky that provided enough light to guide them through the dry-riverbed.

Christopher held up his hand as a bright UE searchlight panned over the landscape.

The warriors dropped onto their stomachs in the ravine as a strafing of random gunfire followed the searchlight. After a few tense moments of the UE searching the gullies with the light, the desert returned to darkness.

"That was close. Let's hope the UE believes they finished the job."

Christopher broke the silence standing in the ravine to watch the headlights of the UE drive into the distance. He waved his hand, watching the others silently fall in behind him as the group made their way toward the Alice Springs Airport.

❧

As the sun illuminated the Australian outback, Christopher's group of operatives reached the Alice Springs Airport's chain-linked outer fence. A broad smile rose on his face, finding no roving security or any heightened activity. He beckoned for the other five members of his team to join him.

"It seems the UE has given up on searching for us. I spotted a maintenance yard over there." Christopher pointed to a few Hilux trucks. "Let's take one and head for Sydney."

"Are you crazy? Your plan was to drive somewhere. That's a two-day drive through UE-held territory," Jackson said.

Christopher's jaw tensed. "You want to walk up to the ticket counter and buy a few first-class tickets?"

"Enough! Jackson has a point." Kerim's stern tone shifted the growing argument toward resolution. "I know of a contact in Adelaide. It's a full-day drive. But if she is alive, it's our best option."

Gilana exploited the break in tension. "I like Kerim's plan."

Christopher tossed his phone to Kerim. "Make the call."

❧

CHAPTER 2

GENERAL HAVID INTIMATELY knew the facility of his detainment between the Dead Sea and the ancient Masada fortress. The Dead Sea Intelligence facility comprised several small rooms built to extract information for a singular purpose. It was here that Israel broke the minds of its enemies. The facility, hidden from public oversight, used pain and isolation to turn the human senses into weapons against a captive's mind.

Terrorists and other threats to the state surrendered knowledge, either freely or unwillingly. General Havid knew of no detainees who departed with their minds intact or lives spared. He feared he would be next on this infamous list.

The brightness of his room blinded him from viewing his tormentors. He knew the authors of his pain would soon visit. The general's experience with the suffering at this site allowed him to walk the path of those holding him prisoner. He knew the chair he sat in monitored his internal vital signs. The UE kept him waiting and anticipating what would come next, as the growing concern in a captive's mind was the first step to breaking them. The general was being studied, and he knew it. The torturer gauged his reaction to the hot room, analyzing potential vulnerabilities every second from a darkened two-way mirrored room next to where he sat. The general prayed for strength, knowing he would now reap the pain he sowed. The UE would keep him as he had done to others, suspended between life and the relief of death to ensure he complied with their wishes.

The sterilized smell of cleaning solutions used after the brutal interrogations of Israel's enemies lingered in the air. It was not a clean scent that brought comfort or reassurance like in a hospital. Instead, his hands twitched, and the general felt a tremendous pressure rising in his chest, understanding for the first time the smell covered evidence of horrors.

Stripped down to only his underwear, General Havid continued to sweat as the heat intensified in the room. Now, the general felt the humiliation witnessed on the faces of the captives he'd ordered brought here. Visions of the torture awaiting him caused the experienced soldier to tremble.

General Havid tried to flush from his mind where he'd watched blood and other body fluids cleaned away from this very room. He often wondered during the interrogations how much pain the person in the chair could take before their mind would break. It varied from person to person, but the end was always the same. He'd inevitably divulge information needed to protect the innocents the detained individual sought to harm. General Havid prayed his mind would hold in the pain's grip.

The first course of pain an electric current sent through the floor into his bare feet broke his thoughts. The hidden female inquisitor's voice blared over loudspeakers, echoing off the walls, causing General Havid to squint his eyes from the pain the noise made.

"General, the electric current was merely an introduction. To help you understand, unless I gain cooperation… well, I need not explain what happens next. Where is Gilana Edri?"

General Havid shook his head. He prepared his mind for an invasion of pain. The room went dark. Two large industrial vents roared to life, forcing a voracious cold rush of air into the room. The sudden shift from extreme heat hit his sweat-soaked body, causing him to shiver uncontrollably. A second and longer-lasting electric shock caused his body to stiffen. He bit his lip, causing warm blood to flow down his bare chest. General Havid vomited, fighting to maintain consciousness as another wave of electricity stung his body.

"God, save me."

The laughter of his tormentor filled his ears. "General, I'm impressed that a man your age has held up this well. Save yourself. Tell me where I can find Gilana Edri?"

The general struggled to lift his blood-soaked face toward the voice in the control room. He flashed his crimson-stained teeth to the void of the darkened mirror.

"Never!"

The female voice replied, "I welcome you resisting the inevitable."

The slam of a metal door followed by the sounds of military boots shuffling across the floor told him what was coming. He braced himself for an imminent attack. The cold air forced heavy breathing from the muscled Mossad agents moving in front of him.

With a flash of blinding light as the room lit up again, General Havid fell over in the chair as a sharp blow landed on his left cheek. The general attempted to adjust his focus on who struck him. However, a second strike to the face rendered the world black as the general faded into unconsciousness.

⤚

General Havid awoke to a splash of liquid on his face. He assumed it was water until the pungent smell of vinegar overwhelmed him. The general's face ached and felt swollen. Throughout his body, muscles cramped from the aftereffects of electrocution. General Havid took inventory of his pains when a new pain flashed on his cheek. His face burned as he blinked at the woman who slapped him, the one who was leading the interrogation now stood in front of him.

"General, are you awake now? Your nap was my last act of mercy. Tell me where Gilana Edri is or prepare to die piece by piece, starting with your fingers."

General Havid squinted with his bloodshot right eye to see the woman, as he had no vision in his left eye. She didn't look like any Mossad agent he had seen. The tall, midnight-haired woman stared at the general through piercing brown eyes that carried darkness. The unknown woman made the combat-steeled general's lip quiver.

He responded in the way he thought would make his late wife Abagail proud. "God, I give you my life."

The woman spat in his face as she grabbed a pair of hedge trimmers. "There is no God to save you."

As General Havid accepted his fate, the room door burst open.

The Israeli Prime Minister screamed, "Stop! This is not what we agreed to, Agent Morozov."

The now-identified UE Unified Russian Nations operative kicked General Havid in his chest, causing the 61-year-old to tumble over in his chair, moaning. She screamed in anger at the Israeli Prime Minister's directive.

General Havid peered up from the floor, watching Morozov stride over to the Israeli Prime Minister, as his security detail flanked him. The woman's Russian accent broke through the English she spoke during the general's torture.

"There is a reason Secretary-General Cross had me fly overnight to this wasteland you call a country. If you don't have the stomach to get the information, then the failure is on you, Prime Minister," Morozov declared.

The Prime Minister said, "I will not allow this man, a hero of our nation, to die this way. Your reputation, Sasha, as an expert in torture techniques is a fraud. You beat the man and having nothing to show for it, that's the report that will reach the Secretary-General's ears."

General Havid looked on as Morozov turned to leave the interrogation room. "It's a shame my country didn't wipe Israel from the map five years ago during the invasion."

General Havid grew tearful, thinking of how the Lord had provided for his safety using the same man who ordered his detainment.

The Prime Minister turned his attention to the general. "Forgive me, Benjamin. I did not know they would go to these measures. I had to—"

General Havid cut him off. "Daniel, you don't need to apologize or explain yourself to me; it is the God of our forefathers that you've offended."

The general let out a low moan as they lifted him from the floor, and his hands and feet were unfettered for the first time in over 24 hours. He looked through his blood-crusted right eye into the sorrowful brown eyes of his former leader. He noticed a look of terror and sorrow fall over the Israeli Prime Minister's face.

"What you've said may be true, Benjamin, but I have the weight of preserving the Jewish people on my shoulders. Cross has protected us, and you will not be the reason for the world to turn against us now. You will live but will never see the hills of Jerusalem again."

General Havid watched as the Prime Minister turned from him to a security staff member. "Treat his wounds and take him to *Hekal Emah,* where he will live out his days."

"So, you will send me to the Temple of Terrors, Daniel. It is of no matter to me. You assume too much in your duties to God's people. Draven will betray you and Israel. It's the God of Abraham, Isaac, and Jacob, not Cross or anyone else, that has always protected Israel."

The general fell silent as they loaded him into a wheelchair destined for the infamous Shin Bet detainment facility, *Hekal Emah.*

CHAPTER 3

DRAVEN RUSHED FROM his press briefing on victory over the Omega Group to the UE HQ command center as the world faced another calamity. As he stood in the command center, the images before Draven's face caused him to pause in awe. The world was on fire. The rambling of the command center briefers failed to register in Draven's mind. Instead, his focus centered on a video loop displaying thousands of vehicle-sized meteoroids racing toward Earth from space. As if programmed, the meteors broke into smaller symmetrical units. Draven watched groups of meteors descend over the globe's vegetated areas while still high in Earth's atmosphere.

The All-News-Network feed in the command center completed the story by showing the meteor impacts that started raging fires from the Amazon in South America to Africa's "green heart."

"Sir, how do you want us to handle the fires?" A UE staff officer's question pierced the hold the visual epic commanded over Draven.

Draven's veins pulsed as he glared at the looping visions of destruction before focusing on the colonel. "What a dumb question. If I need to explain to everyone here how to handle fires, then why do I need you on my staff?"

"Sir, we cannot extinguish the fires. This problem is being reported by all the unified regions. The fires continue until consuming the ablaze vegetation. An additional hazard is a blood-like substance that lingers after the fire. There have been fatalities for those attempting to enter ravaged areas."

"That's absurd. An inextinguishable fire mixed with blood?"

Draven took notice of everyone staring behind him, turning to see his deputy hurrying toward him. "Evan, I assume by your harrowed pace you will only add to the ridiculous explanation for this latest challenge."

"Beyond what you've heard, the fires also don't consume everything in an area, like houses, only vegetation. We'll need to run numbers on how much global flora remains."

Draven sighed with the more ridiculous reporting. "My answer to these 'magical' fires is simple. We will deal with the aftermath. Control the narrative in the media. What you've provided doesn't warrant your presence, Evan."

Evan waved the UE command center personnel away from Draven. "I really came to provide an update on the integrations of General Havid and Gemma."

"Well, get on with it."

"General Havid didn't provide any information before his interrogation concluded."

Draven raised his eyebrows. "Why did Sasha stop?"

"She reported that the Israeli Prime Minister ended the session before she could break the general's mind."

"This is of no consequence. The Omega Team is dead, so who cares where the female Mossad agent is now."

"That's the other problem. John failed to destroy the Omega Team. He's being treated at a UE outpost in Alice Springs for wounds he received during the gunfight with the American terrorists."

Draven swore, causing staffers in the command center to stare at the two senior UE leaders.

"I should have killed that twit John Barnes a long time ago! Where are the Americans now?"

"UE forces in Australia are hunting them down as we speak. I will keep you updated. How do you want to handle Barnes?"

Draven walked out of the UE Command Center, with Evan following. "Tell me, do you think John's life has value?"

The UE Deputy Commander paused and ran his right hand through his salt and pepper-streaked hair. "Yes. John Barnes is an expendable resource. A morally questionable soldier with some niche uses—for example, the Martin Sorenson job allowed you to take control of ANN. Let me bring him in, scuff him up a bit for failing, and then send him back to track down the Omega team."

Draven smiled. "I concur with your plan, especially the part about inflicting pain on John. I hate the man and his abject stupidity. I will use him until he dies, or I grow tired of his incompetence. Now, take me to Gemma. I am sure she is more than pliable at this point."

⁊

Draven and Evan made the short walk across the UE campus to a detainment facility used by the UE to hold threats to the organization from nearby Rome.

They entered a control room that provided hidden observation of Gemma Sutherland's interrogation. A sizeable, tinted pane of glass separated the two rooms. Gemma looked defeated to Draven. She sat in a metal folding chair in her tattered underwear. Her once radiant face now darkened from bruising and swelling. Gemma's eyes, which were as blue as the Adriatic Sea, were now bloodshot and half-closed. Draven felt no remorse as he starred at his long-time assistant, enduring the horror of torture.

Draven turned to Evan. "How long has she been here?"

"For the last day. Her story remains the same, stating she knows nothing of Gabriella's treachery."

Draven smiled as Gemma wailed from a slap by a burly male interrogator. He listened with delight as she screamed. The world leader enjoyed watching Gemma struggle against the torture.

"Tell me Gabriella has provided *some* measure of information that can help us find the rebellious Omega terrorist attacking me at every turn."

Before Evan could answer, Draven held his hand up as if he watched a critical scene in a long-awaited movie. His attention again focused on Gemma's direction, watching her struggle as the guards stripped her naked. Streaks of excitement coursed through his veins as his heart raced, imagining the pain and shame Gemma endured.

Draven grew giddy, as a towel was wrapped around the petite woman's neck. He chuckled as the UE guards yanked Gemma out of her chair. A burly guard used the leverage the towel provided him to sling Gemma against the control room window so hard it reverberated. Draven moved to the front of the control room, so close his breath fogged up the window. He could see fear dilating Gemma's pupils as she wailed in pain before collapsing into a heap on the floor. As she struggled to get to her feet another guard gave her a swift kick to her gut causing her to vomit.

Draven's head nodded, unconscious encouragement to Gemma's tormentors, watching them drag Gemma to a wall before slamming her face first into position. Her hands and feet were placed into restraints. Two UE security guards stood with two bamboo rods behind her. Draven's eyes widened as the first wrap of a guard's cane fell across Gemma's back. He loved watching her writhe against the restraints.

A female guard punched Gemma hard in the kidneys twice, causing her to lose control of her bladder and Draven to laugh harder. No sooner had she caught her breath from wailing than questions on Gabriella's betrayal and Omega's location started.

Gemma screamed, "I don't know!" before being lashed.

Draven laughed as his attention shifted from Gemma's cries of pain. Gabriella instead came to mind. "A part of me wants to allow this delectable pain to continue Evan, but I need your attention elsewhere. So, you can end this. While I am not convinced Gemma did not know of Gabriella's treachery, nor Omega's whereabouts, I am satisfied with her punishment. I am not sure what to do with Gemma in the long-term, shockingly I am hesitant to kill her. And people say,

I am not sentimental. Place her on house arrest until I can decide her fate. Ensure Gabriella faces worse treatment. No more excuses; find Omega."

Evan nodded in agreement and moved toward the control room door.

CHAPTER 4

GABRIELLA DARED NOT call the moments of unconsciousness she cycled through sleep. The time where her body shut down from the shock of physical and mental torture was biological mercy. She was unsure if the vision would ever return to her right eye, and the smell of her own blood dominated all other scents. The UE guards had taken shifts interrogating and thrashing her into unconsciousness. She had been beaten with rods and kicked so hard she was sure multiple ribs were broken. The only mercy afforded to Gabriella was no one had sexually molested her body yet. She pondered her fate as she lay on a dirty cot in the corner of her large cell. The rattle of keys in her cell door brought uncontrollable tremors to Gabriella. The next round of torture was about to begin, and she didn't know how much more she could take. Gabriella prayed for death and the freedom it represented.

She had endured electric shock, physical beatings, and sensory deprivation. However, the sight of a gurney and a water hose curdled Gabriella's blood. Waterboarding would be the next dish served in this nightmare. Gabriella remembered stories from the 'old-timers' at the CIA about waterboarding and its use during the long-forgotten war on terrorism. Gabriella remembered the expressions of pain the grizzled CIA agents had on their faces when they told stories of terrorists begging to be spared from waterboarding. Now it was her turn.

Two female UE guards stripped Gabriella out of her clothes and underwear. Fear drove her to resist, sensing something worse than waterboarding would soon occur. The larger and more muscular woman slapped Gabriella so hard the fight ran from her. Gabriella went limp as the two women dragged her toward a man eyeing her exposed body. Tears streamed from Gabriella's face.

An instinctive scream for help rose from Gabriella. The woman handed her to the man before preparing the gurney's restraints. Gabriella winced and turned her head as the man moved his face close to hers.

The nauseating smell of tobacco rode on the man's breath as he said, "You're beautiful, even if you smell like a pig."

Gabriella turned and spat in the male guard's face, regretting her fury as a slap sent her to the hard concrete floor. She remained dazed as the man spoke, in a Germanic or Dutch sounding language to the two women, who picked her up and strapped her to the cold metal gurney. The UE officers strapped her hands to the board, with her head looking up at her feet and the wooden ceiling beyond. The last image she had before a towel draped over her head was the "German" man turning a spigot and adjusting the water hose's length.

The first splash of the freezing water brought resistance to Gabriella's mind, determined not to betray Omega or herself. She tried to shake herself free from the water, but it bound her body with the gurney. The chill of the water stole her breath, and the first gasp of air brought with it a rush of water overwhelming her gag reflex.

Waterboarding brought on a vicious cycle of gagging and searching for a breath. Swirling in her mind were memories of almost drowning as a child on the James River near Langley Air Force Base in Virginia. The dreadful day in the James River rose in her mind, but Gabriella knew her father couldn't save her this time. The sense of drowning brought on by the torture overwhelmed her despite efforts to calm her mind. Gabriella hoped the water would stop flowing soon. Her nostrils stung, and her lungs burned in pain.

Gabriella's brain created images of white-hot pokers skewing her skull as it demanded oxygen. Finally, as she gave up hope, the water stopped, the towel lifted. Pure air replaced water, and she vomited over herself as the two women sat her up.

"Now, tell me where I can find the Omega team. You should cooperate. That first session was only twenty seconds!" the German yelled.

The shaking of her head was as much defiance as she had strength to offer. The two powerful African-looking women slammed her head down and tilted the gurney where her feet again were above her head. The towel went back on her face, and the pain resumed. This time the drowning sensation seemed worst. Death drew near as Gabriella felt her blood boiling and lungs filling with water.

As Gabriella sat up again and spat water, she screamed, "They're in Australia. Omega is in Australia, at the Ayers Rock IEC. I told you what you wanted. No more, please, no more."

The UE guards began speaking in a still unrecognizable tongue, and Gabriella felt a sense of relief as the male UE officer left her holding cell. The two women guards released her from her restraints. Gabriella collapsed as she tried to stand. She felt the sure grasp of the large women as they scooped her into their arms and carried her to a cot. Wet and covered in filth, Gabriella shivered.

For a few moments, the guards stood over her, staring, and Gabriella grew concerned, expecting more violence.

Instead, one woman spoke in accented English. "Someone will bring you food and clothes. You've earned them."

The words of the woman crystalized the moment for Gabriella. Her battered mind now realized what she had done. Gabriella had sold out Omega to save herself. The anguish filling her mind felt worse than the lack of oxygen minutes ago. She wailed, causing the two UE guards to stare at her as guilt consumed Gabriella's senses.

❧

Gabriella awoke, confused, cold, and naked. Tormented by the thought of trading her friends' lives for hers. She was unsure where she was in the world, physically and mentally. But, as she focused on the sounds, smells, and looks of the UE around her Gabriella began to think she was in Africa. All she knew for certain was the language was different from the English of Australia and she was near the coast. The air held a salty scent that reminded her of the beach as a breeze filtered through her lone barred window. "God, if I am not in Australia how will Christopher find me?"

Time made no sense. The lights had not gone off since she arrived days or weeks ago. She had been foolish and arrogant in her actions, leading her to this point. Worse was the delusion that her own intellect matched Draven's. Knowing Draven, he had played with her like a cat with a mouse. The only person fooled by her game had been Gabriella and those trusting her.

Thoughts of Christopher and the others being tortured caused the tears to flow until she could cry no more. Knowing she had placed the Omega team in danger was too much to bear. The lingering sense of despair and hopelessness brought thoughts of ending her life.

As the door to her cell opened, Gabriella didn't acknowledge whoever was coming through. She remained curled up in her cot facing the wall. If it was her time to die, she felt deserving. However, the presence in the cell felt calming, stirring her inquisitive nature. She tried to focus through her "good" blood-splattered right eye on the face of the woman standing before her.

The voice of the woman brought an immediate sense of peace. "Oh, my dear, death will not take you today. Now, sit up and let's get you cleaned up a bit," the unknown guard said.

Gabriella sat up, encouraged by the gentleness the guard displayed, despite her wearing the UE uniform. The guard placed a bundle of clothes at the end of Gabriella's cot before moving back to the cell door to yell to an unseen guard in the same strange language her tormentors used. Moments later, Gabriella watched a steaming food plate brought in and sat before her on a folding table.

The care being shown by the guard bewildered Gabriella. The woman moved toward her, assisting Gabriella to stand. The nurturing guard then walked with her to a seat at the table with food.

The guard's gestures prompted Gabriella to say, "I know you."

The guard laughed, flashing dazzling white teeth in perfect contrast to her smooth, ebony skin.

"I would hope so, dear. I'm your guardian angel. And you keep me busy."

Gabriella trembled with this revelation. God was still so new in her life. Again, God thought to comfort her in a time of need, despite the chaos around the world. "*God is merciful.*"

"You don't know this verse of scripture," the angel said, pushing Gabriella's blood-matted hair from her face. "However, this verse applies to the thoughts in your heart.

"God's word in the book of Deuteronomy 31:6 says, *Be strong and courageous. Do not be afraid or terrified because of them, for the Lord your God goes with you; he will never leave you nor forsake you.*"

"How did you know what I was thinking?"

The angel kneeled next to her, holding her hand. "The Holy Spirit provides me what I need to know to serve the desires of God. Right now, the desire God has for you is to assure you of his love."

Gabriella's analytic mind still wrestled with matters of faith. "So, how do the guards not hear or see this unusual display of kindness? Where am I? How are you getting me out of here; I mean, they will not let us walk out."

The angel laughed. "You always overthink. Was Peter not freed from prison by the hands of God? Did he not shut the mouth of Zechariah before John the Baptist was born? God can make the guards hear and see anything he wants. Don't trouble yourself over the UE. Rest in what God is providing you."

Gabriella shrugged her shoulders.

The angel laughed. "I guess those Bible stories were not on your reading list at Princeton. The point is there is nothing too hard for God. I look like the South African guards. The last time you saw me, I was an Indonesian police officer. Before that, I was a middle-aged staffer at the UE headquarters. I have taken whatever form God pleases that will serve his purpose for you."

"So, I'm in South Africa. That explains the language; I guess it's Afrikaans, not German, the guards are speaking," Gabriella said.

"Yes, you're in South Africa, on Robben Island to be precise, in a UE prison. God has sent me to aide you in one of your darkest moments," the angel said.

Gabriella stood and fell into the embrace of the angel as her weak legs gave way. "I wish I could hug the Lord."

"Well, the day will come when you will get to embrace God. For now, let's get you cleaned up and fed. You will need your strength when your rescue comes."

"I don't deserve to be saved. I betrayed my friends. They have sacrificed their lives and the fight against Draven."

"You don't have the power you believe you have; only God can determine a man's life or death. All your friends are alive. What happened to you and them is a part of this season in human history. As I told you before, your life had another path for you to follow. Despite your choices, God knew before the founding of this world that you would choose to love Him one day as He loved you. Now eat. My time with you grows short."

"When will I be rescued? Is Christopher—"

"Enough, Gabriella," the angel interrupted, moving Gabriella back to the prepared table. "You can't know everything. Now eat so you can rest. What I will ensure your ever-inquisitive mind of is you will not receive any further torture here."

Gabriella devoured the South African dishes before her: pap, beef bobotie, and a few biltong pieces. The angel then helped change her clothes. Gabriella now sported a bright green jumpsuit with bold dark letters 'UE prisoner' patterned in large circles. The best thing was a pair of oversized black sneakers to complete the look.

The ever-fashionable Gemma would not dare wear such an outfit. The thought of Gemma caused tears to flow.

She turned to her guardian angel. "Thank you. I feel that's not the right sentiment, but it's the best thing I can say, considering all you've done for me. Please tell me your name and when I will see you again."

The angel said nothing, gathering the tray of food and dirty clothes. Reaching the door, the angel turned to Gabriella.

"Gabriella, you're never alone. The Holy Spirit is present. I will come to you as the Lord determines. My name is Abigail, and when I come or go is not important; focusing on God is vital. It is better to call on the name of God than one who serves him. It's written, *Be strong and courageous. Do not be afraid; do not be discouraged, for the Lord, your God will be with you wherever you go.*"

With those words of encouragement, Gabriella watched Abigail the angel depart her cell, leaving behind a sense of peace and the first glimmers of hope for the days ahead.

⁂

CHAPTER 5

IT WAS A horrific sight to witness as Christopher and his team drove into the province of South Australia, 20 miles outside of Adelaide. The area renowned for its wooded foothills and world-class wine was ablaze. Christopher's watch displayed 7 a.m. but the dense smoke and ash that filled the sky hid the sun.

The rancid smoke from burning eucalyptus trees filled his vehicle, causing Christopher's eyes to water and nose to sting. The billowing smoke along the A1 highway leading into Adelaide forced the team to drive at a snail's pace. Christopher urged Jackson to pull over to a scenic overlook for a break. The lookout would've provided a calming vista of Adelaide and the South Indian Ocean beyond in the former world. Now Adelaide sat enveloped in an orange haze, the intermixing of the rising sun and God's judgment.

Christopher donned a keffiyeh to filter the toxic smoke as he took in the surroundings. Christopher admired the warriors fighting through the trials of the tribulation and the UE with him the past few years. Kerim, an ethnic Uyghur who suffered much in his service to God and fighting against the former Chinese government. Ilham the last living operative of Kerim's former resistance group remained loyal to Kerim and his fight against God's enemies the U.E.

Gilana, the Israeli Mossad-hardened warrior who cared deeply for those around her despite her stoic shell. Then there was Jackson. Christopher fought back tears thinking about how much he loved and admired Jackson, the man who was like an older brother to him. The person who had led him to Christ Jesus. Jackson never shied away from a fight for those he cared about or a joke in times of stress. "God, thank you for this team of friends."

Despite being autumn in Australia, the morning should've been warmer, as it had been before the first trumpet judgment. The thick haze created a noticeable chill in the air.

"Hey, everyone, I know this smoke is rough, so I'll be brief. I wanted to make sure we reached Kerim's contact, Alinta, before getting to the city and likely UE forces," Christopher said.

Kerim ignored what Christopher said, speaking of the terrifying scene around the team. "I have seen nothing like this. Did you notice that not all the trees burned despite the firestorm?"

Christopher rolled his head back, soaking in a moment of fresh air as a stiff breeze arose. He knew the answer coming as he watched Jackson pull their former teammate and spiritual mentor's Bible from his backpack. He smiled behind his scarf as Jackson unwrapped a cloth covering Rev's careworn Bible.

"Here we go, Revelation 8:7. The First Trumpet Judgment." Jackson pointed across the road to a reddish substance pooling near a burned eucalyptus tree. "The fire and blood describe what we are seeing. We have entered the next phase of the Tribulation. The world now faces the Wrath of the Lamb."

Gilana asked, "Explain what you mean?"

Jackson closed his Bible and leaned back on the truck. "Many, if they even believe in God, think He is angry because the world is suffering. In this view, there would be no difference between Draven's wrath and God's. However, this assumption of God is wrong. The Bible defines the Wrath of the Lamb many times. The definition rests between the concepts of sin versus revenge.

"In Hosea 9:12, God says, '*Woe to them when I depart from them!*

God separates himself from sin, which is his wrath. God does not seek revenge when we disobey him or reject his guidance for our lives. No, he steps aside in pain and watches as sin leads to its natural conclusion: suffering followed by death. How many times did we see this pattern in the Bible with Israel? They would reject God's teachings and law, and he would step away, leading to the nation's suffering, only to return when the nation repented and cried out.

"The sin of humanity, our desire to rule ourselves rather than submit to a Holy God, is what we see around us. Living apart from God has deadly consequences. Sin is naturally vicious. The essence of God's wrath is He gives people the freedom to leave His side. While we may feel it's unloving for God to let sin take its course, I argue that giving humanity the power of free will was the most loving and heartbreaking act God did. God knew countless numbers of His creation would reject Him and choose to live apart. God knew the consequences of not forcing us to love Him, the suffering it would bring, but love exists by choice. If we had no choice, we never could have loved Him, nor could God love us.

"That, my friends, is the difference between the Wrath of the Lamb and the revenge Draven seeks." Jackson re-wrapped his Bible.

Christopher recognized the same look of acceptance he felt in the rest of the team's eyes. God allowed the world to feel his absence and weight of sin. The Holy Spirit no longer restrained Satan's influence. The only thing positive from Jackson's explanation was Draven's reign of suffering won't last forever. Christopher tossed Kerim his phone to call his contact as Kerim began translating for Ilham. He prayed the Omega team drew closer to God as the world separated from Him in the days ahead.

⌇

CHAPTER 6

KERIM'S OLD FRIEND, Alinta, made Christopher's skin tingle in the way it does during a gunfight, as the last friend of a friend, Noah Brown, had betrayed them. Kerim's assurances that Alinta was trustworthy did nothing to ease his concern. Christopher prayed for God's protection as the two trucks pulled into parking spots next to a two-story industrial warehouse in the Port of Adelaide. The warehouse had a prime location in the port as it sat on a cliff overlooking the St. Vincent Gulf.

The old doubts of trusting God in his life crept into Christopher's mind as he stepped away from the vehicle. He hoped the prayer for protection had gotten through. His attention diverted to a tall Indigenous Australian woman with an uneven mahogany tone that enveloped her skin like the red earth that surrounded Uluru. The woman cast a striking presence as her silky black hair wafted in the rancid air. She held a light machine gun at the top of the warehouse's second-floor landing.

Christopher studied the woman as she offered a broad smile at Kerim who raced up the stairway to greet his ally.

"Alinta, it's great to see you," Kerim said with a deep embrace.

Alinta glared at Christopher, Jackson, Gilana, and Ilham.

"Yes, it's been a while. Who are the people with you?"

Kerim turned and gestured toward Christopher and the others as they walked up the stairs.

"This is my new team; we're fighting for the same thing as you."

As Christopher went to shake Alinta's hand, she ignored him. Instead, she opened the door leading into the warehouse's second floor, motioning for the group to follow.

When the entire group was through the door, Alinta turned to Kerim. "No, we are not fighting for the same thing; we are fighting the same enemy, which is good enough."

Christopher wanted to ask what Alinta was fighting for but held back, given the tension in her response. Alinta led them around the walled entry to a spacious living area framed on its edges by plywood rooms. On crude, handcrafted furniture sat six other Indigenous Australians, a mix of three women and three men who looked military by their clothes. The unknown individuals stood as the Omega team emerged behind Alinta. Christopher watched as Alinta placed the machine gun next to a wall of windows that overlooked the parking lot.

"Kerim, I fight to secure the lost lands of the Wiradjuri, my people. These six are the commanders of the resistance. The UE has created chaos here in Straya, and I will not let it go to waste."

Jackson held his hand up. "I agree with your cause, but what's Straya."

Alinta and her compatriots laughed.

"Straya is the way Australians say the name of this country. So, what do you need, Kerim?"

The abrupt shift in the conversation's tone worried Christopher. Alinta seemed to have a rough edge.

Kerim glanced at Christopher, who offered an awkward nod to proceed. "We need help to get to China. The UE is tracking us."

Alinta spoke in what Christopher assumed was Wiradjuri. He watched one of the yet to be identified men pull out a cell phone and move away from the group.

"Jarrah is calling to see if we can get you on a logistics flight leaving for Cairns this arvo."

"That's great, thanks," Kerim said.

Christopher pulled down Jackson's again raised hand. "Arvo is slang for the afternoon."

Alinta flashed a broad white smile to Christopher before Jarrah ran back to her, screaming.

Christopher watched as Jarrah gathered the other Wiradjuri commanders and began loading weapons as they moved to the windows overlooking the parking lot.

"Is everything okay?" Christopher asked.

Alinta moved toward her machine gun before Christopher grabbed her. She snatched her right arm away from him.

"Hey, Alinta! What's going on?" Christopher shouted.

"You've got no worries about getting to Cairns, then to Port Moresby, Papua New Guinea, but it's iffy if you'll make it to the airport. The UE followed you here."

Alinta sprinted to grab her gun near the warehouse's front as a window exploded, spraying her with glass and killing her instantly.

Christopher stopped Kerim, who was attempting to get to his friend.

"Kerim, focus! We need to get out of here; Alinta's dead!"

A fire erupted, filling the warehouse with smoke. Added urgency came from the growing sound of bullets searching for them. Jarrah's face contorted after running toward Christopher and his team as he glanced at Alinta's bloodied face.

"Follow me," Jarrah said.

Christopher dashed behind Jarrah as they made their way toward a flight of stairs leading down to the first floor. For the first time since his first gun battle in Afghanistan years ago, he froze in panic, surrounded by chaos. The entire first floor of the warehouse was in flames.

Jarrah continued forward, waving for Christopher and the others to follow. But Christopher couldn't move.

"Don't stop moving, soldier; if you want to live, keep moving," came the familiar voice of Jackson.

Christopher felt a tug on his arm. He blinked like a computer screen during rebooting.

"Move! Let's go!" Jackson shouted.

Christopher ran with Jackson through a narrow gap in the firewall between two plywood rooms toward a black hole in the ground. The familiar face of Gilana peered through the utility hole as the loud crack of the collapse of the second floor began. Jackson disappeared into the void, followed by Christopher.

The other Omega members' white tactical flashlights guided him as he crawled behind them toward the unknown. A salty breeze wafted through the claustrophobia-inducing tunnel, a welcoming contrast to the humid and sour air surrounding him. As Christopher watched, the others' silhouettes fade in the bright light ahead of him; the sound of waves crashing rang in his ears. The firm hands of Jackson helped him to his feet as the brisk sea air rushed over him.

Slimy bright-green algae-covered Jackson. Looking at himself and then Jackson provided a visual for the slop Christopher felt sloshing through the tunnel.

"Look at that," Kerim said.

The Omega team watched the warehouse collapse. Jarrah had led everyone to the safety of a sea-cliff crag through an industrial runoff tunnel.

Christopher approached his rescuer. He attempted to console him and the other survivors of Alinta's, now Jarrah's, army. "Jarrah. Thank you for saving us. I'm sorry for your loss today."

Jarrah covered his heart with his right hand as Kerim approached him with tears in his eyes and hugged Jarrah before walking away.

Jarrah turned back to Christopher.

"We are brothers in a war. I promise you the UE will suffer for today. You need to get to the Adelaide airport before 1400. You have a five-mile journey to the north. I think your path should be clear, as the UE will scour the warehouse for hours. Good hunting."

Christopher nodded to Jarrah, glancing at his wristwatch before turning to his team and waving them forward. As Omega started out for the airport, he reflected on Alinta's people losing her. Christopher hoped to find the rest of this team, General Havid and Gabriella, before it was too late.

CHAPTER 7

JACKSON'S SLEEP CAME in tortured spurts since departing Adelaide almost a week ago. The misery the team endured made insomnia logical. Omega experienced delays as the smoke from the global firestorm prevented Adelaide flights to Cairns. Instead of a comfortable flight, the Omega team endured a travel itinerary planned by Satan, or so Jackson thought. Omega's travels included the foul-smelling trailer of a cattle transport truck returning to Cairns, minus its bovine cargo. Jackson would remain forever grateful for the blessing of not riding with the cattle. However, the smell of cow manure was a part of the truck. It made the transport 'UE proof' as no UE guards dared approach the vehicle, given its pungent odor.

Again, poor air conditions forced indignity upon Omega from Cairns to Port Moresby. Omega traveled in the empty cargo hold of a fishing trawler for this leg of the trip. The remnants of dead fish caked to the hull walls seared in Jackson's senses and made seafood an unlikely meal for a while.

In Papua New Guinea, Omega now enjoyed and likely appreciated air travel. Jarrah and his team secured a commercial flight through the Wiradjuri resistance network for the last leg to China. Jackson smiled as the Lord's provision came to mind despite the travel discomforts.

The current flight from Port Moresby to Guangzhou, China, again left Jackson wide-eyed, not only for the break in the smoke but also for God's command over his creation. The power of God, after the disappearances, brought Jackson from unbelief to an evangelist. Jackson thought of all the people in the world whose hearts remained unmoved by God despite all that had occurred. Jackson's protective nature brought feelings of remorse, knowing the judgment the unbelievers would face if they died in their sin. He understood as bad as the past two and half years had been, the worst was yet to come.

God's words regarding the first trumpet judgment became history in precise detail. The hazy light of a new day provided a visual of the landscape, giving credibility to God's prophecies on the Tribulation. 'Hand-carved' sections of smoldering scorched earth scarred the lush jungles and biodiversity of the many Indonesian islands. In contrast, other areas on the same islands were unharmed. The prophesied devastation of Revelation 8:7 now was history, as only a third of Earth's vegetation bore scars. Jackson didn't need official verification of the burned areas to know how much the planet's foliage remained; the view God gave provided the truth.

As the commercial airliner made its way to the Guangzhou Baiyun International Airport gate, a wave of optimism rose within Jackson. His life was in God's hands, and there was no other way he wanted to live. Looking around the plane as people stirred to get off, Jackson was glad the fear from the Pyretos pandemic made public mask-wearing a standard fixture around the world. Thanks to Jarrah's folks, he and the rest of Omega were traveling in costume. A fake gash and bandage on his head distorted Jackson's profile, while Gilana wore a mask, gray-haired wig, and used a cane. Kerim and Ilham, besides a face mask, wore bigger clothes to break up their body signatures.

Looking at Christopher and the extra details provided for his disguise, Jackson laughed. After the Jakarta attack, Christopher's picture rose to the most infamous in the world as the 'Omega terror group leader.' So, Jarrah added unique features to Christopher's body to ensure he passed through Guangzhou's Unified Asian Nations security. Jarrah's team dyed

Christopher's black goatee and eyebrows gray. He wore a back brace, which caused him to bend over, and topping the look was the request for a wheelchair through the airline. With Kerim in agreement, Jarrah explained even post-Rapture, the Asian culture demanded elder respect; thus, they'd scrutinize Christopher less if he looked like an old man.

Jackson grabbed his backpack from the overhead bin before turning to Christopher. "You ready, pa?"

Christopher smacked Jackson in the leg with a backpack, causing Jackson to stop laughing.

Jackson told the flight attendant he would wait with his 'old friend' until the wheelchair arrived. He watched Gilana and the others exit the plane as a wheelchair came aboard for Christopher.

"Easy old-timer," Jackson said as the flight attendant helped him lower Christopher into the wheelchair.

Christopher mumbled. "You're enjoying this too much."

"Speak up."

Christopher remained silent as an attendant wheeled him off the plane into the gate area. Jackson grabbed the wheelchair and provided a few UE dollars to the attendant.

Jackson turned to Kerim. "Where is your ground transport meeting us?"

"Follow me."

Jackson led the group, following Kerim, wheeling Christopher through the airport security with no second looks. Then, as the team emerged, Jackson stopped to let Christopher stand.

"Okay, pa, this is the end of the road. How about a tip for my service?"

"I'll give you a tip, alright. The tip of my boot to—"

A tense discussion between Kerim and Ilham cut Christopher off.

Before Jackson or anyone could respond to the men's disagreement, Kerim hugged Ilham, and Ilham walked off.

"What was that about?" Jackson asked.

"Ilham doesn't want to work with us anymore. Concern over his two younger brothers in Ürümqi drove his decision. Ilham fears losing the ability to care for his brothers by working with us. He told me; he will find his own way home."

Jackson glanced at Christopher as they watched Ilham recede back into the airport, now out of disguise.

"We should go, don't you think?"

Gilana answered, "Yes, let's go before someone questions us."

Jackson watched Christopher stop walking with the group, turning to Kerim. "Are you sure you want to stay with us? I mean, you could reestablish a resistance team of your own here in China."

"I'm grateful to have fought alongside such brave individuals. I owe it to Gabriella to help save her from Draven. I still have a few friends." He pointed to the awaiting van driver. "You're stuck with me at least until we free Gabriella."

Jackson smiled and swatted Kerim's back as they boarded the van for a new safe house.

Christopher's body screamed for him to sleep, but his mind whirled with the scenery. Compared to his recent travel experiences, the drive from Guangzhou to Kerim's safe house in the Jiuzhaigou National Park of north-central China was amazing. The lush forest and terraced hills bore witness to God's judgment, with fire scars canvassing the landscape. However, the same areas displayed God's mercy as farmers tended to their flooded rice paddies that escaped God's judgment. The sharp contrast provided a testament to God's desire for repentance during this time of tribulation to the observant person.

The conversation between Kerim and Adil, the "friend" Kerim asked to pick up the team, was as stimulating as the scenery. Adil served with Kerim in the PLA before the Rapture. Adil converted to Christianity after the Rapture during an experience that changed his views on religion and Jesus. Christopher had grown fond of hearing how other believers accepted Jesus. He never tired of hearing stories of overcoming doubts and cultural obstacles like the Islamic background of Adil to find the truth Jesus offered.

Christopher starred at Adil as he began recounting his journey to Christ.

Adil turned to Christopher, giving him a partial smile.

"The world often views Islam and Muslims as obsessed with violence and oppression. Islam is a worldview that creates a structure to live in a world governed by chaos. Islam provides discipline in all aspects of human existence. I often listened to these words given by my father, the Imam of our village. My father spoke of the moral beauty of living a life dedicated to Allah. He believed the Beijing communists and Westerners lived lustful lives. As our Imam, he often defined Western living as a pursuit of things. In comparison, we lived in simplicity in Xinjiang Province focused on Allah and our community.

"I believed the words of my father until one Friday after *ṣalāt.* Not long before the Rapture, a woman came to our village speaking of Jesus and having a relationship with God. The village men brought the woman, a *murtad or apostate,* to my father for punishment. I can still see her face and hear her wails for mercy. My father's temples pulsed, and he spat on the woman condemning her to die.

"The men of the village gathered stones and began striking her. The woman's last words haunt me, even now, 'forgive them.' I stood in horror as the men I'd known my entire life tossed the woman's lifeless, bloodied body on a rubbish cart. They burned her outside the village. The brutal act served as a warning against trying to convert people in our village to follow Jesus. I asked my father why they treated the woman this way. He grabbed me by the shirt and pulled me close, yelling, 'Christians make the prophet Jesus to be God to enslave others!'"

Christopher could see the pain on Adil's face as he paused, and Kerim spoke to him in Uyghur.

Adil nodded at Kerim before continuing, "The treatment of the woman brought to light the hypocrisy of the many teachings of tolerance I had heard at the mosque. I took a significant risk. But I felt driven to know more about the woman's faith—a person who, despite suffering and facing sure death, held to her beliefs.

"I came to find out the woman's name was Nur. After converting to Christianity during a secret house church meeting, Nur's family disowned her. I sought leaders within the Jiātíng Jiàohuì, or house church, in English. I found a group of church leaders in Ürümqi who knew of Nur's death and mourned her not as if she were dead. Instead, they treated her absence as if she had gone ahead to a distant place that one day they would visit.

"I spent a week with the men wrestling with the beliefs of my father and what my heart was telling me. I knew I wanted to pray for God's forgiveness of my sins and ask God to change my life, but…"

Adil shook his head before continuing.

"I feared to tell my father, but I needed him to hear my reasons for wanting to convert. I no longer saw Jesus as a prophet, but now as my savior. A part of me thought I could convert him. On the day of the Rapture, I made my mind up to not deny Jesus after weeks of hiding my desire to become a Christian. I planned to pray for salvation in front of my father, boldly declaring my decision no matter the cost. However, I didn't get the chance to speak with my father. The chaos of the day, babies, and young children's disappearances brought fear and confusion to the village. By the evening of the Rapture, my father collapsed and died; I think the stress and horror overcame him. I had lost my father and missed, what I now know is the Rapture of the Christians. The words of urgency from the Jiātíng Jiàohuì leaders rang in my ears. I was told that Jesus could return at any moment. That making a decision to receive Jesus as my savior shouldn't be put off for another day. I lay on my father's bed with shame and pain filling me and I started praying for God to save me. It was hours too late, but I am grateful that Jesus accepted me."

Adil fell silent, and Christopher could see the tears creating wet trails down his tan face. Christopher noticed Gilana was awake and staring at Adil; interest and sympathy filled her eyes. He prayed to himself that the impact of Adil's story would push Gilana toward the Lord.

᪥

CHAPTER 8

PONTIFF CONTI FINISHED a daily Interfaith mass for his triune's chapel staff. The sanctuary went as the Santa Marta chapel in the former Catholic Church era. The church dedicated the chapel to the third member of the trinity, the Holy Spirit, with a Latin inscription above the altar, "Come, Holy Spirit, fill the hearts of your faithful."

Conti viewed the chapel as a fitting celebration of the Interfaith religion, the third point in the universe's supreme trinity. The name correlated with the triangular motif throughout the chapel as a visional representation of the Interfaith trinity of the Prince of World, the Interfaith religion, and the Prince's earthly representative Draven Cross. The latter Pontiff Conti hoped to dispose of, so he could become the new head of the world.

This thought of ridding the world of Draven made the Pontiff happy as he beckoned his trusted aide Giuseppe toward the altar. "I'm surprised to find you at my mass. I didn't take you as a religious man."

Giuseppe looked around the chapel, allowing a few stragglers to leave before speaking. "I didn't attend mass. I'm here to provide an update from Ayatollah al-Farshid. The *Ḥashashiyan* is ready."

Pontiff Conti steepled his hands and took a seat on a nearby pew.

"I have longed for this moment; the chance to rid myself of Draven and assume my rightful place in this world."

Giuseppe sat next to the Pontiff. "There are many steps that we will need to take before we can think of attacking Draven."

The Pontiff tried to contain his excitement around Giuseppe's announcement. The plan he formed with Al-Farshid conceived in a lie that Draven attempted to kill the two leaders now was ready for birth.

"We have all we need. We have an assassin."

Giuseppe stood and let out a heavy sigh. "*Il pontefice.* You're a man of faith, not a military man. An assassin is a unique weapon for a unique purpose. If we rush and miss our chance, we will *essere uccisi.* I'm not ready to die."

Conti asked, "So, what do we do with this special weapon, Giuseppe?"

"A security detail hand-picked by Evan Mallory surrounds Cross. We need to replace one man in that detail with our assassin."

Conti stood with a wide smile, staring at Giuseppe.

Giuseppe raised his eyebrows. "*Che Cosa?*"

" I know the answer to our problem. Gemma Sutherland. Draven placed her on house arrest, until he can come to the inevitable conclusion to kill his long-time aide and brief lover. Every Beast has his beauty."

Conti paused as his comments caused Giuseppe's eyebrows to raise. He enjoyed the shock flowing from his aide witnessing a different side to him.

The Pontiff continued, "Considering Draven subjected her to torture, revenge will be a vibrant thought for Ms. Sutherland. I will push her to vengeance and then offer her a path to regain Draven's trust. We need only test her willingness to help us get the assassin in place, but leave that to me. Your role will be to free up a spot on Draven's protection detail."

Giuseppe ran his right hand over his thick black beard. "This is dangerous. Gemma could sell you out to improve her relationship with Cross."

"You underestimate a woman scorned." Conti laughed. "She will side with us, trust me."

"I hope you're right about Gemma. But I don't want to kill again, Pontiff. Let me find out if there's an opening on the security detail. It might be easier to blackmail a guard than—"

The Pontiff held up his hands, interrupting. "Giuseppe, blackmail won't work. We can't leave a trail of people that will know our plans."

Giuseppe shook his head as he left the chapel.

✖

Gemma wiped the moisture from the steamed-over mirror in her new UE campus apartment bathroom to see a face unrecognizable staring back. The bruises would heal. Gemma was unsure if the anger and pain in her heart would ever go away. She fought to focus on gratitude for God sparring her life over the details of her ordeal. *Why did God want me to live?"* was the thought that ran through Gemma's head.

Gemma wrapped herself in a towel, moving to her bed where she lay staring at the ceiling. Thoughts of revenge filled her. She had traded one prison for another and still had no idea if Draven would keep her alive until tomorrow. She desired more than living to enact the pain and humiliation she felt in Draven's life. However, glancing at her Bible on a nightstand brought on a churning stomach and a tightening in her chest. She wrestled between thoughts of revenge and forgiveness. A loud knock on her apartment door interrupted her feelings about what emotion to yield.

Changing into a sweatshirt and leggings before answering the door, she asked. "Who is it?"

"Gemma, it is Pontiff Conti's assistant, Giuseppe."

Her eyebrows raised, and her face furrowed at hearing Giuseppe's name. Peering through the door hold, she asked, "What do you want?"

Giuseppe looked around the UE apartment complex as if being watched. "Ms. Sutherland, Pontiff Conti wants to speak to you. He heard of your recent experience and wants to provide some spiritual guidance, if you're willing."

Gemma laughed to herself. Conti's spiritual guidance was as profound as watching cartoons. She felt there was an alternative motive. "Thank you, Giuseppe, but I decline the invitation. Good day."

"You should know Pontiff Conti insisted your torture stop once he found out."

Gemma watched Giuseppe turn down the stairs leading to the parking lot. Now, she felt compelled to give the Pontiff an audience based on him helping her. What could it hurt to express gratitude in person?

Gemma opened her apartment door. "Giuseppe, wait. I will meet with the Pontiff. I would like to thank him in person. Please give me a moment to change."

"Excellent. I will wait for you here."

Gemma ran back to her bedroom and threw on a navy A-line dress and matching heels. She moved to her bathroom and applied foundation to minimize the discoloration of her bruised face. She used a subtle lip gloss to provide a healthy sheen to otherwise cracked and swollen lips. Gemma formed her blonde locks into an elegant bun, completing her transformation. As she headed for the door, Gabriella's communicator caught her eye from the living room coffee table. She went over and grabbed it. The phone had a minor charge remaining. Unsure what she could use the mobile for, she took the device for comfort and the help it represented and walked out the door.

Pontiff Conti enjoyed the late spring afternoon in Rome. The view of the Adrian Park ornamental pond calmed him. The air sat heavy with the fragrant and tranquil scent of jasmine. Star Jasmine vines covered the stonework around the pond and climbed the rear wall of Castel Sant'Angelo. It was a mesmerizing environment the Pontiff savored as the Star Jasmine competed with the manicured gardens and pond for lead attraction in the park.

Conti loved the reflective thoughts this location invoked. Giuseppe called earlier, notifying him that Gemma Sutherland agreed to meet him under the pretense of thanking him for freeing her from Draven. He loved the embellishment Giuseppe improvised, as it ensured his ability to manipulate Gemma.

The sound of the Pontiff's sedan coming to a stop atop the graveled drive caused him to turn. He watched Gemma emerge from the vehicle, where she hesitated at the head of the path which led to the pond and him. He watched Gemma fidget with her dress while staring at rows of iconic stone pine trees along the trail. It was apparent to the Pontiff that Gemma seemed on edge, creating a perfect mental state for the suggestion he had in mind.

As Gemma drew near, Pontiff Conti stood and enveloped both of Gemma's hands in his own. "It is so good to see you. I have prayed without ceasing since learning of your ordeal. Please sit."

"Thank you, Pontiff Conti." Gemma's emotions caused tears to flow. "I'm indebted to you for helping free me from Draven's torture."

Conti raised his hands to his mouth and attempted to wave off Gemma's compliment, despite her release being an act absent of his actions. "I'm a servant of the people, and my goal is only to ease suffering in this world."

Gemma sat on the bench next to Pontiff Conti, staring at the pond in front of her. "I've known for years Draven was heartless, but torturing me... Pontiff, I don't understand all the emotions I have right now."

Pontiff Conti grew elated by Gemma's confusion. He let her words hang without response until the awkward silence brought her to speak. Conti took this moment to respond, interrupting her. "Gemma, what if I told you I'm conflicted about watching Secretary Cross lead the world? You know he didn't even check on my welfare after the attack by the Two Witnesses?"

Gemma turned toward the Pontiff. "I didn't know that Pontiff, but hearing you say Draven didn't show concern for someone is not surprising. Draven attended a business conference on the day of his father's funeral."

Pontiff Conti assumed that such a personal revelation by Draven's trusted assistant meant she would receive his plan. Conti stood pacing in front of Gemma. "Let me be clear on how I feel about our mutual employer. Draven Cross is not fit to lead the world. He is a brute who only serves himself. I guarantee you will have vindication for the suffering you've endured with the death of Draven Cross. What do you think?"

Gemma's eyes lost focus before she said, "Your assessment of Draven only scratches the surface. You need to be careful. Draven's cunning is second only to his ruthlessness; if he even suspects your treachery, you and all involved, including me, are dead."

Conti watched Gemma's gaze darting around the park. She was nervous, but also considering his proposal. The afternoon sun created long shadows across the lush surroundings, reflecting the shift in his conversation with Gemma.

The Pontiff sought to seal Gemma's support. "What I offer is an obscure role in ending the terror that is Draven's reign over the world. However, if you want no part in this plot, you can leave now."

"Pontiff Conti." Gemma shook her head. "I've been around powerful men long enough to know you would never let me live without committing to your plan. A plan that puts you in charge of the world. I'm upset and want revenge. I am not a moron."

"We have a mutual enemy. Which makes your willingness to work toward an agreeable situation regarding Secretary-General Cross vital."

"An 'agreeable' situation. That's a fascinating way of describing what you're planning for Draven. Pontiff, can I have a few hours to consider everything we've discussed?"

Conti stood over Gemma. "You have until midnight to decide. I am sure you understand the sensitive nature of our discussion. I will leave you with a final thought. I can bring you back into the graces of Draven or ensure your demise. Choose wisely."

Gemma stood and faced him. "A threat is unbecoming of you, Pontiff; it reeks of desperation. As I stated, I've lived amongst the powerful for a while now. Even those that mask their ambition behind religion. You will have your answer soon. Thank you for helping me and good day."

Pontiff Conti nodded and watched with cautious optimism as Gemma strolled back toward Giuseppe. He pulled out his cell phone calling his aide. "Giuseppe, Ms. Sutherland is not a willing participant in my plan, yet. You know your tasks. Eliminate the guard and prepare the documents that will aid Gemma once she accepts her fate to help me. Expect my call, directing you to deliver the documents to Gemma."

Conti listened as Giuseppe sighed. "I understand, Pontiff."

Conti allowed a broad smile to rise on his face as he ended the call with Giuseppe. He enjoyed the irony of the short walk he undertook toward a centuries-old papal escape passage within Castel Sant'Angelo. Previous pontiffs had used the hidden tunnel to escape uprisings against the church's rule. He now used the route to plot his global ascension.

❧

Gemma felt unsettled for the first time since her early nerve-racking days at Cross Industries as the new aid to the dashing Draven Cross. Sitting in the backseat of Pontiff Conti's luxury sedan now seemed wrong. Gemma stared at the empty, ravished Roman streets to take her mind off the deal she made with the devil's henchmen.

Praying had become difficult, as her mind would drift toward being tortured and away from seeking God. Gemma knew she needed God more than ever. She faced certain death if she didn't help Conti. What she was less sure about was her potential role in the assassination of Draven. *Perhaps, this is why I am alive, to serve as a vessel for God's revenge on Draven.* Gemma, wanted to scream as she tried to suppress her desire for revenge and align with the ever-ambitious Pontiff Conti.

The weight of the situation pressed on her, and a headache grew as Giuseppe crossed the Tiber River. She needed a sense of direction. She needed God, but wanted revenge. *What am I going to do?*

As Gemma's mind raced, Giuseppe interrupted her thoughts. "We have arrived at your home. I encourage you to think about the Pontiff's offer. When you make your choice, contact the Pontiff.

❧

43

CHAPTER 9

GIUSEPPE LOOKED AT his reflection in his rearview mirror. "You must do this. This time is different. You're helping the world and the Pontiff and besides *God owes me*." The memory of losing his adored wife Maria and their twin toddler boys during the disappearances left Giuseppe hollow and angry with God.

Giuseppe wrestled with his past and appointed future, awaiting him outside of a brothel minutes away. Giuseppe was a hitman for a Roman crime family before the disappearances. His wife, Maria, who had terminal pancreatic cancer had asked him for years to walk away from crime and dedicate himself to serving God. He loved Maria more than his own life but found her faith in God crazy. She was dying and leaving her family, but trusted God. To the astonishment of the Roman medical community, three months before the disappearances, God granted Maria a miracle by eliminating any trace of cancer in her body. After learning of her healing, Giuseppe promised his wife in the doctor's office that he would never kill another person.

He shook his head, trying to push his promise away. Yet, eliminating one of Draven's bodyguards opened the door to the UE Secretary-General's death. The guilt of killing one man to kill another pushed Maria and his promise to her into every thought in his mind.

Giuseppe pulled into an alleyway across the street from a bordello disguised as an apartment building. Watching "Johns" patronize the seedy establishment, Giuseppe ended the debate between his past promises and the present situation of killing a man.

Giuseppe closed his eyes before speaking aloud. "Forgive me, Maria. I must do this."

The tall, well-built Alberto Bianchi became the target of choice because of the rumor floating within the UE security staff; he was an adulterer. Alberto, like many men in UE service, had a secret vice. Alberto's deadly sin was his lust for women. Every Friday the Secretary-General was in Rome, Bianchi would come to this bordello for two hours, then head home. Giuseppe confirmed Alberto's habit last week after the Pontiff made his assassination plan known. He determined with a sense of moral satisfaction that the killing of a wayward husband was justice being served. At least, it eased his soul for failing the promise made to Maria.

Tonight, would be the last time Alberto would see his favorite prostitute. Giuseppe glanced at his watch. He had 15 minutes before his target would exit and cross the street, walking toward his car parked for discretion, or so Alberto thought, in a vacant parking lot near the bordello. Giuseppe put his murderous talent into action. He popped the sedan's trunk and used his smartphone flashlight to find a small block of plastic explosives. Using his criminal connections, he'd acquired the plastic explosives from a construction firm working to rebuild the UE campus.

Ten minutes remained before Alberto departed. Giuseppe ran behind the building, spotting Alberto's black Alpha Romero sport coupe sitting vulnerable. Giuseppe attached a small cellular transmitter to the explosive block before wedging the mass under the driver's seat on the car's frame. He raced back into his car and pulled out of the alleyway as Alberto exited and made his way toward his car. The two men whose lives were about to interweave made brief eye contact as Bianchi left the house of ill repute.

As he looked back at Alberto entering the alley, Giuseppe was grateful for removing the Pontiff's religious markings from the vehicle. Even the hapless Alberto would be leery if he noticed the Pontiff's vehicle so near his sordid secret. Giuseppe had already made a U-turn to follow Alberto to the top of a nearby hill. The deserted hilltop would ensure Giuseppe minimized collateral damage and the investigations such damage incurred. While he didn't want to kill Alberto's wife with the explosion, if Alberto made it home somehow—well, he would not fail his mission. Giuseppe hoped no cars would be at the stoplight on the hill for Alberto's wife's sake.

Trailing Alberto from a safe distance of four hundred meters, Giuseppe sighed. He observed an empty roadway as Alberto arrived at the stoplight atop the hill. Giuseppe hit send on his phone, and Alberto became an afterthought seconds later. Giuseppe turned around in the street, heading for Gemma's home as bright orange flames leaped from Alberto's car. "*Per'dónami*, Maria."

Pontiff Conti waved an attendant out of the room as his cell phone rang. He expected this call but wanted to make the dialer linger for a moment longer. Conti took another sip of a Tuscan Merlot savoring his luxury appointments while the world suffered. "Life will only get better once I am the Secretary-General," Conti thought before answering his cell phone.

"Gemma. I hoped you would call. Have you thought about the offer I?"

"Yes, Pontiff, I have. I want to help you in return for you saving my life."

"Excellent choice, Gemma. The documents for Deputy Secretary-General Mallory will be under your door by sunrise. One document will contain names of candidates for replacing a member of Draven's security detail. I will also include a memo with the name of a UE staff member, indicating this person has been funneling money to resistance organizations. I want you to take the documents to Evan Mallory tomorrow."

"What am I going to tell Evan? I magically found these documents?" Gemma chided.

"Make the following your own voice and story. Say, sir, I've come to my senses and I am her to beg for my life. I am grateful to serve the Secretary-General and you. I do have proof of traitors in the UE ranks, that will prove I can be trusted."

"Are you serious? You want me to grovel!" Gemma shouted into Conti's ear, causing him to pull the phone away.

"If you want to live, you will appeal to Evan's ego. Stop at your desk, then pull the traitor's file and plead your case. If you live through the moment, then later in the day present the document with the candidates, one of which will be the assassin, a Demir Ersoy."

The phone was silent for so long that Conti asked if Gemma was still there.

"I'm here. The way you phrased the point of me living through pleading with Evan scares me," Gemma said.

"You have no choice. I expect to hear a report tomorrow that you're back on the staff. Get some rest, tomorrow's a big day for us."

Conti hung up the phone smiling. He called Giuseppe with a brief message. "Take the documents to Ms. Sutherland's home."

CHAPTER 10

GENERAL HAVID REFLECTED on the small mercies God granted him each day, turning the *Hekal Emah* or "Temple of Terror" into a mere inconvenience. The prison superintendent was a former *Shayetet 13* member who received a commendation from Havid for bravery. Thus, General Havid enjoyed a cell away from the other prisoners. Prisoners he'd ordered captured and would be glad to have a chance at revenge.

General Havid most wanted to exploit the privilege of having visitors and uncensored reading materials. He grew excited in the superintendent's reception room, with the potential this privilege afforded. General Havid couldn't sit still. The thought of his long-time aide, Jonathan, bringing his study Bible, had him as excited as the first date with his beloved Abagail.

However, as Jonathan entered the room, General Havid's elation turned to sadness as he watched the young man hobbling toward him, leaning on a hardwood cane.

Havid rushed to help his former assistant. "Jonathan, what has come of you? You did not describe your condition to me over the phone. If I knew your condition, I would not have asked you to come."

"General, it is an honor to serve you, and my wounds are a small price to pay for what I've gained."

After helping his aide into his seat, General Havid sat opposite Jonathan. "You speak like a madman."

Jonathan's started his reply by pulling a wrapped Bible from his backpack. "General, your faith led me to understand who the Messiah of our people was. I know it was Jesus."

General Havid's eyes filled with water. He'd hoped that his prayer for salvation of this man, once stricken by the skin plague of the Witnesses, would come to pass.

"I am happy for you," Havid said, embracing Jonathan.

"I am glad to know who Jesus Christ is and what he means in my life. I broke my leg when the UE torched your home, fighting to save your Bible, and this."

Jonathan pulled a picture of a young General Havid and his departed and cherished wife, Abagail, from his backpack.

General Havid held the photo and his Bible close to his chest as tears streamed down his face. "Thank you for coming here today and bringing such valuable items."

Havid squeezed Jonathan's hands discreetly, passing him a note he had already written in his cell. He nodded to Jonathan and watched his aid return the nod, showing he understood the note's contents were to be read later.

"I need to go now, General Havid, but I will be in touch soon."

General Havid stood and walked to the door with Jonathan. He realized that passing Jonathan a note to contact Gemma Sutherland and Omega was risky, but he'd grown desperate.

"I look forward to hearing from you soon."

Jonathan smiled at General Havid as two guards escorted him from the *Hekal Emah* prison.

General Havid returned a false smile as Jonathan's footsteps faded away. *God, please forgive me placing lives in danger.*

⋖

Christopher felt a deceptive sense of calm. It was unsettling to be heading for a new safe house knowing General Havid and Gabriella sat in confinement or worse. As the van entered the Rize Valley in Central China, he decided the team's stay needed to be short. He would not cower in hiding while Draven killed innocents.

The Rize Valley's remoteness matched its stunning beauty. This section of the Jiuzhaigou National Park, Five Flower Lake, concealed the rebel outpost that would soon be home. The area stood picturesque in stark contrast to the burned-tree patchwork that weaved through the valley. Three gigantic mountains surrounded the clear lake, invoking feelings of a fantasy world.

The beleaguered Omega team traveled the winding road to an abrupt end near a massive granite cave entrance. Dozens of burned vehicles and military hardware littered the road in front of the cave entrance, resembling a deserted battlefield. Adil drove the van between a destroyed commercial truck and an army transport vehicle parking alongside the mountain.

Before Christopher asked questions about the facility, Adil leaped from the vehicle. "We walk from here."

Christopher watched Kerim get out of the van as he nodded to Gilana.

Christopher then grabbed a half-empty water bottle, and threw it at the sleeping Jackson. "Hey, old man, time to get up."

Jackson mumbled before pulling his "woobie" or poncho liner as civilians called the beloved piece of military gear over his head. Christopher upped his harassment by taking a full water bottle and dumping it on Jackson.

"Hey, what's going on?"

"We're waiting on you." Christopher laughed. "We're at the new safe house, so pick up your gear and get moving."

Christopher exited the van as Jackson grumbled, grabbed his bags and slid out of the vehicle to join Gilana, Kerim, and Adil. He nodded to Adil and walked through the vehicle graveyard with the others. Their destination was a vine-covered crease in the mountain face.

Christopher entered a sophisticated underground facility as he came through the other side of the single-person wide crack.

Adil moved beside Christopher, triggering a lever along the rock wall that slid a sizeable faux-rock, steel blast door over the entrance. Christopher watched Adil open a metal box near the blast door lever and push an intercom before speaking Mandarin.

Adil turned to the Omega team. "I needed to let the others know it was me and not the UE."

Christopher took in his surroundings. He had trained in underground complexes, but his new temporary home was cleaner than those sites. The air carried a metallic scent, signaling heavy filtration and some level of environmental control. There were no signs of moisture problems, identifiable by the lack of mineral deposits on the walls and no noticeable humid-musty smell in the air.

As the group descended a flight of stairs two stories, they walked through a second blast door and into a large room resembling a luxury resort lobby. It confirmed Christopher's observations that the site was not a simple underground training facility.

Jackson approached Christopher as he continued absorbing everything. "Impressive facility, huh? This had to be a PLA senior leader's bunker."

"I agree." Christopher redirected the conversation with Jackson. "But where is Gilana going?"

"I don't know, but I'll find out."

"No, I'll keep up with her." Christopher pointed to Kerim and Adil speaking with six other people dressed in camouflaged clothes. "Find out more about our new roommates."

Christopher pursued Gilana through a corridor where the sound of water thundered around him. As he turned a right corner, a rush of cool air scented by wet vegetation met him. Given that Christopher was meters below the ground, the noises and smells seemed out of place, causing his heart rate to rise. He moved his pistol to the ready position as he approached a doorway that sounded like a train was on the other side. Gilana, standing on an observation deck behind a waterfall, broke the tension. Christopher holstered his pistol in shame, after his arch nemesis, trust, had made him overreact.

Christopher moved slowly toward Gilana to not startle her, given the roar of the water ten meters ahead of them. The deafening cascade of water made subtlety useless as he shouted, "Gilana, how did you know this was here?"

"My nose led me. The artificial air of the command bunker couldn't hide the freshly flowing water!" Gilana shouted.

Christopher half-smiled at her. The team all felt the facility was too luxurious and clean for everyday soldier use. Gilana pointed to the door. He walked back into the hallway, where the waterfall's rumble lessened.

"You worry easily, don't you, Christopher?" Gilana asked.

"What makes you say that?"

Gilana pointed to his holstered pistol. "What were you going to shoot?"

"I was ready for whatever, the motto for my life. What's on your mind?"

Gilana's hands covered her face as she let a loud sigh out. "I've been thinking about who God is to me. I continue to replay Adil's story. He turned away from all he knew after watching a stranger sacrifice their life to Jesus."

Christopher nodded, not wanting to rush the conversation, like a hunter hurrying a shot of a deer in the open, scaring Gilana away from committing to Christ.

"Jimbo gave his life protecting followers of Jesus." Gilana crossed her arms. "He never wavered in wanting to save Christians, people who didn't know him. I think about General Havid likely dead; his country turned against him because of his commitment to serve Jesus. How can I forget surviving the Inverness lab mission and Jackson leading strangers to Jesus after the attack? I can't deny any longer what

I've seen, Christopher. If such talented people will sacrifice everything for Jesus, how can I not accept him?"

Christopher felt a sense of nervous electric energy flowing through him. He thought. *God, is it possible you're going to answer a prayer and Gilana is ready to accept Jesus as her savior.*

"What's stopping you?"

Gilana squeezed her left arm with her right arm. "My father served in the Israeli Defense Force during a turbulent period for Israel. Bombings in the cities, rockets rained down everywhere; the terrorists killed without mercy. So, the government attacked the terror camps in Syria and Palestine. The operation failed from the start, and many Israelis died. My father lost his older brother and received a gunshot wound. He left the IDF as a hollow man. My father's IDF service shattered his perception of Israel and God. He thought Yahweh abandoned us. My mother tried to take my brother and me to the synagogue during Passover one year, and my father erupted. He slapped my mother and threw her to the ground. I can still see him standing over her, screaming, 'God was for the weak; the strong take care of themselves.' I joined the military as soon as I could, never looking back. A part of me hoped me serving would change things at home, but it didn't."

Gilana's story painted the picture for Christopher of why she kept her emotions hidden.

When Gilana collapsed onto the black-tiled floor, crying, Christopher joined her on the cool tile.

Christopher felt it was time to make a confession of his own. "I've only known Jesus as my Lord and Savior for a year now, so I'm no expert. I struggle to this day with trusting God, but it's a choice I'm learning to make. The people you know on this team have faith built on their relationship with Jesus. Trusting God strengthened them; it didn't make them weaker. I know firsthand that Jesus will walk through the fires of life with you, even to your last breath; I believe that with all of me. My advice is to follow King David's words in Psalm 34, *Taste and see that the Lord is good; blessed is the one who takes refuge in him.* Take a chance and get to know God and see how your life changes."

Christopher's eyes met the tear-filled eyes of Gilana, who nodded her head, acknowledging the desire to find Jesus.

"Gilana, repeat after me."

And she did.

"Dear heavenly Father, I come to You as a broken person looking for peace. My desires guide my life, and I have turned away from You at every opportunity. Now, I realize I am a sinner and that You have provided a way, Your son Jesus, for me to be reconciled to You. Father, I believe Jesus died on the cross for my sins and rose to life again, giving me victory over death. Please forgive me for my sins, as I accept Jesus Christ as my Lord and Savior. In Jesus's name, Amen."

The two friends embraced, and Christopher thanked God for answering his prayers for Gilana's salvation. The moment ended with Christopher's phone vibrating in his pocket, signaling a missed call. Gemma needed him. He pulled back from Gilana's embrace, glancing at the phone's display, which showed one service bar.

Christopher turned from Gilana. "Gemma tried to reach us. I need to call her back. We will celebrate your salvation after the call."

CHAPTER 11

GEMMA FOUND SLEEP impossible between the bruises and mental anguish of siding with Pontiff Conti. She was awake when Giuseppe slid the "documents of death" under her door around 1:30 a.m. It was now 4:30 a.m. *God, what have I gotten myself into.* Her fate hung in the plot against Draven. The first obstacle to clear would be ensuring she wasn't dragged back to the UE detention center or shot upon entering the headquarters.

Gemma eased out of her bed, sore and stiff from the beatings to open her bedroom window. It was a smoky night, a lingering effect of God's recent judgment of the world. She wanted to grab the phone and call Christopher asking him to save her. Omega was the only insurance against Draven available, given the uncertainty of her employment going forward. Gemma picked up the only phone in the world that could reach Christopher and Omega and placed a call. She hoped to find a friendly voice and reassurance, instead the call went to voicemail. She placed the phone on the charger and climbed back into bed, praying she found a few hours of sleep before facing the unknown.

❧

The dread of returning to the command suite of the UE eased when Gemma discovered Draven out of the office. The other executive suite staffers peered above computer monitors. She heard faint whispers condemning her as she strode to her desk. Gemma placed her personal effects on her desk and retrieved the folder with the traitor memo from an envelope. She held her head up, striding toward Evan Mallory's office as the sound of keystrokes returned to the rest of the cubicles. Fighting to maintain her composure, she knocked on Evan's door.

Evan was watching his office television. A look of shock rose on his face as he noticed it was Gemma. Instead of acknowledging her presence, Evan picked up a memo pretending to be busy while holding up a hand. Gemma knew he meant to insult her as she suffered more indignity watching Evan arranging papers on his desk.

Gemma hugged her arms over her chest. *I should leave. Run away before it's too late.*

Evan waved her into his office before Gemma could act on her thoughts. "Gemma, you're either really brave or really stupid for coming back to the headquarters. I'm not sure yet which description fits you."

Gemma pushed every ounce of dignity and pride from her body as she began to plead as Conti had directed. "Sir, I love my job. I love serving the Secretary-General and you. I realize that I was wrong not to inform the Secretary-General or you that something was off with Gabriella. I assure you I had no idea of the details of her activities. I accept my punishment, but I wanted to prove to the Secretary-General that he could have confidence in me. I want to turn over a document that I discovered in some of my personal effects. Michael Sutton in the UE resource office has been smuggling funds to resistance groups."

Gemma slid the memo Conti had prepared to Evan. He stared at her longer than she desired before reading the memo.

"Where did you get this?" Evan questioned.

"I had it—"

Evan cut off Gemma. "I understand what you've told me, but I know for a fact that UE security officers tore through everything you owned and your old apartment."

"Sir, I hid the document in a false pocket within my Bible. I figured I could use it as leverage against Michael if I ever need something."

Gemma tried to keep her composure, but she felt Evan was not buying the story. She silently prayed, *God help me.*

Evan ran his hands through his grayer than usual hair before hitting his intercom. "Jenny, get security up to my office immediately and patch me through to the Secretary-General."

"Sir, please I am telling you the truth," Gemma shouted.

"Don't move, Gemma, or it will be your last steps," Evan said as he placed his office phone on speaker while it rang for Draven Cross.

Gemma almost fainted at Draven's voice. "Evan, what do you want?"

"Sir, Gemma is standing in my office begging for me not to kill her and to welcome her back into the inner circle."

Gemma began crying as Draven swore, calling her horrible names. "This is trivial, Evan. Kill her and move on to important matters like improving my global image."

"Well, sir, it's not that easy. Gemma produced a memo outlining Gabriella working with Michael Sutton from UE resources supporting terror groups like Omega."

Gemma winced as the fury of Draven streamed across the phone in colorful words. "Check the veracity of the memo. If Gemma is proven right, then she can have her old job back. If she lied, kill her where she stands. Keep me on speaker; I don't want to miss this."

Evan directed Gemma to sit in one of his office chairs as he entered an account number from the memo into the UE data network.

Gemma prayed Conti had not set her up. *I swear I will take that pompous man down with me.*

Gemma began to sweat and felt ill when UE security arrived as Evan finished reading over the details of the account provided.

A shout from Draven over the phone caused Gemma to jump. "Get on with it, Evan. Did you confirm the truth of the memo?"

"Sir, Gemma was telling the truth. Sutton diverted millions of UE dollars to various off-shore accounts."

Gemma heard Draven call her name for the first time in almost a month. "Gemma, my dear, I hope you've learned a valuable lesson. Your only loyalty is to me. The reason you're alive now is linked to you providing something useful. Remember, Gemma, I never keep things that have no value. You've earned my mercy by exposing the depths of Gabriella's treachery. I permit you to serve me once more."

Gemma could only nod acceptance. The tears and sobs overtook any sense of dignity she had remaining. The realization she had been spared from the hands of the UE broke the emotional shackles she was bound by for the past 24 hours. She also felt shame knowing that whoever Michael Sutton was, he faced his final moments of life. Evan thankfully took her emotion as gratitude.

God, thank you and forgive me, Gemma prayed silently.

"Sir, Gemma is a little overwhelmed with your mercy. I know she is glad to be back with us. I will eliminate Sutton right now."

Gemma watched as the UE security team departed to find Michael Sutton. She regained her composure as Evan turned his attention back to her.

"I am glad you proved your loyalty. Though, you're a bad judge of character and it cost you. You should have turned in Gabriella and saved yourself this pain. Back to work."

"Thank you, sir," Gemma said.

As Gemma returned to her desk between Draven's office and Evan's within the UE command suite, she found taped to her computer monitor a "welcome back gift" from her coworkers. Written in red marker, a piece of printer paper read, "TRAITOR." Gemma grew warm, and her face flushed. She fought an urge to run from the office and crawl into her bed, never to return. Instead, she pulled the paper from her monitor and ripped it into small pieces, announcing her thoughts on the matter.

Before Gemma could get settled in, Evan hovered in front of her desk. "Gemma, I will need you to compile a list of candidates to replace a security member from the Secretary-General's detail. It seems he had a secret life that caught up to him in a violent way last night."

Gemma wanted to say Alberto's death ensured Draven's. Instead, she said, "Yes, sir, you will have the list within the hour."

Evan said, "Excellent. I am sure your colleagues have given you a proper reception. I know we're all thrilled you're back in the fold."

The loud volume and tone Evan took told Gemma all she need to know about the office environment. She refused to give Evan or anyone in the headquarters the satisfaction of seeing her in pain. "It was good to see all the old smiling faces."

A smirk rose on Evan's fake-tanned face. "Get that list to me as soon as possible. I don't like the boss to have less than a full complement of security."

Gemma delayed long enough to make it seem like she put together a list of security team replacements. After twenty minutes of going through folders on her computer and a backlogged email inbox, she pulled out the three dossiers that Pontiff Conti provided and added a few files from the initial security team candidate pool that did not make the cut. Gemma then walked to Evan's office for the second time today.

She knocked on Evan's door. "Sir, I'm bringing you a list of candidates to replace the slain security team member for the Secretary-General."

"Gemma come in. The Secretary-General was not pleased to begin his travel itinerary today, minus a security officer. Proactive work is why I missed you. The efficiency you operate with is unmatched. Where did the candidates come from?"

Gemma paused, as Evan's question pierced her soul. She understood from this day forward she would always need to lie, to cover every step to stay alive. *This is going to be exhausting.*

"Sir, I used the alternate list from the initial selection of the security team, as we've already vetted these men. I assumed you would want to pick a replacement before the Secretary-General returned."

For the second time in a still early day, Gemma studied Evan as he sat back in his oversized brown leather chair reviewing a document that if its origins were discovered would mean the end of her life.

Gemma watched Evan flash a porcelain-veneered fake smile. "Nice work, Gemma. Sit for a moment as I look at the candidates."

"Sir, I should get back to my desk; I'm sure I have thousands of emails awaiting me."

Evan said, "Nonsense. Have a seat; this won't take long."

Gemma squeezed her hands as she sat in front of Evan. She felt beads of sweat forming on her forehead as Evan scoured the dossiers. She expected Evan would scream obscenities at her any moment, exposing the deceit she supplied in the documents.

"Gemma," Evan said.

The sound of her name caused her to flinch.

"This is our man. Demir Ersoy. Born in London to Turkish immigrant parents. He studied at Sandhurst and served in the SAS. He even received the Victoria Cross for action in the Middle East; I'm lost in why we didn't pick this guy from the beginning. Demir makes the other two candidates look like amateurs."

"I'm sure that was the point," Gemma murmured a bit too loud.

"What did you say?" Evan challenged.

"It sounds like I was on point with the selections."

"Yes, you nailed the candidate pool."

Evan read "Demir works as a grounds security guard here at headquarters. Mindboggling that even within the greatest organization in human history, we cannot get talent management right. What a waste of talent, checking identification as people enter the building. Let the grounds security supervisor know that effective today, Demir will work on the Secretary-General's security detail."

Gemma stood to take the dossiers from Evan when she noticed a partially obscured document on his cluttered desk that read, "Gabriella, no change in status. Robben Island, South Africa."

Evan stood at his desk. "Go. Let me know if the security folks give you any trouble about Demir."

Gemma wanted to smile based on what she glimpsed but chose a simple head nod instead. "I have all I need to get the job done."

She hurried back to her desk, pulling her phone from her purse. Christopher needed to know where Gabriella was located. Gemma prayed as she walked toward the elevator for the lobby floor. *"God, keep Gabriella safe until Christopher can get there.*

After Gemma entered the UE gardens, she looked around, attempting to be cautious as Gabriella had instructed. She glanced at the note, thought of her dear friend imprisoned, and made the call to Christopher.

The phone rang, but he didn't pick up. "Oh, Christopher, where are you?"

The beep of the incoming text message brought a spike to her heart rate, anticipating Christopher's response.

Instead, the text read: *I am a friend of General Havid.*

Gemma clicked the phone display and began reading the message. *Good day, Ms. Sutherland. My name is Jonathan. I serve as General Benjamin Havid's aide. He's detained at a maximum-security Israeli prison named* Hekal Emah. *Gilana can provide details of the prison. General Havid wants Christopher and the others to know he is well and his location. While the general did not ask for rescue, I ask that Omega do all possible to free the general from such an undignified place. Don't respond to my messages. I will contact you in the future.*

Gemma deleted the text message and switched to the keypad on her phone to call Christopher. The phone went straight to voicemail. She reopened the text app on her phone to send Christopher a message, hoping it would reach him.

Gemma felt relief and worry at the same time. She had knowledge that two vital people in the fight against Draven were alive and had their locations. Gemma began walking back to her desk, hoping the man who could change the fates of Gabriella and the general got the message.

CHAPTER 12

JACKSON COULD TELL by the expression on Christopher and Gilana's faces he had missed something important. He excused himself from Kerim and Adil, walking over to Christopher and Gilana.

However, Christopher waved him off. "Give Gilana a second."

Jackson raised his hands in mocking surrender. "Hold your horses, college boy. I can see that something is wrong, and I'm concerned. Gilana, I'm here for you when you want to talk."

Jackson watched a smile break across Christopher's and Gilana's faces.

"What's got you two so tickled?" Jackson asked.

Gilana wrapped her arms around Jackson's neck and shouted, "I accepted Jesus!"

Jackson twirled the powerful physique of Gilana through the air as if she were a child in the arms of her father. The scene caused the others in the expansive room to move toward Jackson, Gilana, and Christopher. "Oh, man. I've prayed for this moment for what feels like forever."

"Put me down, Jackson." Gilana laughed. "But thank you for praying for me."

Jackson stood back and smiled as Kerim, Adil, and the others enveloped Gilana, welcoming her to the family of Jesus Christ.

When Jackson turned and saw the face of Christopher, his smile faded. "I thought you would be happier."

Jackson acknowledged Christopher's head nod, leading him to follow his friend. They walked toward the corridor where Jackson had watched Gilana and Christopher emerge from moments ago.

"Hey, what's up with the sound of rushing water?"

Jackson's question met with silence as Christopher held open a door that led to a deck. Jackson peered through the door to see a waterfall shimmering in the fading sunlight. The spectacular view ended as Christopher closed the door.

Jackson said, "That was amazing, but I'm sure that's not why you brought me back here."

Christopher's shoulders dropped. "I think Gemma tried to reach us. I'm heading outside where I can get better satellite coverage to call her back. Let's pray that whatever Gemma has to say is not bad news about Gabriella or General Havid."

Jackson ran his hands through his auburn-brown hair. "I could kill that son of the devil Draven, when I think about everything Gabriella and General Havid are going through. Well, get up top and call Gemma back and let's find out what's going on. I will stand by with the rest of the team."

Jackson turned and followed Christopher back into the corridor leading to the main area of the facility when he almost fell down after Christopher made an abrupt stop in front of him. "What's the problem?"

Christopher moved by Jackson. "I received a text message from Gemma. Follow me out to the deck so I can try to get a better signal."

While the men opened the door to the deck, Gilana shouted after them, with Kerim and Adil following her, "Hey, what are you two doing?"

Jackson waved for them to follow.

Christopher read Gemma's note as the group formed near him to hear the message over the raging water.

It read: *Christopher and team. I've discovered that both General Havid and Gabriella are alive. The general is at an Israeli prison,* Hekal Emah. *Jonathan, the general's aide, told me that Gilana would understand the details of this location. Draven detained Gabriella at a UE political prison on Robben Island, South Africa. It's been a rough go for me here. Draven tried to get information on Gabriella and you, but I resisted and remain committed to serve. There's much more going on, but I don't have the time to discuss now. I hope this information allows you to plan the respective rescues. Respond by text, but don't call me as I may be in the UE HQ. God Bless you. I am praying for you, Gemma.*

The revelation stunned the group of covert warriors.

Jackson broke the silence. "Gemma is in more trouble than a cow that wandered into a butcher shop. Let's head back inside and talk about our next move."

CHAPTER 13

As KERIM, ADIL, and Gilana discussed the news of Gemma's text, Christopher pulled Jackson aside. "Before we jump into Gemma's note, who are the other six people working with Adil?"

Jackson pursed his lips. "They're not soldiers. Adil rescued them from the UE and brought them here. The most relevant skill set anyone in the group has is cooking."

"Well, that leaves us short on... " Christopher didn't finish his thought. His heart sunk. The realization that having only five, including himself, military-trained personnel meant either Gabriella or General Havid would remain in UE custody longer than desired.

Christopher and Jackson rejoined Kerim, Adil, Gilana, and the now six identified civilians. He tapped Adil on his narrow shoulders. "Could you ask the non-military folks to give us a moment?"

Adil nodded, speaking in Mandarin, before returning his attention to Christopher. "They will get the evening meal started."

Christopher affirmed Adil's gesture. "We face a hard truth. We cannot save Gabriella and General Havid simultaneously with our personnel. It will take—"

Christopher saw the hope fall from Gilana's face as she cut him off. "How can you say that? We can get help to rescue the general. There are five of us standing here, all trained in irregular warfare. If we can't free them both simultaneously, then the general must be our focus."

Before Christopher could respond, Adil spoke up, "Please forgive my intrusion; I cannot leave my people to fight in this struggle. Many need me here; my fight is against the UE in China."

Christopher struggled to gain control of the meeting as Gilana shouted, "Fine, we don't need Adil. We can find others to help us fight. Jarrah has fighters in Australia. Call him!"

The tears racing down Gilana's olive-toned face made the dejection of Christopher's announcement palpable amongst the warriors. Christopher forced himself to speak the truth. "Gilana, I feel your pain. I'm not saying we won't try to free the general first. However, the information surrounding the prisons and given by the general, not emotion, should guide our decision. This is a team decision. Robben Island has always been a formidable location for a prison. It's remote, surrounded by shark-infested waters and doesn't take a lot of men to hold off an assault. I trained with African Union nation special forces there in the pre-Rapture world. My guess, given the UE like everyone is short on personnel, Robben Island will be our easiest attempt at a rescue."

Christopher cleared his throat. "Jonathan relayed a key message from the general. First, the general mentioned Gilana knew some of the details of the prison where he's being held. The most critical thing from the general was the fact he didn't say plan for his escape. My last point like Adil, Jarrah has a fight he must wage and can't help us. Freeing our friends will fall on our shoulders."

Christopher took a step back as Gilana closed the distance between them, drawing near his face. "I see. So, you want all of us to save your girlfriend, Gabriella, but the general whose life hangs in the balance because he protected you, you will do nothing."

"Who do you think you are, Gilana? I've bled for you, the general, everyone! Yes, I want to save Gabriella, but she is not my girlfriend. And I would take the same approach if you were in her place. I want the general back, but not at the cost of anyone's life! Gabriella and General Havid are both believers. We are at war; they both accepted the risk of fighting Draven. If you want to be mad about the general, look in the mirror; he's in prison for not selling you out, not me!"

The anger subsided to regret as Christopher watched Gilana retreat from the argument, standing away from the group of men but within earshot, staring daggers at Christopher.

Before Christopher could say anything, Jackson whispered aloud, "Brother, you went too far there. You need to make it right before we can move forward."

Christopher starred at Jackson and the others. "I'm not trying to be mean or show favor to Gabriella. My assumption is General Havid's location is more secure than Robben Island, based on my limited experience with Robben Island. Am I correct, Gilana?"

The group turned to Gilana, who refused to acknowledge the question.

Jackson walked over to Gilana. "I know the college boy got a little personal in what he said, but the only way we get the general and Gabriella back is by working together. I know deep down you want both of them back alive, so please help us figure out the next move."

"Gilana, I'm sorry if I hurt you. That was not my intent. Please forgive me," Christopher added.

Everyone watched as Gilana wiped her face and approached Christopher, slugging his right arm.

"Ouch, I take that punch as forgiveness."

Gilana half-smiled. "*Hekal Emah* is the most secure prison in Israel. The facility houses dangerous terrorists and hardened criminals. Each guard is selected from Israeli special operations units. There is a rotation for the guards to mitigate sympathizing with a prisoner.

"I once debriefed a terrorist there, and I can tell you it will take luck to get by the guards. If we get through, we will need God to bypass the technology that locks the cell doors. If all of that is not enough for an added layer of trouble, a nearby IDF garrison directly supports the prison. I doubt Gabriella's facility is more secure; if it is, then we have little hope of saving either of them."

Even with Gilana's detailed description of *Hekal Emah*, Christopher wanted more information to decide who to rescue first. He hated to say it aloud. "We need to ask Gemma for help. I will ask her for the schematics of the facilities. Kerim and Adil start identifying any potential resistance elements willing to give us a hand. Jackson and Gilana work on a tentative plan of getting the general out, based on Gilana's description. I'm going to send a message to Gemma. But before I head up to talk to her, Jackson, is there anything with the second trumpet judgment we can leverage?"

Jackson sucked air into his cheeks before exhaling loudly. "The hard thing about these judgments is knowing when the next one will start. The Bible doesn't lay out a timeline for between the judgments. I will say the UE will be busy with the next judgment that will turn a sea to blood. We may have a window for a rescue once the UE is distracted."

Christopher said, "I agree that based on what the second trumpet judgment will bring, we need to plan to be in position to rescue either the general or Gabriella once the event happens."

Christopher watched with faint hope as his ragtag and fragile team moved to save their dear friends. Besides speaking with Gemma, Christopher needed a moment to hear from God. He walked back toward the underground facility entrance instead of the waterfall deck, hoping for a better signal on his phone and with God outside.

After emerging from the underground shelter, Christopher took a moment to soak in his surroundings. From the first trumpet judgment, a mix of the burned vegetation and surviving wildflowers scented the cool night air refreshing Christopher's warm face. He thanked God for his mercy and prayed that the Omega members with him and those detained by the enemy would live until Jesus's return.

Christopher pulled out his cell phone and sent Gemma a text message: *I hate to ask you, but I need more information on the Robben Island detention facility and* Hekal Emah *prison. I need the structural layout, the number of guards, and where Gabriella and General Havid are located, if possible, in their respective prisons. This may seem overwhelming, but it's vital information. Follow up with me if you have questions.*

After Christopher finished his message to Gemma, Gilana called out from the bunker entrance, "Christopher, the Two Witnesses made an announcement on the next judgment."

Christopher thought, *I hope this is an opportunity, Lord.* He walked back toward the facility entrance, wondering what challenges the latest judgment of God would bring for his team and him.

❧

Christopher followed Gilana into a media room next to the main hall. Kerim, Adil, Jackson, and the six civilians were sitting on plush loungers, watching ANN's coverage of Reuel and Eliyahu's proclamation of a pending judgment from Jerusalem.

Christopher first noticed the right image on the split-screen view of the ANN report. "Is that asteroid a part of the judgment?"

His question drew a loud "shish" from the group in the room. He took the hint to be quiet and pay attention.

As Christopher took a seat next to Jackson, Jackson leaned over and whispered, "The Witnesses announced the second trumpet judgment almost an hour ago. The asteroid *is* a part of the judgment. They're about to run a replay so listen."

Reuel and Eliyahu began a late evening sermon, pointing to a mega screen in the Wailing Wall Plaza that broadcast the Witnesses to the world.

"Israel, hear the words of the Lord and witness his judgment on those unwilling to repent of their sins and accept Jesus Christ. *The second angel sounded his trumpet, and something like an immense mountain, all ablaze, was thrown into the sea. A third of the sea turned into blood, a third of the living creatures in the sea died, and a third of the ships were destroyed.*"

As the Two Witnesses finished speaking, the ANN camera feed moved from the two men to a massive fireball racing from deep space toward the Earth.

Christopher had more questions racing through his mind, but held back. Instead, he turned his focus to the ANN reporter covering the event.

"Good afternoon from Jerusalem; I am Sam Morrow, ANN's lead for covering the Two Witnesses. An hour ago, local time, The Witnesses decreed the asteroid bound for Earth is the next event in an ongoing saga of God's wrath on the world. However, UE Deputy Secretary-General Evan Mallory released the following statement:

'The UE Space Consortium has been tracking this object for months. The asteroid's course tracked toward Earth only in the last 24 hours, with confirmation it would strike the planet coming hours ago. Remember, it's the Two Witnesses who continue to spread hate. The UE refuses to yield. Peace will reign on Earth."

Sam Morrow continued reading as Draven's recorded image popped up on screen. "In his televised remarks, Secretary-General Cross stated that this is a natural event and not a supposed God's purposeful act. The UE is taking action now to mitigate the loss of life in the Mediterranean region."

The camera snapped back to the live scene. "It seems the Two Witnesses fabricated natural events to support their claims. I am Sam Morrow, returning you to the ANN center in Rome."

Adil stood and turned off the TV while speaking Mandarin to the six civilians who departed the room. He turned to the remaining group of operatives. "So, what will you do? What do I need to do with my people now?"

Silence settled into the media room. Christopher knew nothing to do but wait for the literal and proverbial dust to relax after the second trumpet judgment. "We will need to wait for any rescues until after this upcoming judgment. I have sent a message to Gemma asking for more info on Robben Island. Gemma's update in the best-case scenario provides an informed decision on who to rescue. The second judgment may give a window to save either General Havid or Gabriella."

"I am glad to hear you've not decided who to rescue yet," Gilana said.

"Let's hope that time improves the decision. I pray Gemma gives us what we need, and our friends survive until we can save them."

❧

Gabriella felt a weight rise from her mind with each day passing regarding the angel's words about not being tortured, holding true. She had found a rugged sense of normalcy for prison life. The Lord's mercy extended to a guard assigned to her, a Zulu woman named Amahle. A smile rose on Gabriella's face, lying on her cot, thinking of Amahle. The two women discovered a set of shared secrets that bound them together; they were both Christians and hated the UE.

The rattle of keys in Gabriella's cell door caused her to sit up. Sweat under her arms and the churning of her stomach rose over her each time the cell door opened. The wave of terror faded as she took in the smiling face of Amahle. Amahle's always cheerful ebony complexion radiated joy as she hurried toward Gabriella with a tray of food.

"It looks like pure happiness is bursting from you today."

Amahle sat next to Gabriella, pulling a chair from the small card table where Gabriella ate what the UE described as meals.

Amahle smiled, watching Gabriella eat. "I could finally do it."

"Do what?" Gabriella asked between bites of biltong.

Amahle pulled a sweat-covered, linen-wrapped book from under her uniform blouse, laying it on Gabriella's bunk.

Gabriella grabbed Amahle's hand. "Thank you for thinking about me."

Gabriella pulled the wet linen off the book to reveal a Bible Amahle provided. She hid it under a blanket, fearing someone would see it.

The strong-calloused hands of Amahle squeezed Gabriella's shoulders. "Let me remind you again, there are no cameras here. I also knew that the 'scheduled random' searching of guards entering the facility would not occur today. I'm not foolish."

"Thank you. This means more to me than I can tell you."

"This is a small gift. I wish I could free you. If my brother Nkosinathi… " She paused, staring at Gabriella.

"What is it? Why are you staring at me?"

Gabriella said, "His name is Nkosiany?"

Amahle laughed. "Good try, but we call him Nkoie."

"Yes, the pronouncing of your brother's name was at the front of my mind."

Gabriella used the moment of levity as a break before verbalizing the crazy idea racing through her mind. "Amahle, I want to ask you to do something. This thing is dangerous. I can help your wish to free me become a reality. It's okay to refuse my request. I value your life more than my freedom."

Amahle flashed a bright smile. "What did the Lord Jesus tell us about being a friend?"

Gabriella's cheeks flushed, as she didn't know the answer, and she shook her head.

Amahle continued smiling. "You can look this up later in your new gift. In John 15:13, Jesus says, '*Greater love has no one than this: to lay down one's life for one's friends.*' If Nkoie's resistance group were better equipped, I would ask him to free you."

As she lifted her head to meet the gentle eyes of Amahle. Gabriella said, "Thanks, Amahle. I have a group of friends who can help your brother's team become better fighters against the UE and save me. I want you to text this number a message detailing my location. Do you think you can memorize the number?"

Amahle studied the phone number Gabriella scribbled on her hand for a few minutes, before saying, "I got it."

"Amahle, be careful and never call this number, only text. Thank you," Gabriella said.

Excitement rose on Amahle's face and in her voice, as she said, "I will go now and send the message. Don't lose hope in God; you will be free soon."

Gabriella stood and watched her friend depart the cell, carrying a prospect for freedom. She prayed Christopher saved her before the UE killed her.

❧

CHAPTER 14

DRAVEN GREW ANGRY thinking about his tarnished global image as UE One taxied across the Buenos Aires Ezeiza International Airport tarmac in the shadows of the late afternoon sun. Buenos Aires was the latest stop in his effort to reshape his public perception against the onslaught by the Two Witnesses, Reuel and Eliyahu, and from the Interfaith religion. He created a rival in a twist of irony by using the Interfaith religion to unify the world to his vision. Now he had to play a dangerous game of promoting himself over the newfound religious beliefs of billions.

The world expected Draven to coddle their fears, leading them toward a reality where all was well. It was exhausting trying to garner public support. He'd rather the world fear than love him any day, but his hidden mentor, the Prince of This World, had never guided him wrong. Conti's ruse of using rallies potently combined religion and in-person charisma to woo the weak-minded rabble searching for hope. He appreciated the power false hope gave him over the world. What he didn't care for was Conti's attempts to elevate himself above him as the source of hope.

As the plane came to a stop and a band played, Draven resigned himself to the duty of winning the war for the hearts and minds of the world over the Interfaith religion and the Two Witnesses' attacks on him. He knew the day would come when fear would be all he needed for control. He stood atop the mobile airstairs, waving to the ANN cameras and a crowd. People hand-selected for loyalty by the office of Unified Latin America States Ambassador Matías Fernández. Draven bounded down the stairs and along the deep red carpet, shaking hands with Fernández before approaching a lectern stuffed with microphones.

Draven held his hands up to calm the adoring crowd, before saying in flawless Spanish, "Ambassador Fernández, your region shines. A golden example of the UE's future. So, to the Unified Latin America States people, rest easy. The world is getting better by the day."

A security guard rushed onto the stage, cutting off Draven's speech. The guard covered the microphones. "The massive asteroid's impact is imminent; we need to get you to safety now."

Draven struggled against the tugs of his security detail, dragging him to Matías Fernández's up-armored sedan and on to El Palomar Military Air Base outside of Buenos Aires. He paused as shrieks rose from the fleeing crowd as all eyes turned to the sizeable high-definition video monitor that displayed what looked like a burning mountain racing toward the planet. As security shoved Draven into the sedan, he pulled out his cell phone and dialed Evan Mallory.

Evan enjoyed seeing the arrogant John Barnes writhe under the torment of waterboarding. Barnes had been a source of misery for Evan from the moment he joined the UE. The torture Evan scheduled for failing to eliminate the Omega team had been underway for two hours when Draven rang his phone.

"Sir, I am enjoying punishing Barnes—"

Draven interrupted Evan, swearing. "Get to the command center and find out where the asteroid is going to impact."

"I'm not tracking the asteroid, sir."

Draven swore again. "Are you daft? My initial statement would have been different if I realized you were tracking the asteroid. Call me back when you get in the command center with my desired answer."

Evan's phone went dead. He banged on the two-way mirrored glass separating him from Barnes's debriefing session. As Evan stepped out of the observation room to brief the guards assaulting Barnes, his phone rang again.

"Yes, Gemma. I know there is a crisis. I'm on my way."

He turned his attention to the guard assailing John Barnes moments ago.

"Slap Barnes around for an hour longer, then send him to the infirmary. I will deal with him later. Ensure you don't break any bones. I will need to put him in the field soon."

Evan jogged toward the central UE HQ building and the command center to determine the extent of the latest disaster facing the world.

⚚

The UE command center was a cauldron of chaos as Evan entered. Phones across the center were ringing unanswered as the understaffed UE headquarters attempted to better understand the threat racing toward the world. Evan noticed next to the massive central video monitor, which displayed the impending flaming doom, was a small bank of monitors replaying the message of the Two Witnesses. He ignored Gemma and the other senior staffers, clamoring for his attention, all seeking answers he couldn't provide.

He held up his hands. "One at a time, I can't hear you babbling all at once."

Evan pointed to the liver-spotted face of the chief UE scientist, Dr. Gerrit Jacobsen, for the critical answer of what options were available. "Dr. Jacobson, we can stop this thing, correct?"

Dr. Gerrit Jacobsen adjusted his wired-framed bifocals and ruffled his snow-white hair. A lower pitch fell over the command center as he answered, "There is no need to stop the asteroid. The 350 meters in diameter asteroid hurtling toward us is, moving at a speed of 31,000 miles per hour, placing impact in 45 mins. The asteroid will land between Italy, Sardinia, and Sicily in the Tyrrhenian Sea. Most of the impact energy will vaporize the surrounding ocean. The resulting wave will be minor by the time it reaches any coastline. It will be an unprecedented event in modern human history, but the world will be fine."

Dr. Jacobsen's decree sent UE staff officers scrambling. Some raced toward their desk to start the emergency warning system for the unsuspecting global population, while others froze in shock.

Before Evan could respond to the surrounding panic, his phone rang, displaying Draven's phone number. "Dr. Jacobsen, your life hangs on the Secretary-General accepting that answer."

"Provide me an update," Draven ordered.

"Sir, the asteroid will land in the Mediterranean, 500 miles southwest of Rome. We expect minor damage at the headquarters, as the impact is in the middle of the ocean. However, we expect a massive tsunami to produce localized flooding and lost vessels across the region within the hour," Evan said.

Draven challenged. "Is there nothing we can launch to destroy the asteroid? A nuclear weapon, perhaps?"

"I'm afraid not, sir. It's moving too fast."

"Fine. The end state will produce fewer people for me to concern myself over. I will be on the television in five minutes." Draven ended the call.

Evan returned his attention to Dr. Jacobsen. He watched the doctor wipe his brow with a linen handkerchief as he wrote something at a fevered pace.

The doctor's demeanor prompted Evan to ask, "Dr. Jacobson, what are you doing? How can you sit and work a mathematics equation during the present situation, given I hold your life in my hands?"

Dr. Jacobson held up a hand as he finished working the math. The doctor then stepped back and steepled his hands. "Mr. Mallory, math and science provide the truth and clarity in moments of disorder. I wanted to have precise assurance if you failed to convince the Secretary-General of my situation estimation. My calculations confirm that neither you nor I have anything to fear."

Evan said, "Lucky for you, the Secretary-General accepted your conclusions." He then turned to Gemma, who looked mesmerized by the loop of Reuel and Eliyahu. "Don't worry about those two fools. By this time tomorrow, the media will counter their narrative that this is another judgment of God."

⌇

Now back at her desk in the UE command suite, Gemma pulled her cell phone out to update Christopher and Omega on the pending doom, when the noise of a scuffle stopped her. She stood to see two UE security guards dragging John Barnes into Evan's office. Her curiosity pushed her to delay updating the Omega team to discover the fate of John Barnes.

Gemma burst into Evan's office to find Barnes huddled in a chair in front of Evan's desk with the two guards on either side of him. She did little to hide the shock of seeing Barnes's face swollen and bloody. Barnes's clothes were filthy with sweat, tears, and by the smell attacking Gemma's nose, his own waste. The once-arrogant man looked broken and near death.

Evan's sharp tone snapped Gemma from staring at Barnes. "Gemma, I'm glad you're here. It seems Mr. Barnes had a run of bad luck, failing several key missions. The good news is I've provided him the guidance he needs to move forward. I need you to secure lodging for him until the Secretary-General decides his fate."

Gemma looked at Barnes, who didn't respond. In shame, the disgraced man kept his head down. Barnes must have received the similar "guidance" she had for being a friend of Gabriella.

"I will take care of the lodging for John. But, sir, I also wanted to determine what we needed, what final preparations before the asteroid arrives?"

Evan propped his feet on his desk, smiling as he clicked on his large television. "Gemma, lose that worry from your lovely face. There is nothing to fear. I expect some localized flooding along the coast, but the headquarters complex is safe. And you two"—Evan's attention shifted to the guards with John Barnes—"get him out of here. He smells like an animal."

Gemma pursed her lips, conflicted in thought as a humiliated and defeated Barnes was paraded through the UE HQ. Draven and Evan enjoyed shaming others, something she had lived through; at the moment, a part of her wanted Barnes to find Christ and help fight against Draven.

As Gemma turned to leave the office, Evan stopped her. "Stay and watch the show. I may need to task you after the big splash."

Gemma failed to find humor in the imminent judgment of God against a rebellious world. Countless people would die or suffer in the days ahead. She sat in a chair watching the ANN coverage as a timer showed 18 minutes to impact. As the minutes to impact dwindled, Gemma's anxiety grew. There was also a red banner displaying cities and countries under tsunami evacuation orders rolling across the bottom of the screen. The callousness of the UE staff members gathering to watch the nightmare was unbearable. Yet, Gemma was not surprised by blindness of others to God's plan unfolding before their very eyes. She had been unconcerned with religion and especially Christianity, but despite serving so near the center of evil, she was eternally grateful she accepted Jesus Christ as her savior. Gemma, considered it a blessing as Evan turned up the volume over narrating imminent disaster.

The local ANN Media Center began coverage of the asteroid's last moments as other staffers gathered near his office door. "Good day, I am Stewart Davis. ANN's Sam Morrow joins us from Jerusalem, reporting on the Two Witnesses. The senior member of our panel is the UE lead science advisor, Dr. Gerrit Jacobsen. Thank you to my guest for helping our viewing audience understand this historic event. We are now less than 15 minutes away from the asteroid splashing down. Sam, have the Two Witnesses said anything further?"

On the split screen, Sam Morrow adjusted her sandy brown hair from her face at the Wailing Wall Plaza. "No new statements. They continue calls for repentance and acceptance of Jesus Christ."

The picture on the television moved back to the ANN Rome studios and Stewart Davis. "Dr. Jacobsen, we are receiving reports from the UE that their unmanned drones in the area show fragments have fallen in the impact zone. I understand one of your degrees is in astrophysics. Can you describe for the viewing audience what to expect in the last minutes before impact?"

The screen filled with Dr. Jacobsen's face, with the UE Command Center behind him. "The fragment impacts our drones are observing show the asteroid is disintegrating in the upper atmosphere. The viewing audience along the Mediterranean coastline may experience flooding based on elevation, but no significant threat beyond the immediate impact area. These religious zealots in Jerusalem don't understand science; this asteroid will not produce the damage they've predicted."

Gemma tried to block out the curses against God and the Witnesses from a few staff members after Dr. Jacobsen's announcement. She didn't fight the tears back, knowing that the second trumpet judgment was far worse than what Dr. Jacobsen envisioned. Gemma's attention returned to the television as Stewart Davis announced the impact.

Her heart skipped a beat watching a three-mile-high column of seawater envelope the fireball as the asteroid struck the sea, turning the bright morning scene dark as night. The subsequent violent explosion waves raced away from the center of impact, like the results from rocks Gemma had thrown in a pond near her home as a child. The energy waves destroyed the nearby camera drones, causing a blackout. ANN diverted the live event to drones farther away, as technology attempted to keep up with tragedy.

ANN then switched coverage 400 miles away to Tortoli, Sardinia. Gemma looked on in awe as disaster gawkers turned into a sizeable crowd gathered at the edge of turquoise waters and powder-white beaches to experience whatever the asteroid held for them. ANN cameras panned the shimmering waves of the Mediterranean for any signs of increased activity.

Moments later, as the first impact waves reached the Sardinian coast, screams rose from the crowd, and ANN broke away to the media center in Rome.

"This is Stewart Davis, back here at the ANN media center in Rome. We seemed to have some difficulties in Sardinia but will have an update from there soon."

Gemma watched panic rise on Evan's face as his cell and office phones began ringing. He yelled at Gemma to answer his office phone as he put his cell phone to his ear.

Gemma responded to the UE command center on his office phone. "Please hold."

She knew Evan was trying to appease Draven on his cell phone, based on his apologies and vows to get an answer.

Gemma and everyone else in Evan's office paused as ANN moved back to Sardinia. The screams and blaring of emergency signals made it hard to understand the ANN reporter.

"Good afternoon. This is Francisco Serra. It's hard to describe what we see here on Tortoli beach. The waves grew to about 10 feet high and turned from water to blood. Spilling on the beachfront, sweeping many out to sea."

Stewart Davis interrupted Francesco, "Did you say blood?"

"Yes, the sea has turned to blood. Ships are sinking in the harbor, and the people exposed to the waves are dying. The stench is unbearable. I will try to continue to report later; I am sending coverage back to you in Rome."

Evan screamed expletives. He threw the television remote at the TV cracking the screen. "Someone get me an answer now."

Gemma attempted to hand him his office phone, but Evan waved her off. "Put it on speaker."

Gemma hit the speaker button. "Go ahead; Deputy Mallory is listening."

"Sir, reports are flooding in that the entire Mediterranean Sea is turning to blood," a UE Command Center Officer said.

Gemma stepped back from Evan's desk as he fumed, interrupting the UE officer. "Stop saying the water is blood. That's impossible. It makes no sense. Get samples of this stuff and figure it out."

Gemma almost felt sorry for Evan as his cell phone rang. She watched Evan attempt to smooth his graying hair with his hands before answering Draven again. Gemma took Evan's distraction and the growing pandemonium from the second trumpet judgment to leave and update those depending on her.

CHAPTER 15

GEMMA HURRIED BACK to her desk and grabbed her cellphone. There were two text messages. One from Christopher and the second from an unknown sender with the subject header, "Friend of Gabriella."

Gemma opened the friend of Gabriella's message first. She began reading: *Hello. My name is Amahle, and I serve as a guard at the Robben Island UE prison. I have become friends with Gabriella as we share a love for Jesus Christ. My brother Nkoie leads a UE resistance group here in South Africa. Gabriella's idea is to introduce Nkoie's group to her 'military friends.' I am sure you know what Gabriella means by military friends. I want to add that time is running out for Gabriella. Execution occurs for prisoners within three months of arriving at Robben Island. The UE lies about the rehabilitation of prisoners here. Therefore, there is only a month remaining before Gabriella's execution date. I dare not tell her, as she has endured much already. I will look for your response soon, Amahle."*

Gemma had to calm herself as autocorrect kept changing her excited mistakes during her response to Amahle: *Thank you for taking the risk of passing this message. I, too, share a love for Jesus. I will ensure that the right people get this message and start planning to free Gabriella. Your sister in Christ Jesus, Gemma."*

Gemma scrolled to Christopher's message.

She murmured, "Thank you, God." The focus of Christopher's note centered on saving Gabriella and General Havid.

She wrote back: *Christopher, as sad as it's been watching the second trumpet judgment, the situation creates a tremendous opportunity for Omega to save Gabriella. I say, Gabriella, as she has a scheduled execution date. I would not know where to find the general's prison plans and might die trying. I am in contact with a guard at the Robben Island facility whose brother, Nkoie, is the local resistance group leader. My guess is the UE has a distraction for the next few weeks or more. Gabriella, in my opinion, should be Omega's focus, so please waste no time on her rescue. We can expect to receive the details of Robben Island through our new friend Amahle. I will be in touch soon, Gemma."*

For the first time since being tortured, Gemma smiled at her position in life. She had a sense of purpose in God's Kingdom, minimizing Draven's effect on believers. Gemma let a smile grow as she searched for files on the Robben Island prison.

Christopher sat alone in the media room of a former Chinese military leadership bunker, trying to make sense of what he had witnessed. He thought about how he would answer what he saw if asked. The iconic blue waters of the Mediterranean Sea turning crimson red had happened. Still, he would be hard-pressed to explain the event. Christopher was unsettled and felt vulnerable by this subsequent judgment of God, despite having accepted Jesus as his savior.

There were more significant problems for him to solve than his fear of tribulation, like rescuing General Havid and Gabriella. Christopher ran his hands over his cell phone and headed outside to check for messages from Gemma.

Jackson almost ran into Christopher. "I thought you would come to eat. Those folks may not know how to shoot a weapon, but they make some amazing beef and noodles."

"I can't shake the image of the Med turning into blood," Christopher said.

"It's one of those things in life that unless you experience the event, you won't believe it. So where are you going?"

"Outside to check in with Gemma. I'll eat when I get back."

Jackson laughed. "You might not eat tonight. Don't expect any food left when you get in here."

Christopher shot back as he began climbing the stairs to exit the bunker. "You've always told me that officers eat last. So, consider me an excellent officer. Eat up, big boy."

Christopher watched Jackson laugh, wiping tears from his eyes as he returned to the communal dining space. He prayed to himself for more days with laughter, but he knew the truth. More sorrow was coming.

⍋

Darkness overtook the Rize Valley as Christopher emerged from the command bunker for a second time this evening. The cool air felt nice. The sounds of the night reminded him of camping as a Boy Scout. But as Christopher's ears attuned to the chorus of nocturnal sounds, he felt transported far away from what he knew was reality.

Christopher shook his childhood memories from his mind, pulling out his phone and dampening the backlight, which had attracted various bugs. He was excited to find an update from Gemma pointing Omega toward rescuing Gabriella first.

Christopher hit the text message icon on the phone display and responded: Gemma, I am happy that you've provided Omega a sense of direction regarding who to rescue first. I also look forward to linking up with Nkoie and his resistance group. I hate to ask more of you but welcome to supporting the team. You will need to set up air transport to South Africa for us, under the guise of the team being UE operatives. Ensure the transport carries plenty of 5.56- and 7.62-mm ammo and hand grenades for the mission ahead. Let me know when and where the transport will be located. Guangzhou was 'friendly' for covert transit, so plan for there first. Be careful. I will be in touch soon, Christopher.

Christopher turned his phone off to enjoy the evening for a

minute before returning to the bunker. The sudden stillness of the night made him uneasy. It had become too quiet. His face wrinkled, realizing he left his rifle in the bunker, leaving him with a 45 pistol and night vision goggles, if needed for protection.

At least I will see anything coming, Christopher thought.

He drew his pistol to the ready, hearing a rustling behind him, but relaxed after picking up the repetitive clicking noise that he knew came from Jackson. It was a low-visibility patrolling technique Jackson developed when they were both in the 5th Special Forces Group. Christopher repeated the tongue clicks and watched as Jackson, Gilana, Kerim, and Adil approached him.

"What's going on?" Christopher asked. "Why are you all here?"

Jackson passed Christopher's M4 assault rifle. "You're going to need this in about five minutes."

Before Christopher could ask, Adil added, "We lost power in the bunker. However, our security cameras along the road leading to the bunker alerted before the power failure. The UE is sending a three-gun truck patrol."

Christopher's heart raced as he peered down the access road leading away from the bunker to see distant white lights. "We're going to ambush the UE. Gilana and Kerim, I want you to move toward the riverside of the road and try to center yourselves on the second truck when it stops. Then, when you hear us open fire, you do the same cleaning up anybody we miss. Jackson, Adil, and I will take positions behind the front of two destroyed vehicles here at the end of the road. I will be behind the troop carrier near the mountain face, and you two by the carrier near the riverside. Now go!"

Adil approached Christopher as the others ran into the darkness. "I don't have night-vision goggles."

Christopher handed his high-tech night-vision goggles to Adil. "Take these. Tell Jackson not to fire until I do. I will target the UE soldiers' silhouettes in their vehicles' lights. You hit the ones I miss."

Relief filled Adil's eyes as he ran off to join Jackson. Moments later, the UE patrol pulled up to the destroyed obstacles, stopping their advance. He heard the truck doors open. The rushed tones of Mandarin filled the night air. Two UE soldiers stood in front of the lead vehicle, and Christopher knew they were waiting for the patrol leader to join them. He squinted against the vehicle's headlights, focusing on the UE soldiers through his riflescope, glad for the thermal capacity on the device.

As the UE patrol commander joined the two soldiers near the front vehicle, Christopher took aim. He squeezed the trigger, watching the UE commander fall from his sight. A scan of the lead vehicle found the other two soldiers were down. Additional shots rang out a few meters down the road.

Christopher stood and waited for a moment after the last shots echoed through the valley. He heard a UE soldier screaming in pain down the road, and then a rifle retort brought a stillness again to the area.

Christopher called out to the ragtag team that had again thwarted the UE. "Hey, let's go."

Christopher walked up to the lead vehicle, where the UE soldiers slumped on the ground. He found a fourth soldier collapsed back into the truck after being shot while standing in the gun turret. The steady breeze cooled him as it blew across his sweat-soaked shirt. He thanked God they had survived the moment, but he knew they were still in danger.

Christopher waited for Gilana and Kerim to join Jackson, Adil, and himself. "Is everyone okay?"

Everyone acknowledged they were fine.

Christopher then added, "We need to leave here before reinforcements come looking for this patrol and for who was using this bunker. It's time to move."

Adil spoke out, "I can't leave here. I have to look out for my people."

Christopher recognized the burden of leadership. He knew Adil was not thinking like a soldier. "Adil, I understand your feelings, but you can't stay here. The UE will send another patrol looking for this one. You're not safe."

"So, what do you suggest?" Gilana asked.

"We leave two UE gun-trucks for Adil and the six civilians. Gilana, Jackson, Kerim, and I will take the third truck. In a few minutes, I will give Gemma a call and ask her to provide some transportation to South Africa sooner rather than later," Christopher responded.

"South Africa?" Jackson questioned. "So we've settled on who we're saving first?"

Christopher held up a hand to Jackson's question waiting for Gilana and Kerim to draw close after sweeping through the falling UE for weapons and ammo. He explained to everyone that Gemma provided a critical element in their decision on who to save. Gabriella would be executed in a month if they didn't attempt a rescue. Even in the limited light of the UE vehicles, Christopher could tell that everyone took the news on Gabriella to heart. Christopher tried to summarize what he thought were the feelings of the team. "I hoped we would have a few days to plan our exit, but time is not a luxury now."

In the scattered light of vehicle headlights, Christopher attempted to study the faces of the other operatives. The decision on who to rescue first earlier was an emotional event he hoped never to repeat.

Christopher grew nervous, as Gilana was the first to speak after his explanation.

"The decision to save Gabriella is logical. There is an active UE resistance there, and the facility has less security than General Havid's prison. Plus, she is facing an execution date."

Christopher realized Gilana was speaking more to herself than to the group at the moment. He exhaled at her acceptance of the decision to rescue Gabriella first.

"Okay, let's get the civilians and whatever gear we need and get out of here," Christopher said.

Adil turned to Christopher with the night vision goggles in hand. "I pray God watches over you in the days ahead."

Christopher pushed the goggles back. "You keep those. You will need to watch over those in your care, even in the dark."

When the UE vehicle headlights illuminated a smile on Adil's face, he nodded and ran back toward the bunker, along with Gilana, Kerim, and Jackson. Christopher had a renewed sense of urgency and purpose after the violent near miss with the UE. He appreciated the mercy and provision of God. Composed and focused, Christopher pulled out his phone and texted Gemma for the next steps.

CHAPTER 16

GEMMA STOOD AMONG several staffers, taking commands from Evan. She watched the beleaguered UE deputy attempt to gain control over a situation that God ordained, when her phone vibrated in her blazer pocket. She knew it was a message from Christopher and grew distracted from the demands of Evan.

Evan yelled at Gemma. "Well, are you listening Gemma or am I boring you?"

"I am sorry, sir, please excuse me for a moment. I need to visit the loo." Gemma put on a show squirming as if she had been waiting for a while.

Evan shouted after her, "Hurry back!"

Gemma rushed to the elevators and hit the ground floor button. Once the doors opened, she moved through the UE cafeteria and into the gardens. The sun shone brightly against a brilliant blue late afternoon sky fading into the warm hues of sunset. It was 4 p.m. in Rome, meaning it was 10 p.m. for Christopher in China.

She hit the dial button to call Christopher back. "Hello, Christopher. My apologies for sending your call to voicemail. I was in Evan's office when you texted. It sounds like you're driving. Where are you?"

"Yes. We're on the move. The UE sent a patrol to our safe house. We're heading back toward Guangzhou in one of the UE vehicles."

"It sounds like you've had a dreadful time. How can I help?"

"Well, from your question, I know you didn't get the chance to read my text, but I understand. For time's sake, I won't repeat what I sent you. Can you have an airplane transport us to South Africa? And, please ensure the items in the text are on the plane. What's the situation at UE HQ?" Christopher asked.

"I promise you a plane and those items will be waiting for you in Guangzhou by tomorrow. I will send you Amahle's info. It's better to go direct to her if you have technical questions and it limits people contacting me. As far as the situation here, it's frantic. Draven will hold a press conference from Naples tomorrow, and I'm lost for words describing the devastation from the judgment."

"Thanks, Gemma, for all you're doing for us. Be safe."

"I will. Expect flight details in the next couple of hours. Goodbye."

Gemma ended the call, excited about developing a plan to save Gabriella. However, she was unsure on how to secure a plane and military item for Omega. She sent Amahle a note saying Christopher and his team would go to Cape Town tomorrow and to expect direct contact from Christopher going forward.

As she put her phone away to return to the office, it rang. The display indicated it was a UE headquarters number. Gemma felt the world stop, as she answered, "Hello."

"Ms. Sutherland, I hope you're well. The UE has a crisis on its hands," Pontiff Conti said.

"Pontiff, you're a part of the UE. And, yes, things are busy. How did you get my number?"

"I called your office. The UE directory lists the number."

Gemma forgot she forwarded her office calls to her cell phone, something she didn't want Conti to know. "I'm busy, Pontiff, and I don't want to be rude, but Deputy Mallory is demanding the world right now."

"Yes, I understand. I want you to ensure that our 'mutual friend' joins Draven's security detail tomorrow."

"How am I supposed to accomplish that feat? Evan, not me, makes that call."

"Gemma, I expect you to uphold your end of the agreement. I would hate for you to suffer any further harm."

The phone went silent as the Pontiff hung up. Gemma ran her hands through her blonde hair. Being stressed out was an understatement. Omega needed her, and her foolish alliance with the pompous Pontiff Conti could soon end her life.

Gemma prayed aloud as she began walking back to the UE command suite. "God, please help me. I am in trouble."

❧

It surprised Gabriella to hear a noise at her cell door. She looked up to see Amahle. Gabriella could see from Amahle's bright smile she had good news for her.

"What brings you back so soon? I thought you were heading home for the day."

Amahle spoke quickly and in hushed tones. "I heard from Gemma."

"Wow!"

Amahle waved off Gabriella. "Calm down. Yes, I got the message as I was leaving to catch the ferry back to Cape Town. I made up an excuse that I had forgotten something. Gemma's message was too good to hold until tomorrow."

"Okay, so what's her message?"

Amahle looked at her watch and then at Gabriella's cell door. "I can't get into the details right now. Your friends are flying to South Africa tomorrow. Before you ask a million questions, I need to go. I can't stay with you for too long."

Gabriella reached through the bars grabbing Amahle as she tried to leave. "Please tell me more."

Amahle took Gabriella's hand. "As I always tell you before I leave. Keep praying and trust God. I will see you tomorrow during my routine visit. We will discuss the details. I promise."

Gabriella's eyes filled with tears as she watched Amahle walk away from her cell door. She went back to her cot and lay staring through the barred window as stars began dotting the new night sky.

She prayed, "God, please watch over my friends."

꙰

Gemma reentered the UE command suite to find staffers back within their cubicles, attempting to make Draven's desires a reality. She walked toward Evan's office to determine her next task. Compared to Christopher's daunting list, which she had no idea on how to meet, Evan's orders would be easy. The fear of overpromising to Christopher and Omega seemed real as she stood outside Evan's office. Gemma gathered herself and knocked on Evan's door.

"How can I be of service, sir?"

Evan looked up from his computer for a moment while typing. "It's a madhouse around here. It's hard to keep track of everything flooding in."

Gemma was glad that the chaos from the recent judgment provided her cover to talk to Christopher.

Evan continued his rant, "I need you to schedule three flights for tomorrow. Take this." Evan pointed to a memo on his desk. "It will overcome the stubbornness of the UE logistics director."

Gemma walked to Evan's desk and picked up the note, giving her carte blanche authority to commandeer flights to support the UE Secretary-General. As she read the message, she felt like shouting thanks to God.

Instead, she said, "Will there be anything else, sir?"

Evan stopped typing. "Yes. I need you to contact Demir Ersoy. Let him know he will accompany us to Naples tomorrow morning on his first assignment on the Secretary-General's detail. Also, contact John Barnes and let him know he is flying out to Israel tomorrow. I will contact him upon his arrival with instructions."

Gemma couldn't stop the smile that formed at the way God had worked things together for her, solving the Pontiff Conti and Christopher task with a single document. Gemma acknowledged Evan's orders by turning to leave his office.

"I will complete your request. I suggest a 6 a.m. departure for Naples to ensure arrival ahead of the Secretary-General."

Gemma didn't expect nor receive any acknowledgment from Evan as she left his office. She didn't care about the slights and disrespect anymore; she had a higher purpose. Gemma entered the elevator and pushed the button for the basement level where the UE logistics division operated.

Now alone, she said aloud, "God, thank you. You're amazing."

⤚⟨⟩⤙

As Gemma walked into the giant underground labyrinth of the UE headquarters, the logistics division resembled a beehive as people, equipment, and machine blurred into a single mass of movement. The basement of the UE headquarters was a series of interconnected passageways with massive warehouses interspersed. Given the activity level, she was pleased with herself for taking the personal approach to getting flights scheduled instead of over email.

Gemma approached a man climbing onto a forklift. "Excuse me, sir. Please tell me where I can find Hank Mankenson."

The man starred at Gemma for a moment and then yelled, "P4, Warehouse 2!"

Before Gemma could say thank you, the man started the large forklift and headed toward Warehouse 3. She got her bearing using the worker's information and realized she was in P3, which meant she was one passageway over from her destination. A quarter of a mile later, she arrived with her heels in hand and less pleased with the decision to seek Mr. Mankenson in person.

Gemma walked through the plate-glass suite entrance for the UE logistics division, where she greeted Mr. Mankenson's executive assistant, Brian Francis. "Brian, please tell me Mr. Mankenson is in his office."

"No, you just missed him. He went to the UE command suite looking for Deputy Mallory."

"I am going to die, right here at your desk." Gemma dropped her shoes.

Brian laughed as he stood, grabbing a bottle of water from a mini-refrigerator next to his desk. "I'm kidding, Gemma. He's in his office and in a terrible mood, I might add. What brings you here? You could have sent him or me an email."

"Why am I standing here? I have questioned that choice many times in the past 45 minutes. Deputy Mallory wants some flights scheduled. I figured that an in-person discussion might go over better given the massive push to get aid across the region."

"Good luck." Brian shook his head. "I will announce you."

Gemma watched as Brian walked around the corner and knocked on the closed door of Hank Mankenson. She foresaw a trying conversation as she overheard the man yelling at Brian.

Mankenson swore and then shouted, "Well, send her in; it's not like I'm busy or anything!"

Gemma stood and walked toward Mankenson's office as Brian gave her a closed-mouth smile. She put on her best English charm and entered Mankenson's office.

"Good evening, Mr. Mankenson. Thank you for taking time out of your busy schedule to accommodate Deputy Mallory's request."

Mankenson pushed back from his desk and stood, walking over to a series of pictures. "Did I have a choice?"

Gemma refrained from answering Mankenson's question, while he continued ranting, "I've been in the logistics business for over 40 years. I was the CEO of one of the largest transportation companies in the world. I have never seen the entire global supply chain brought to its knees. Since the disappearances, it has been one disaster after another. I can't see the Secretary-General's vision for peace coming to pass."

Gemma felt bad for Mankenson. She could see the crisis weighing him down, coupled with his waning faith in Draven. However, Gemma didn't feel the Holy Spirit leading her to discuss the source of genuine hope.

She watched Mankenson return to his desk and rub his balding head. "So, what miracle does Deputy Mallory expect?"

"Nothing major, only scheduling three dedicated flights departing tomorrow."

Mankenson laughed. "I know the Deputy realizes that most commercial flights under our command and even some private flights are all heading this direction. We lost over a third of global maritime transportation when the Mediterranean turned to blood or whatever out there. I can't send a ship anywhere in the region right now, or it sinks. So, air transport is a little light."

"I understand, sir, but these flights support the Secretary-General's initiatives. There is little we can do but find a way."

Mankenson studied Gemma and the memo she gave him from Evan. "So, where are these flights going?"

Gemma smiled. "I need a helicopter dedicated to Deputy Mallory for a 6 a.m. departure to Naples. I need the UE Special Activities Group Commander, John Barnes, flown to Jerusalem. We consider the last flight UE Top Secret."

Mankenson stopped typing the flight request to look up at Gemma. "Top Secret, huh? I've been in this business long enough to know that anything secret relates to moving military personnel and equipment to places they shouldn't be located. Am I right?"

Gemma smiled, playing to the ego of Mankenson as she hoped not to arouse suspicion about the unauthorized third flight. "Mr. Mankenson, you're astute on all accounts. The Secretary-General is dispatching some elite operatives to deal with a matter. You need to have a transport aircraft at Guangzhou International bound for Cape Town, South Africa, loaded with enough 5.56- and 7.62-mm ammo and hand grenades for 20 men for 20 days. I also need five pairs of the most advanced night vision goggles in the UE inventory aboard the craft for the operatives. The details of this request should not leave this room in any regard."

Mankenson held his hands to his mouth as he studied Gemma.

"It sounds like the Secretary-General is sending a deadly message to someone."

Gemma ignored Mankenson's assessment of the request. "I assume you allocated all three flights and necessary equipment?"

"Yes. There are two flights scheduled in the UE system. I scheduled the third flight and equipment via a unique system, which uses military aircraft. The operatives in China will fly a UE military aircraft to South Africa."

Gemma squirmed in her seat, hearing that Omega would have to ride with the enemy. "Make a note that the operatives will not be in uniform, nor should their purpose elicit questions. The group leader is a UE Colonel. The operatives' mission and the fact they're working directly for the Secretary-General demands respect. No flight crew or UE personnel should question the colonel's directives."

Mankenson began typing. "No problem. I've added the note about the Secretary-General's team. I've also added a care package of advanced military gear, including the night vision devices. Is there anything else I can help you with tonight?"

Gemma smiled with the thought that Omega was on Draven's team. "No, Mr. Mankenson, you have been generous with your time and expertise. I will relay your loyalty and professionalism to Deputy Mallory."

Mankenson perked up with Gemma's comments. "You're too kind. If there is anything I can ever do to support the Secretary-General, let me know."

Gemma nodded and departed Mankenson's office, stopping at Brian's desk.

"I guess it went well. I didn't hear any swearing or things breaking."

"A lady can soothe a savage beast." Gemma laughed.

Brian dipped his head and smiled as his intercom buzzed with the angry voice of Hank Mankenson. Gemma waved goodbye and began the journey back to the command suite of elevators.

❦

CHAPTER 17

THE PRINCE OF This World flooded Draven's mind with messages that time was running out. Draven tossed and turned during the overnight flight from Buenos Aires to Naples, terrified by a recurring announcement and the lifelike dreams of death and suffering. Finally, a loud knock at the door of the executive suite of UE One caused Draven to shoot up in bed, drenched in sweat.

Draven shouted, "What do you want?"

Draven's aide said, "Sir, you requested a wake-up call two hours ahead of arrival in Naples."

Draven replied, "Yes, I'm awake. You can leave now."

The Prince of This World's message—time is running out—would not leave Draven's head. He turned his attention to preparation for his appearance, entering his bathroom and turning on his shower, hoping to wash away his night terror.

Minutes later, Draven emerged from the UE One executive suite, portraying his trademark confidence. Inside, however, he fought to uphold his calm demeanor over his worries as he prepared to spin another disaster in a positive light.

Draven walked over to a window, glancing at the endless expanse of churning red liquid in the Mediterranean Sea. "What is the latest on determining the cause of this?"

One of the UE staffers said, "Sir, all the testing we've been able to conduct from across the Mediterranean region concludes the water is now blood. We don't have a logical explanation for why this occurred."

Draven grew agitated as he sat in a plush executive chair around a conference table with liaisons from each significant UE division. "So, you're telling me, I should go on camera in an hour and tell the world that those two fools in Jerusalem's claim that God turned the sea to blood is correct? I will do no such thing."

"Sir, I see no other option," a UE staffer said.

Draven grabbed the conference room television remote and turned the TV to ANN. "Let's watch for a moment."

Draven turned the volume up and stood behind his chair, as everyone focused on the screen.

"Good morning, everyone. This is Sam Morrow for ANN here in Jerusalem. The Two Witnesses, long demonized here in Israel, are now drawing sizeable crowds. The correlation between their predictions of the Mediterranean Sea becoming blood after the asteroid strike and the reality of what happened draws many to hear their daily messages. Here's a brief sample from this morning's message."

Draven and the others watched as the television monitor went to a pre-recorded, subtitled segment.

Reuel was the first witness to speak. "Israel, for three years, you've watched God's hand move against the Beast and his followers. How long will your hearts deny what your eyes and ears tell you? The God of Abraham, Isaac, and Jacob lives, and his son Jesus is your messiah. Repent now."

Eliyahu said, "The shadow of the Great Tribulation is growing. The wrath of God's judgment is yet to come. If you have heard our voices, then you will have no excuse in God's presence. Woe to those that accept the Beast Mark. Woe to women who will bring forth children during this time. Woe to the Beast. Repent and accept Jesus Christ today."

The screen returned to the ANN reporter, Sam Marrow. "In the last month, the overall sentiment in the crowds here in the Wailing Wall Plaza has shifted from hating the Two Witnesses to begging for salvation. With the growing presence of UE-troops and the increasing numbers of Witness converts, tension is high. Back to Rome."

Draven threw the TV remote, cracking the television screen and sending the liaisons scrambling away from the conference table.

Draven screamed, "Do you know how this situation makes me look, debating if a body of water turned to blood? We are fighting against fanaticism. The heart of this world is at stake. The superstitious beliefs of those two idiots in Jerusalem and their followers are a ruse. Humanity's best days are ahead of it, and I will lead the way."

While Draven finished his rant, the UE One captain announced the final descent into Naples, Italy. Draven watched the staff leave, preparing for the landing. For the first time since the asteroid strike, Draven's stomach rolled and his head throbbed in waves of pain, signs of emotions unfamiliar to him.

For the first time in a long time, Draven felt unsure about his future.

As the sun rose over the Pearl River delta and the outskirts of Guangzhou emerged through a humid haze, Christopher glanced from the driver's seat at Jackson, Kerim, and Gilana, deep in sleep. He was grateful that Kerim was forward-thinking, grabbing a purchase card from the uniform of the UE commander before they departed. Without Kerim's quick thinking, they would have been without gas hours ago. The operatives and friends took turns making the eight-hour drive from the safe house back to Guangzhou.

Gemma called earlier, giving him the flight details and expectations upon arrival in Cape Town. He was glad to hear Nkoie provided detailed link-up instructions. The level of detail given was a sign that Nkoie had some military skills or criminal background. Time would tell which of those skill sets Nkoie used.

Christopher swerved the gun truck to the side of the road breaking hard as he took the off-ramp to Guangzhou international airport.

"Oh man, that was close!"

In the passenger seat, Jackson shouted, "What's going on? You alright over there?"

Christopher could see Kerim and Gilana's eyes popping open. "I'm fine, but we need to get ready for what's coming up."

Jackson punched Christopher in his left arm. "What's wrong with you? The next time you think you're at Talladega and slam the brakes like that don't. There's a better way to get us ready, speed racer."

Christopher laughed. "I'm tired, and we're almost there. It seemed like the best way to wake all of you up."

"Americans have a weird sense of humor," Kerim said. "Remember the plan; I will speak when we arrive. Let's hope Gemma's assurance that you, as a UE Colonel reporting direct to Draven, is enough to fool the UE."

"I have faith. We will be fine. Worst case, we get a promotion to heaven today," Gilana said.

Christopher and the others all looked at Gilana with furrowed eyes, puzzled by the mix of her still new faith and typical bluntness.

"Let's pray we don't get promoted today," Christopher responded.

"Kerim, I want you to drive. Your driving will ease our access to the military hangar. Jackson, switch seats with me. It will seem out of place for a colonel to be sitting in the back."

Christopher, now in the passenger seat, began praying to himself. *God, give us your favor. Let us safely reach South Africa.* He directed Kerim to the airline service entrance as Gemma instructed. As the team approached the gate, he saw many UE soldiers moving on the busy airport tarmac.

Jackson said, "Lord, we need you now."

Jackson's words echoed in Christopher's mind.

Kerim stopped behind a fuel truck. "Let me do all the talking."

"Is there any choice? We don't speak Chinese," Jackson quipped.

Christopher wanted to laugh but hid the emotion behind a stern face and sunglasses. He listened as Kerim drove up to the gate guard and began an animated discussion. The guard ducked his head, staring through Kerim's open window at himself and Jackson and Gilana. Another UE soldier walked out of a nearby guard shack with a clipboard. The two soldiers moved out of earshot, but Christopher saw them pointing at the truck and then the clipboard.

Christopher couldn't explain nor stop the sudden urge to speak; as the guard approached Kerim's open window, he shouted, "Gǎnkuài!"

The guards stopped speaking and looked at each other. Then they starred at Christopher. It was the same reaction Christopher found from Kerim, Jackson, and Gilana. The guards snapped a salute and lifted the gate, begging Kerim to drive.

After a few awkward moments of silence, Christopher said, "I don't know why I spoke, but I couldn't help it; sorry."

Kerim laughed as Christopher, Jackson, and Gilana stared at him. "You told them to hurry. I didn't know you knew any Mandarin."

"That's the thing. I don't. I tried fighting the urge to speak, but it came out."

"God is amazing. If God can make a donkey talk to Balaam, he can make the college boy speak Mandarin," Jackson said.

"I told you to have faith," Gilana added.

Christopher laughed with his team. "Kerim, head for that big transport plane at the end of the north runway. That's our ride."

As Kerim pulled up to the open rear ramp of a Y-20 transport, Christopher watched as military personnel awaited their arrival. It was apparent by the lined-up, three-person flight crew rendering salutes that the gate guards passed the message that an important visitor was coming.

Christopher's attention turned to the person who broke from saluting, who he assumed was the captain, running toward Kerim's side of the truck. Kerim and the UE officer had a quick exchange in Mandarin. Christopher was only slightly disappointed that he didn't understand a word.

Kerim turned back to Christopher as the UE officer returned to the plane. "Captain Kelly Liu says she is ready for departure after you inspect the equipment."

"An inspection? What do I need to do?"

"Look over the supplies in the cargo hold. It should be the ammo and other items requested through Gemma. Give me a sign of approval, and I will tell her we are ready to depart. Simple."

Christopher nodded and exited the vehicle, grabbing his rifle and assault pack. He moved to the front of the gun truck, where Captain Liu saluted, then bowed to him before pointing and leading him toward the cargo hold. He glanced at Kerim, who gave him a head tilt to follow Captain Liu.

The captain led Christopher and the others into the cavernous cargo hold of the UE transport. Christopher stood in front of a two-meter-high stack of ammo crates, marked 5.56 enhanced and hand grenades.

After Christopher waved over Jackson, Gilana, and Kerim to the crates, Captain Liu approached him, wheeling a large storage box. "Some special equipment from the UE logistics division. There is one more box," Captain Liu said in non-accented English.

In keeping up his stern appearance, Christopher did not acknowledge the captain. Instead, he pointed to Jackson to open the box.

"Yes, sir," Jackson said with an added over-the-top salute.

Christopher and the others gathered around Jackson.

"Looks like Christmas came early for us," Jackson said.

Jackson held up one of five sets of advanced U.S. night vision goggles. Also in the box were five enhanced individual weapon sights and high-cut ballistic helmets. He wondered, *How did the UE get their hands on this equipment?* Omega intended to field test the night vision goggles and weapon sights three years ago. However, the Rapture changed many things.

Captain Liu's return pulled Christopher from thoughts of the pre-Rapture world as she opened the second storage box.

Before Christopher could say anything, Jackson shouted, "Is that what I think it is? It is. Team, this is Nemean body armor. While it's lightweight, reports say it can stop sniper rounds. I'd heard the Army was testing this stuff, but that was before—"

Christopher cut Jackson off. "Before the disappearances. We know."

Captain Liu turned to Christopher. "Are you pleased, sir, or should I request the UE logistics representative to return?"

"The equipment is fine. Let's depart as soon as possible."

Captain Liu saluted Christopher and turned, speaking in Mandarin to the other two UE officers in flight suits as they moved toward the flight deck.

As Kerim and Gilana claimed their new gear, Christopher's mind wandered to Gemma. His eyes watered, knowing the risk she took in providing Omega the equipment and transport for the journey ahead.

Jackson patted Christopher on the back whispering. "We could fight Satan himself with this gear. It's better than even what General Havid provided." Jackson's joy faded looking at Christopher. "I expected more happiness on your face."

Christopher half-smiled. "I'm thinking about the fight that lies ahead."

His long-time friend Jackson moved in front of him.

"It's not our battle, little brother. God has the situation under control. Remember that before you worry yourself to death. I'm going to go find a place to sleep. We got a long flight."

Christopher chuckled as he watched Jackson walk over to one of the six rows of jump seats the crew had installed and pulled out his 'woobie.'

He prayed God would grant them success in the moments to come.

✧

Gemma pictured the many times her family had taken a holiday to the white, sandy shores and turquoise waters of the Mediterranean. The view below the helicopter now was horrific. Crimson waves crashed onto blackened beaches, where droves of dead fish and sea creatures littered the shore. Half sunken vessels listed in the mire, while others ran aground on once-crowded beaches.

Tears began racing down Gemma's cheeks. She glanced at the other occupants of the helicopter: Evan, Pontiff Conti, and the future assassin of Draven, Demir Ersoy, who seemed unfazed by the "sea of blood."

Gemma knew the Pontiff's presence annoyed and perplexed Evan. However, the day's events stole Evan's time and energy to resist his nemesis.

Evan had told her before they boarded for Naples, "Keep that pompous idiot away from the Secretary-General and me."

Gemma knew that would be impossible and looked forward to the drama to come. Pontiff Conti could not stay away from this moment like a child eager to play with a new toy Christmas morning. The arrogant priest had been plotting for who knew how long for Demir to become the harbinger of Draven's death.

As the whirl of the helicopter circulated, the pungent humid air over the Ovo Castle in Naples, the smell of decay and death was overpowering. Gemma donned a mask that did little to filter acrid air.

Gemma watched as UE security personnel opened the helicopter door for Evan. He moved toward a makeshift platform that over-looked the Mediterranean from the castle walls at a frenzied pace. Draven was due to speak in two hours. She approached Pontiff Conti after he whispered to Demir. As she walked toward the Pontiff, she couldn't help but admire the seamless transition of the assassin into the ranks of the UE security. The role seemed to be Demir's destiny.

Gemma stepped into the path of the Pontiff. "A word of advice. Tread carefully. Neither Evan nor Draven will be in any mood for Interfaith upstaging. I recommend you admire your new toy from the shadows."

"You sound like Giuseppe. However, you both underestimate me. I long for the day when Demir ushers me into power. Now, if you will excuse me."

Gemma shook her head, watching the flowing purple and gold robe of the Pontiff flutter in the early morning breeze. She fought against her own feelings of wanting Draven dead and her growing new faith in the God of the Bible. It seemed wrong to hope for the death of the Antichrist.

Evan and a gaggle of people rushing in her direction interrupted Gemma's thoughts. "Sir, what's wrong? Where are you going?" Gemma asked.

Evan swore. "We're leaving this place right now. There is no chance the Secretary-General speaks from here. I know he wanted a dramatic backdrop for his speech, but that water is rancid. We're going to move further inland and hope for the best."

Gemma turned to follow Evan and the Pontiff to the awaiting helicopter. However, she glanced back at the UE security detail, now scrambling to secure a new venue. The shadowy Demir Ersoy no longer stood out as Gemma searched for him. She wondered when the fateful day for Draven would come. Gemma and the Pontiff knew the deathly task the assassin waited to execute. Boarding the helicopter, Gemma prayed God would allow her to see the moment life departed from Draven Cross.

⤨

John Barnes tried to hide his shame. He tried to focus on the task given to him by Evan Mallory, hours earlier before departing Rome; debrief General Havid, find and destroy Omega. However, as he walked through a Ben Gurion International Airport hangar toward an awaiting SUV, he could sense his presence became the focus for the dozens of UE soldiers and personnel. The whispers and judgment filling the eyes of the UE soldiers told him that his humiliating torture had become public knowledge. He knew Draven and Evan prompted the sharing of his treatment, which caused John to sweat with fury. How was he going to be able to command respect amongst the growing UE military presence in Israel, if the soldiers viewed him as weak.

John's pride filled his mind, as his thoughts reminded him of his previous role as the once-feared UE Special Activities Group Commander. His name now reeked of disgrace. As a driver opened an SUV door, pride overtook him as he heard laughing and pointing from a group of UE soldiers.

"Make an example out of them," a distant voice echoed in John's mind.

John walked over to two soldiers in a group, pointing and laughing at him. A tense stillness filled the UE hangar as the activity came to a stop and the focus turned to John Barnes.

John felt his blood boiling when he questioned the taller, more muscular of the two jeering soldiers. "Do you think I'm a joke, or am I dangerous?"

As the tall soldier spoke, John punched him so hard he felt his hand sink deep into the man's jaw. Teeth and blood flooded from the soldier's mouth as he collapsed, wailing at John's feet. The screams and gasps from the crowd fueled him as he enjoyed the fear that filled the eyes of those watching and his victims. He stomped the tall soldier in a blind rage with his right combat boot until the soldier lay motionless in a growing puddle of blood.

John turned his attention to the tall soldier's whimpering friend. He grabbed the glasses-wearing, tiny soldier by the throat, causing blood vessels to appear around his brown eyes.

The demure young soldier struggled in John's grasp before being thrown to the ground, causing his glasses to break as the frames splashed into his friend's blood. The small soldier cried, covered in his dying friend's blood.

John screamed, "Clean off my boots!"

As the soldier's bottom lip trembled while he performed the degrading task with his uniform shirt, John Barnes kicked him in the face. The blow caused the soldier to writhe in pain across the blood-soaked floor.

John ran his hands through his black hair and gazed around at the stunned UE contingent in the hangar. John felt his muscle pulse as the waves of adrenalin flowed through his veins. The fact that no one challenged his actions or spoke to him as the crowd parted before him meant his message was effective. He strode toward the SUV as silence filled the hangar. The wake of Barnes's fury caused a standstill.

Barnes smiled, entering the vehicle. Pride filled Barnes's heart at the savagery and fear he generated.

⋅⋙⋅

John Barnes's reception at *Hekal Emah*, the maximum-security facility for the most dangerous prisoners in Israel, provided him more respect than his arrival in Israel. A small group of leaders emerged from the facility when he arrived.

John watched who he assumed was the prison superintendent open his vehicle door and greet him, "Welcome to *Hekal Emah*, Commander Barnes. I am Colonel Yair Ohayon. I will escort you to the prisoner."

John said, "Colonel Ohayon, I appreciate the respect you've given me. Lead on."

John followed Colonel Ohayon and four other security guards entering the prison. Colonel Ohayon boasted of the history and security of *Hekal Emah* as they made their way to a debriefing cell.

Colonel Ohayon said, "This prison detains the most dangerous terrorist for the rest of their lives. We do not execute the prisoners as their deaths would make them martyrs for their networks. We extract what information we can from the willing and weaker prisoners that come here, but these terrorists are not dumb."

John nodded in agreement. "Colonel, I expected to debrief General Havid alone. I realize you will listen and watch us, but you will not interrupt me no matter what happens."

From the change in demeanor and Colonel Ohayon's eyes, John could see that his shift in tone caught the man off guard.

Colonel Ohayon stopped in front of the debriefing chamber and saluted. "Commander, I will leave you with the prisoner."

John entered the briefing chamber without acknowledging Colonel Ohayon's fealty. His attention went to the haggard face of the once-famous General Havid. The sunken look of General Havid's face added to the emaciated look of his arms resting on the table before him. But John could still see some life and passion in the general's eyes as they met his. The once-proud warrior was still alive, somewhere in that shell the prison created.

John said, "General Havid, what an honor it is to meet you. You're a legend in the special operations community. But you know, civilians are never comfortable with folks like me and you; I mean, look where a national hero of Israel is spending his last days. It is a shame."

General Havid glared at him. "Mr. Barnes, we are nothing alike. I am a man who loves a country that betrayed him; you're a man who betrayed his country for the love of himself."

John punched the general in the face, causing the older man to tumble off his chair.

John said, standing over General Havid, "I would be a careful, old man. You have no power here. You no longer hold influence in Israel. I can kill you and sleep well tonight."

Barnes thought the general had lost his mind when he began laughing. Slowly, General Havid rose from the floor and sat again, staring at Barnes the entire time.

General Havid said, "Mr. Barnes, death comes to us all. I know what awaits me on the other side, but I am afraid you do not know. You didn't come here to check on my health, so get on with your questions."

John wanted to strike General Havid again, but worried the corrections officers would interrupt his debriefing. He knew enough about this prison to understand that most of the staff worked for General Havid during their careers. They would only let the physical abuse go so far.

Instead, John attempted to manipulate the general's mind. "Would you like to know what has become of your rogue team of operatives?"

"I assume they remain a thorn in the UE's side, else you wouldn't be here."

John's eyes narrowed as he tried to think of his response. "Omega is far from being a problem for the UE. Where was Omega's last mission?"

John was shocked at General Havid's response as the general began laughing. "You're not an intelligent man. How you made it through the U.S. special forces selection course is beyond me. You're a savage, a sociopath. First, I am unsure where Omega is or what they're doing. Second, if I did know, you would have to kill me before I told you. Third, the UE's far more talented operative attempted to get this information from me and failed. Good day."

Stunned by the blunt assessment, John watched General Havid leave the table and begin banging on the door, asking to return to his cell.

As a guard opened the door for the famed Israeli General, John made a desperate inquiry, "Will they come for you?"

General Havid stopped in the doorway and looked back at John. "Christopher is smarter than you think. If Omega needed me, then the UE wouldn't have sent you here hoping to find something that would lead to Omega."

After the general had left, John sat in the room with his thoughts. Perhaps the general was correct. He reflected back on his source development training, *"Once a source is compromised, they have no more value. You never go back to them."* Omega doesn't value the once-powerful general.

But as John stood to leave *Hekal Emah*, he thought, *The general is more than a source of information for Christopher, it's deeper. I need to be ready for Omega.*

CHAPTER 18

As UE ONE taxied to an awaiting convoy of black SUVs, Draven understood why Evan had pushed the speech from Castel Ovo near the ocean to the Piazza del Plebiscito. The air circulating in the plane carried death's scent. As the air stairs wheeled into place and a red carpet unrolled, Draven donned a UE logo adorned facemask and braced himself for the world's attention.

Draven gave the nod to an aide for the main cabin door of UE One to open. Draven's legs wobbled for a moment as he descended the stairs. Those watching his arrival released a loud gasp after he almost collapsed. The stench of decay overwhelmed his senses. With the movement by security personnel down the red carpet toward him, Draven regained his composure. He paused at the bottom of the stairs before waving to cameras and the small crowd of airport personnel now fixated on his every step. He resumed his regal appearance all the way to an awaiting Evan Mallory and an open SUV door.

Draven whispered, "Get me out of here. I can't breathe."

Evan helped Draven into the SUV, where Gemma awaited the two world leaders.

Draven ripped the mask away from his face as the SUV drove away. "Gemma, I see your bruises are healing. Tell me, you helped

Evan determine a way for me to give this speech without vomiting on international television."

"Sir, there is no venue where the smell will not affect you. It will be less pungent at Piazza del Plebiscito, but not by much."

"Thanks for nothing. I am tired of people not fulfilling my wishes. Evan, I will only speak for five minutes, and then I plan to return to my plane and on to Rome," Draven replied.

"I understand, sir. Five minutes with you will be more than enough to reassure the world," Evan said.

Draven adjusted his tie and fidgeted with the air vents before cursing and shouting, "Turn the air off. It's allowing the foulness to seep into the vehicle!"

He ignored Gemma and Evan for the rest of the short drive to the piazza.

Out of patience for formality or protocol, Draven opened his own door as soon the car stopped. He ran to the podium set up for him and began speaking without greeting the Neapolitan dignitaries assembled or waiting for an introduction.

"My heart pours out to everyone who suffers through this horror engulfing the Mediterranean region. Worldwide request to aid the wonderful people who call this beautiful land home has overwhelmed the UE. I will limit my speech to minimize the exposure to the noxious air for those attending locally. The UE will rise to this challenge as we have since the disappearances three years ago."

Draven felt warm as a tremble rose within him. He stopped speaking as a picture of him suffering a gruesome death flashed into his mind, along with the voice of the Prince of This World, who said, "Time is short."

Draven shook his head, continuing, "The Two Witnesses claim the world suffers at God's command. A God they say we should worship. We are the gods and make our destiny. In me, you have life, not suffering. I don't judge your lives as sinful, but I see each life in this world as unique and valuable."

Draven paused as he began looking at his wrists that felt bound to massive golden chains. The podium faded before him. His knees burned from the pressure of kneeling. Draven was bound between an unseen man to his right and Evan on his left, both of whom were similarly restrained. In front of them sat what looked like a man on a throne of dazzling light, whose eyes burned like a roaring fireplace. The mysterious figure faded as the Piazza del Plebiscito came back into focus.

The clicks of the press's cameras brought on some composure as Draven attempted to remember what he'd been talking about. Draven waved away Evan's concern, determined to finish his speech. "In closing, please understand the asteroid that crashed into the Mediterranean Sea two days ago caused a chain reaction. The impact produced an unprecedented red tide, which killed countless sea creatures. My explanation is backed by scientific research, not religious fable. The event was not at the hands of a vengeful God. And I have good news to add, with my staff telling me the Mediterranean is returning to normal."

Before Draven could finish, he returned to the "dream" and message haunting him. He couldn't contain his terror this time. He shouted, "Why are you torturing me? I serve only you."

Then he went limp, and a wide-eyed Evan caught him before he hit the stage. Gasps and quickened shutter clicks filled the void left by the sudden madness that overtook Draven.

Draven felt the hands of Evan grab him and pull him off the stage and toward his SUV. Pontiff Conti emerged from one of the SUVs and moved toward the podium. Despair rose in his heart at the last sight of the stage. Conti speaking at the lectern caused an extra wave of fear to engulf Draven.

He thought to himself, *Master, are you replacing me?*

⤝

Gemma had never seen Draven look so vulnerable and human. A man who obsessed over every detail of his image now sat disheveled and near mad. She wondered if it was possible that Draven, the Biblical Antichrist in her mind, felt fearful and guilt-ridden. Gemma knew Draven was human, but he always came across as a step ahead, near-superhuman in everything he set his mind to accomplish. Her faith in Jesus had opened her eyes to the authentic man. Gemma now knew Satan ruled Draven, which gave him these superhuman abilities.

She looked on at Draven as he stared out the window mumbling over and over the phrase, "Time is short."

Despite her attempts to push it from her mind, she felt a wave of concern rise for Draven. Being compassionate was her nature. But she had always wondered, did Judas have a choice in not betraying Jesus? Did Draven have an option not to become the Antichrist?

Evan's concern was not on his boss as his demand moved Gemma away from her worry over Draven's soul. "Gemma, give us some background noise. Turn on ANN. I want to hear what that arrogant peacock Conti concluded."

Gemma did as instructed and pushed the remote for the small-mounted television. Gemma didn't envision Draven would turn violent at the sound of Conti's voice. She screamed as Draven sat up from his trance and kicked the small television screen. Conti announced before the destruction of the television that the Interfaith religious organization would lead a cleanup effort and food-aid campaign throughout the Mediterranean region.

Gemma remained alone on her side of the limo as she prayed that Draven would not turn his violence on her. She watched as Draven's wrath fell on Evan as he grabbed his deputy by the suit jacket. "I am growing tired of that idiot not knowing his place."

Evan blinked at Draven. "You need some rest, sir, and we need to be patient. The Prince of This World has told me—"

Gemma had never seen Draven so out of control. She trembled not knowing what to do or what would come next. She watched Draven release Evan and collapse back into the seat.

Draven looked at her and Evan. "His time is short. I have little patience for Conti undermining my efforts."

Gemma sighed as the convoy arrived back at the airport. There was an increasing sense of heaviness following Draven. She assumed it was Satan. The uncomfortable feeling exited with Draven.

Evan turned to Gemma before scrambling after Draven. "I will return to Rome on UE One with the Secretary-General. Return to headquarters with that fool Conti as soon as possible via the helicopter."

Gemma nodded and watched Evan help Draven to UE One. She wished the world saw their beloved leader at this moment. The tribulation exposed limits and vulnerabilities despite the lavish praise of Draven being superior to anyone. However, few witnessed the weaker side of Draven's persona. Gemma saw for the first time in the many years of knowing Draven, a regular person. She wondered what the media would make of Draven's manic speech if a free press existed, like before the Rapture.

While she took a last glimpse of Draven and Evan boarding UE One, Gemma longed for the day the two men would receive the punishment they both deserved.

⸎

Christopher had slept in fitful spurts. The flight from Guangzhou to Cape Town took over 24 hours with the refuel stops. As Captain Liu announced the final descent moments ago, he grew warm as tingles raced through his limbs. Christopher looked forward to a hot meal and an actual bed. He laughed, looking around the vast cargo hold, observing Jackson, Kerim, and Gilana having little trouble sleeping.

Christopher's stomach churned as the UE transport plane skipped off the Cape Town International Airport tarmac and the powerful engines slowed. During a refueling stop in Seychelles four hours ago, he spoke to Gemma's second-hand contact in Cape Town, Nkoie; trustworthiness did not come to mind. Nkoie said he wouldn't be at the airport, but assured his representatives would transport the Omega team and their gear to his safe house. When Captain Liu dropped the back ramp to the plane, a cold rush of water-laden wind raced through the aircraft.

Jackson's sleepy response to the cold air, "Somebody close that window," made Christopher laugh.

"Get up," Christopher replied. "We're in Cape Town. It's time to get to work."

Christopher watched Jackson sit up from his "bed" of ammo boxes. His red-brown hair looked like he touched a static ball. The thought took Christopher back to his childhood and the fondness for playing with the static ball novelty at the local mall back in his Texas hometown. Nothing would ever be that simple again. Gilana's laughter at Jackson's wild look added to Christopher's thoughts, and he joined her in laughter.

"What are you two laughing at?" Jackson asked.

Christopher said, "You look like a mad scientist from a low-budget movie. That's what's so funny."

The screeching of four large vehicles near the cargo ramp brought the harassment of Jackson to an end. Nkoie had taken the first step in earning Christopher's trust as his transportation option arrived as promised. He watched a tall, slender man move confidently up the ramp toward him.

"I am Solomon Dube," the tall man said. "I am here to pick up a UE Colonel and his team."

Christopher nodded his head, assessing Nkoie's representative was smart enough not to name Nkoie or use Christopher's name.

"I am the colonel you're looking for, Solomon," Christopher said.

"Welcome to South Africa, Colonel. Please gather your belongings and follow me."

Christopher turned to Jackson, Kerim, and Gilana. "Let's go."

The Omega team nodded to Christopher and began walking with Solomon when Christopher stopped at the voice of Captain Liu. "Colonel, please wait."

Christopher turned to his Omega team. "I'll catch up."

Christopher watched Captain Liu's eyes darting between the others and him until they departed the aircraft.

Captain Liu looked around, ensuring that her crew members were helping Solomon's men unload Omega's equipment. "I wanted to tell you I am praying for your success, Christopher Barrett."

Captain Liu's words caused Christopher to stiffen. He responded, "Listen—"

Captain Liu interrupted, "I am a follower of Jesus Christ. I understand you were attempting to be a stern UE Colonel, but despite your best efforts, I think God allowed me to see through your disguise. I also know they detained the former UE Intelligence Director at Robben Island. The rumor floating through the UE ranks is Dr. Gabriella Costa was assisting your group. I assume you're here to rescue her, based on the ammo. Please know your team is brave to fight for God and his followers. I wanted you to know believers are praying for you, as you head into battle."

Christopher's muscles relaxed. The comfort God had provided him, knowing the apprehension he felt minutes ago as Omega landed in South Africa, caused his eyes to water. Though he thought it wise not to disclose the accuracy of Captain Liu's assessment of why Omega was in South Africa.

"Thank you, Captain Liu. While, I am surprised and grateful at the same time to find another follower of Christ amongst the UE; I need to work on my disguises. I pray for your safety in the days ahead. Until we meet again, take care."

Christopher watched Captain Liu bow slightly before turning and walking toward the plane's cockpit. He turned and joined Jackson, Gilana, and Kerim in Solomon's truck.

No sooner had Christopher sat in the front seat, than Jackson asked, "What was that all about?"

"Let's say a small blessing for the days ahead." Christopher smiled.

❧

CHAPTER 19

THE EFFICIENCY AND command that Nkoie's "welcome team" demonstrated impressed Christopher. Nkoie's crew loaded two cargo trucks with the UE-supplied ammo within twenty minutes. It seemed strange that the UE presence at the airport was indifferent to Solomon and his team.

Christopher's curiosity got the best of him. He asked, "How are you able to move about without restriction. Why doesn't the UE harass you?"

Solomon laughed, before saying in accented English, "The UE fears the boss man Nkoie. Everyone respects him in the Cape. The UE working here today are *boets*. They help us conspire against the UE government when and where needed, like today."

"Are *boets* guards in Afrikaans?" Christopher asked.

"No, it's close to the English word brother or close friend. Those men are family. We only trust family in the Cape. While we can speak Afrikaans, we're Zulu and so if you hear us speaking amongst ourselves, most times it's Zulu."

Before Christopher could ask more questions, Jackson jumped into the conversation. "Hey, Solomon, can you turn on the heat? It's freezing."

"Sure thing. I will get you all a jacket when we get to the safe house."

Christopher said, "Since you brought up the safe house, will we meet Nkoie there?"

"He will be there just now," Solomon said.

"What do you mean?" Christopher shook his head. "Is he already there?"

"Forgive me. My South African slang is confusing you. Nkoie will be there later. I will do my best to use English," Solomon said.

Christopher nodded, appreciative Solomon would ease up on the slang. However, his attention moved toward an endless sea of tin roofs dotted with vibrant colored cloths draped from the awnings. As the vehicle merged on the southbound N2 freeway driving toward the famous Tabletop Mountain overlooking the city, the scene before Christopher reminded him of the nightmare that was the Jakarta mission.

"This reminds me of Jakarta," Gilana stated, also noticing the stark change in scenery.

For Christopher, it became clear the impact Indonesia had on his team.

Jackson agreed, "Yeah, I was thinking the same thing."

Christopher knew the long stares and silence of everyone observing the shantytown outside the vehicle windows prompted Solomon to say, "The safe house is in the Khayelitsha Township. This impoverished area rose during the Apartheid era many years ago. Change never came here despite the end of Apartheid, so it serves as a safe area for our group as the non-African UE will not enter here."

Silence dominated the vehicle. Christopher sensed his Omega teammates were soaking in their new surroundings, especially Kerim, who had not spoken since they left the airport. During the Indonesia mission, Christopher and Omega only glimpsed the desperation of a shantytown like Khayelitsha Township. However, one of the clearest signatures of absolute poverty, the smell of decay and detritus filled the vehicle as they moved deeper into the shantytown. As Solomon wove through open sewer-lined streets littered with human and animal waste, Christopher saw the gaunt faces of the sparse residents. These people suffered not only from poverty but also from the mental assault of the Tribulation.

This is as close to Hell as I ever want to come, Christopher thought, as Solomon pulled up to one of the few stucco-walled homes in the area. The safe house was a complex of two homes and had several cars parked near it. Armed men and women patrolled around a six-foot wrought-iron fence. The bright peach roof and green walls seemed warmer than the faces guarding the place.

"Great. Nkoie is here. Let's not keep him waiting." Solomon's announcement drew Christopher's attention back to meeting the man who would help him save Gabriella.

Christopher and the Omega team followed Solomon's lead and exited the vehicle. Christopher fought the urge to grab his nose as the soured-milk sting of a nearby open-sewage trough assaulted him. Omega watched and waited as Solomon talked to the driver of the second cargo truck carrying the ammo. The other ammo-laden trucks followed the second cargo truck, bypassing the safe house, driving toward a nearby stadium.

Christopher asked Solomon, "Where is the ammo going?"

Solomon said, "We use the maintenance storage sheds at the Mandela Park Stadium for our needs. So, the ammo will be safe there."

Christopher nodded and walked behind Solomon. The eyes of the guards followed every step Omega made. It was a look of mistrust etched into the faces of the men and women of Nkoie's resistance. Christopher had little doubt they'd kill every member of Omega and not lose any sleep over the matter if given the word.

Solomon led Christopher and Omega toward the larger of the two homes in the complex. They entered a sitting room furnished better than he expected. The safe house was warm enough, as the winter breeze snaked through cracks in the aged home. The air was mildly less rancid inside as out on the street. Still, the air carried a musty smell that reminded Christopher of his wife's parent's farmhouse attic during the summer. Nkoie's team dotted the white walls with picture tributes to former apartheid resistance leaders like Nelson Mandela, Archbishop Desmond Tutu, and others less familiar to Christopher.

Solomon said, "Excuse me. I will let Nkoie know you're ready to meet him. I will be back."

Christopher took the pause in their schedule as an opportunity to speak with Kerim as Jackson and Gilana soaked up the history on the walls. "Kerim, can I talk to you for a minute?"

Kerim said, "What's on your mind?"

Christopher replied, "You're on my mind. You've been quiet since we left Guangzhou. Anything you want to talk about?"

Kerim sighed. "Coming to South Africa reminds me of the struggles my family faced back in Xinjiang. The poverty and the political oppression take me back to when my parents were alive."

Christopher said, "I won't pretend to understand how you're feeling. What I want you to know is I am glad you're here with us, and we're all here for you."

Kerim smiled. "And I thought I was going to kill you when I first met you."

Christopher shrugged his shoulders at Kerim's remark.

Before he could reply, Solomon returned without Nkoie. "My friends, Nkoie wants you to join him in the courtyard. Follow me."

Christopher, Kerim, Jackson, and Gilana followed Solomon from the sitting room down a dim hallway and through a well-worn door. A rush of vinegary air and sunlight welcomed Omega into a spacious open-air courtyard that separated the two homes of the complex.

Christopher's eyes met those of a short onyx-complexed man with open arms and a broad white smile, made brighter against the contrast of his skin. The man stood next to a woman with a fierce stare and ebony skin that towered over him. The woman's scowl diverged from the man's broad smile he assumed was Nkoie. The scene before him was reminiscent of a mafia movie where the cold-hearted boss smiles at a hapless victim while the henchmen glare.

As the man approached, Christopher's concerns over Nkoie remained.

The smiling man awkwardly embraced Christopher. Because of his small stature the man squeezed Christopher around his chest. "Welcome, my brother. I am Nkoie. I have longed to meet you for days now."

Before Christopher could respond, Nkoie turned and gestured for the physically imposing woman to come over to them both. "Christopher, I want to introduce to you and your team my younger sister Amahle. Amahle knows well your friend Gabriella."

Christopher created a small gap between himself and Nkoie by shaking Nkoie's hand and nodding to the stoic Amahle, who withheld her right hand.

Christopher said, "Nkoie and Amahle, I am pleased to meet you."

Turning toward his team, Christopher waved over Jackson, Gilana, and Kerim. "This is the Omega team. Jackson, Gilana, and Kerim."

Nkoie said, "Now that we've met, how about we get to know each other South African style. I have prepared for you a *braai*. I assume you're hungry?"

As Christopher went to reply, Jackson said, "I know *braai* means barbeque, and I could eat everything on that table and two horses."

Nkoie laughed, and Christopher watched Amahle's rigid exterior crack into a brief, toothy grin.

Nkoie replied, "There is plenty of food and much to discuss."

Nkoie stood in front of the table where the Omega team and Nkoie's closest associates, Amahle and Solomon, sat and announced, "Let me describe the South African delights for our guest. The *braai* meats include *boerewors* or 'Farmer's sausages,' a mix of beef and pork. There are also lamb chops and kudu steaks. Enjoy."

Nkoie passed Christopher a plate filled with sausages, lamb chops, and Kudu. The first meat he had seen in days carried a smell that reminded him of long past Memorial Day weekends with friends and family. The pleasant aroma of grilled meat overpowered the stench of death and suffering that wafted through the courtyard with each breeze. A bowl of mashed potatoes and a second plate with warm bread followed the barbequed delights.

Christopher guessed the puzzled look on his face led Nkoie to explain, "This bread is *Roosterkoek* or 'grill cake.' It goes with the meat."

Jackson blurted out, "I love mashed potatoes at a barbeque."

Nkoie and his team laughed at Jackson's response, causing Christopher and others to smile in awkward confusion before Nkoie replied, "Those are not potatoes, but mielie pap. Similar to your grits."

Christopher grew impatient with the food tour and asked Nkoie, "How soon can we get to Robben Island?"

Christopher saw the smile fall from Nkoie's face and tense silence filled the courtyard.

Nkoie said, "We are not ready to attack Robben Island."

Christopher replied, "Time is not on our side. The UE will execute my friend soon. Right, Amahle?"

Christopher could see his shift to Nkoie's sister caught her off guard as she hesitated. "You're right. Gabriella has about two weeks before her execution date."

Christopher said, "So, what do you need to get ready, Nkoie?"

Nkoie looked at his sister and Solomon, running his hands over his face. "My fighters have heart. They are brave. I want you to understand; we are not cowards. We are also not good shooters. The UE has picked us apart in previous encounters. Can you fix that in such a short time?"

Christopher looked down the table at Jackson, Gilana, and Kerim in the fading evening light. The trio nodded at him.

"We can improve your shooting skills. They will not be perfect, but better. When the times comes to attack Robben Island, we will develop a plan that doesn't require your team to confront the UE."

Nkoie turned and raised his eyebrows at Christopher. "What's your plan?"

As Christopher prepared to respond, Jackson interrupted saying, "Let's eat first?"

The entire group erupted with laughter and agreed, "Amen!"

❧

CHAPTER 20

CHRISTOPHER AWOKE TO a scratchy throat. His stomach bulged from the feast last night. The stale air in the small room he shared with Kerim and Jackson brought on the rawness of his throat. As Christopher wiped the sleep from his eyes, he noticed Jackson was not in the room. However, the laughter coming from the nearby courtyard pinned Jackson's location.

After Christopher pushed himself up from the pallet of blankets that made up his bed on the floor, his stiff back and knees reminded him why he hated camping. His Raptured wife Erin had forced him on annual camping trips, but Christopher longed now to experience those trips.

He pushed Erin and the past from his mind, as he woke Kerim up. "Hey, Kerim, it's time to get to work."

Kerim groaned and stretched. "Where are Jackson and Gilana?"

"From the laughter, I think they're in the courtyard. Let's get cleaned up and join them."

Before Christopher and Kerim walked out the door leading to the courtyard, Christopher's eyes watered as the pungent aroma of decay filled his nose. He walked toward Jackson, Gilana, and Nkoie as they sat sipping coffee at the table from yesterday's feast. The coffee provided moments of relief as its sweet aroma battled the stench in the damp air.

"Good morning. I hope you two are ready to work," Jackson said.

Christopher started to answer, "We're ready. I need—"

But Nkoie interrupted him, "Great, let us go. My team awaits our arrival at the gun range."

Christopher stared at the coffeepot. As Nkoie rushed him to the marksmanship training, he thought, *It's going to be a long day.*

꿍

Christopher didn't realize how much help Nkoie's resistance needed a week ago. Three days remained before Gabriella's scheduled execution date. The time required to turn the resistance members into soldiers didn't exist. He slung a drop of rain off his nose as shots rang across the "gun range" Nkoie constructed.

The scene before Christopher reminded him of training Iraqi and Afghani security teams. Nkoie's fighters, good enough, would still cost lives. He hoped any loss of life would not come from someone close. The vision of Jimbo's lifeless body lying on a stage in Jakarta flashed in his mind. Each day since last week, the former section of the winery in Stellenbosch he stood upon echoed with the effort to make Nkoie's team an asset instead of a liability. The Omega team waged an uphill battle to make marksmen out of a group of homemakers, construction workers, and not one former soldier. Jackson, Kerim, and Gilana mixed their sharp corrections with the intermittent gunfire.

As Nkoie approached him, Christopher hoped his face showed confidence in the training his heart lacked. Nkoie extended a steaming cup of coffee toward Christopher.

"I figured this would help ease the burden you're carrying."

Christopher sipped the warm coffee and relished the comfort the liquid offered as it coursed through his body.

"Christopher, my fighters and I appreciate all that your team is doing. However, I know the truth you will not speak. My team is not ready to support the rescue."

"No, they are not ready, and I fear the worst sending them into harm's way."

Nkoie turned away from Christopher. He watched his resistance fighters attempt to apply the rifle training provided by some of the best soldiers in the world.

Nkoie spoke without looking at Christopher, "So you remain confident your plan will work?"

Christopher had given plenty of thought to answering the question over the past week, drawing on experiences of working with resistance groups worldwide that the American government deemed to be an ally. He turned his head away from the steady sounds of gunfire and Jackson's voice looking Nkoie in the eyes. "Yes, my faith in God is what I am trusting not what I am seeing with the training. We stick to the plan of having your team helping us infil/exfil and creating a distraction while we get Gabriella. If all goes well, your team will never be in danger. Let's wrap up the training and meet with the others to go over the details."

"Yes, let's go."

"Nkoie, one more thing. Call Amahle and have her meet us at the safe house. I want to ensure she is comfortable with the plan and explaining it to Gabriella. I also want to ensure she doesn't have any last-minute updates for us.

Amahle stood outside the safe house, awaiting Christopher and Nkoie's return from the range. A broad smile crested her broad face as she swayed in the damp winter air.

As soon as Christopher entered the gate to the safe house, Amahle asked, "So, tomorrow is the day. We're going to save Gabriella?"

Christopher smiled. "We're about to finalize the plan. I wanted to make sure you were here in case you had questions or updates."

The rest of Omega and Nkoie joined the conversation between Christopher and Amahle as she replied, "Well, let's not waste time."

Christopher felt Nkoie pat him on the back, waving him forward into the safe house's living room. As Christopher entered the musty and cramped space, the environment added weight to the decisions about to be made. He waited for Nkoie, Amahle, and his Omega team to settle in before starting. "Tomorrow night, we will free Gabriella from the UE."

Christopher unrolled a map of the Cape on the floor that Nkoie had provided not long after Omega's arrival a few weeks ago. "The plan remains the same as briefed before start of training. I want to go over one last time to lock in the details. We will use boats to—"

Jackson interrupted Christopher. "Before we head to crazytown, like the HALO jump into the lab in Scotland, let me remind you again the waters around here are full of great white sharks. I'm not trying to be in the next 'When Sharks Attack' documentary."

Christopher shook his head at Jackson's wisecrack, but Nkoie erupted into laughter. Nkoie's laughing caused the others to join and pushed the tension out of the room. Christopher admired Jackson's gift of humor to lessen the pressure of a pending operation.

Nevertheless, he retook control of the mission brief. "Now that we're aware of Jackson's fear of sharks. We have other dangers to worry about, like the UE."

The Omega team, Nkoie, and Amahle focused on Christopher, and the map unrolled across the grimy living room floor.

"Nkoie, do you have the twenty-foot boats ready?"

"There will be no problems."

"Great. Nkoie, your two boats will serve as a distraction force. This reduces the risk to your group and provides early warning when the UE attempt to bring reinforcements," Christopher said.

Nkoie interjected, "What kind of distraction are you expecting?"

"I don't want you getting into a gunfight with the UE. Think of Molotov cocktails to set fire to the UE patrol boats docked, then harassing gunfire to keep the UE focused on the front of the island while we make landfall. For drawing attention to the right area of the island, I still recommend, your group begins the mission from the V&A Waterfront harbor."

Christopher watched Nkoie nod his head before continuing, "Amahle, do you have what you need to mark an entry point on the outside of Gabriella's cell?"

Christopher watched as Amahle produced a small black square of infrared-reflective material that, to the eye, looked like a black piece of tape. Yet, it would shine like a beacon when spotted through their night vision devices.

"I am ready. I will make sure I put this at the far end of Gabriella's cell block and tell her to stay at the opposite end."

Christopher replied. "That's exactly what I wanted to hear Amahle. You're ready."

Amahle nodded her head, affirming Christopher's encouragement.

Christopher turned the meeting's attention back to Nkoie once again. "Nkoie, have you verified that your night vision devices for your resistance members are operational?"

"We have five pairs in total and all are ready to go. I will make sure each boat driver has an extra set of batteries."

"Thanks again for providing operators for the boats." Christopher continued, "Kerim, Gilana, Jackson, and I will launch from Little Bay Beach, which is seven kilometers away from the north side of Robben Island. Omega will stage a mile away from the island, awaiting the fire of the UE boats to signal our infiltration.

"Do we have an updated count on how many boats and guards we should expect?" Kerim asked.

Amahle spoke up. "Tomorrow, there will be two patrol boats armed with machine guns and five UE guards each. There will also be thirty extra UE soldiers at the prison."

"That is not what we expected last week. We are out-manned.," Gilana stood and pointed to Robben Island. "I can go to the island tonight and set up a sniper overwatch. It will lessen the odds of us getting promoted to Heaven tomorrow."

Christopher and Jackson shook their heads.

"We don't have a sniper rifle," Christopher said.

"We also don't have a quick reserve force or fast exfil for you if you're compromised," Jackson added.

Gilana smirked. "Only Americans need so much care when doing a sniper mission. I dare you to be within 300 meters of me and say not having a sniper rifle makes a difference."

"Okay, Gilana. If you want the challenge, I will accept the risk." Christopher pointed to Nkoie. "Can you get her to Robben Island tonight?"

"Can you swim, Gilana?" Nkoie asked.

"As far as needed."

Gilana stood and grabbed her rifle, ready to begin her dangerous task.

Kerim stood next to Gilana. "I will also go." He turned to Gilana. "I can watch your back."

The two talented and deadly operatives held an awkward stare before Gilana nodded.

"Knowing you two"—Christopher pointed to Kerim and Gilana—"it won't do me any good to argue. Let's all be careful and good hunting."

❦

CHAPTER 21

GILANA HAD SPENT a cold and wet night overlooking the Robben Island prison in a hedgerow. The new day was dreary, making for excellent conditions to rescue Gabriella, but horrible for a reconnaissance mission. Gilana was grateful that Nkoie supplied the two of them with thermal blankets, wet-weather gear, camouflage netting, and a UHF radio. As Gilana watched the UE soldiers do more sleeping than patrolling, her thoughts shifted toward the sleeping Kerim. Though she wouldn't tell anyone, Kerim reminded her of Uri, her first and only love. Kerim was quiet and confident, but a fierce warrior. Traits she'd admired in Uri. Almost two years ago, she lost Uri and first met Omega. Now, at the worst possible time, she felt the pull of attraction toward Kerim. Why did he want to come on this mission with her? Was it possible he had feelings for her?

Lost in her thoughts, Gilana accidentally nudged Kerim's leg, startling him awake.

"What's wrong?" Kerim asked.

Without taking her gaze from a set of high-power binoculars, Gilana mumbled back, "Nothing. I thought I felt something crawling on my leg."

"Let me take over watching the UE. You need rest. There are many hours before the mission begins, and you'll need your strength."

Gilana found Kerim's worries endearing. The sight of UE activity through the binoculars drew her attention from Kerim and his offer.

"Did you hear me? I am—"

Gilana stopped Kerim. "Look at that gas tank. It will prove useful if this weather continues. Let's hope the UE soldiers seek warmth over ensuring security. Now you can take over. We see things in the same way. What a talented team we make."

She handed the binoculars over, pointing to a gathering of UE soldiers near a large white building. Kerim adjusted the binoculars. He looked at the fueling of a large propane tank. Cold UE soldiers scurried into the building, seeking shelter from the dreary South African winter day.

Gilana chided herself for her last comment. She tucked herself into her thermal blanket and camouflage, unwilling to make eye contact with Kerim as he provided a radio update to Christopher.

❧

No sooner had Christopher finished receiving a radio update from Kerim and Gilana, than his phone chirped, announcing a text message.

The message from Gemma read: *I pray that your mission finds success tonight, as Draven is looking forward to Gabriella's execution tomorrow. He plans to watch via video, so I hope you put on a good show for him. The Two Witnesses have announced the next trumpet judgment, so prepare yourselves.*

"Everything okay?" Jackson asked.

Christopher used the abrasive metallic clicks from the ammo speed loader filling a rifle magazine to mask Jackson's question for a moment as he tried to find a response.

"Kerim and Gilana are okay. They acknowledged seeing Amahle place the infrared marker outside Gabriella's cell."

Christopher paused and loaded up his assault pack with the magazine and bundle of grenades for the rescue mission.

"What's up? You're more worried than a dad who left his daughter home by herself, only to find her boyfriend there when he gets back."

Jackson's attempt at humor missed this time. "Gemma says the Two Witnesses announced the third trumpet judgment."

Christopher could see the confession of his troubles now weighed on Jackson as his friend sat holding his assault pack.

"The good news, if we can have any with this judgment, is we won't have to deal with fire like the second trumpet, but we might be thirsty," Jackson said.

"Hey, are you guys ready to go?" Nkoie asked, entering the living room.

Christopher held up his hand. "Explain what you mean, Jackson."

Jackson ran a callous-lined hand through his auburn hair. "The third trumpet judgment says a star named wormwood would fall to the Earth, affecting freshwater. What I am not sure about is how this judgment will affect believers."

"What's going on?" Nkoie asked.

"We need to get to the boat ramp. Jackson can fill you in on the way. Regardless of what God has in store for us, Gabriella won't see sunset tomorrow if we fail."

Christopher prayed to himself as he climbed into a truck with Nkoie and Jackson, *God, watch over your followers around the world in the hours ahead and bring us success tonight.*

Gabriella grew anxious as her cell filled with the light of a rising sun. Yesterday, Amahle had explained the rescue Christopher was leading to save her life. She fought against waves of excitement and dread, knowing that the most important people in the world to her were placing their lives on the line.

"Oh, how much longer must I wait?" Gabriella grew manic as she overheard the guards' laughter as they discussed having the rest of the day off tomorrow after her scheduled execution.

God, please save me?

❧

Gemma found focusing on work the past few weeks a tough chore, knowing Gabriella's execution date approached. The only shimmer of good news during this time had been the easing of the second trumpet judgment's effects in the Mediterranean region. However, as the Mediterranean returned to normal each day, she knew the more the UE's attention and resources would turn toward Draven's enemies. Christopher's reports that the resistance element would not be as helpful as hoped only added to her fears of the mission to save Gabriella.

The unusually cool summer breeze rushing through the pre-dawn UE gardens felt like the icy fingers of her thoughts. She knew that by the end of the day, Gabriella and others she cared about could be dead. She prayed as the sun rose over the Tiber River, *God, please surround Omega with your holy angels. Protect the team as they rescue Gabriella. Save them to fight another day against your enemies.*

After Gemma ended the prayer, her phone rang, displaying Evan's office number. She was glad her words of encouragement for Omega had been sent, knowing Evan's call meant stress.

"Good morning, sir."

"I need you in the office now. I want a run down on the setup for the Secretary-General's viewing of Gabriella's execution later today. There is also a supposed bold announcement from those two fools in Jerusalem coming soon. The Secretary-General wants the staff to be prepared to counter whatever lies are forthcoming."

"Understood, sir."

There was no further response from Evan as her phone went dead. Gemma knew what Reuel and Eliyahu were about to proclaim. The next of God's judgments was coming. As she walked toward the UE HQ, she texted Christopher to prepare Omega for the wrath to come.

❧

Gemma rushed to Evan's office, only to find him absent. She instinctively followed the torrent of expletives, filling the air to Draven's

132

office. As Gemma walked through the large glass doors, the intense, now ever-present, malevolence surrounding Draven caused her to pause, drawing Draven and Evan's attention.

"Don't stand there looking lost. Sit and start taking notes," Draven ordered.

Gemma wanted to scream back. Instead, she prepared to write the horrors that would come from Draven's mind. She watched the global dictator pace between his massive desk and near-wall-sized television. Draven fixated on ANN's broadcast coverage of the Two Witnesses.

Draven swore. "I really hate these men. I will celebrate the day they die. Evan, don't miss a thing they say regarding a pending disaster. I don't know how these old fools know what's coming next, but we're getting ahead of them this time."

Gemma wanted to laugh when Evan nodded. He had finally learned when Draven was in such moods that non-verbal acknowledgment of his orders was the safest way to steer clear of his anger.

"Gemma, make yourself useful and turn up the television while you make me a cup of coffee." Draven's demand ended the moment of joy Gemma found watching Evan squirm. She moved toward Draven's desk, grabbed a remote, and turned the volume higher.

"Good day, I am Sam Morrow here in Jerusalem covering the Two Witnesses who earlier today proclaimed to have a bold announcement for the world. We have been awaiting something from the men, as they have not stirred since making that statement. Wait, the Two Witnesses have stood. It seems they're preparing to speak. I will—"

The booming voice of Reuel cut Sam Morrow off. "Each day, we proclaim God's word. Telling the world that God sent his only son Jesus into this world to become a sacrifice to redeem you from sin. Like a dog that returns to its vomit or a fool to his folly, you will not heed the voice of reason. The Beast and his False Prophet lure their followers toward eternal separation from God. God's judgments should soften your hearts and lead you to seek Heaven's mercy and offer of salvation. Instead, your hearts harden. Repent and accept God as your savior as his judgment draws near."

Reuel went silent as Eliyahu spoke, *"The third angel blew his trumpet, and a great star fell from heaven, blazing like a torch, and it fell on a third of the rivers and on the springs of water. The name of the star is Wormwood. A third of the waters became wormwood, and many people died from the water, because it had been made bitter."*

Gemma fiddled with the coffee maker as Draven cursed the two men of God while turning off the TV. His office phone rang, causing the stream of blasphemes from Draven's mouth to dry up.

She quickly answered it, hoping to dodge Draven's ire. "Good morning, Secretary Cross's office."

"Gemma, let the Secretary-General know we have another asteroid heading our way."

Before Gemma could respond to General Quan, the UE Command Center director, Draven imposed his will. "Gemma, put it on speaker."

Gemma tapped the speaker button and moved away from Draven. "What is the issue?"

"Sir, General Quan here."

Draven waved away his introduction as if the man stood in the room. "I know to whom I am speaking. What's the problem prompting your call?"

"There is a large comet heading toward Earth."

"What have you done to ensure it doesn't reach us?"

"Sir—"

"Shut up, General. My question was rhetorical. You should have called me after you acted. I want you to launch a nuclear weapon and destroy this threat now. Am I clear?"

"Yes, sir."

Draven hung up the phone and turned to Gemma and Evan.

"Gemma, I want a press conference ready in 30 minutes. Evan, make sure the nuclear strike happens, and any failure lands in the laps of those fools and their God in Jerusalem. Now go!"

While Gemma gathered herself to prepare for the looming press conference, Draven stopped her. "I assume you have everything ready for this evening's festivities. I would hate to miss watching the demise of that traitor Gabriella. It's too bad Gabriella refused to give up the location of the Omega terrorists. Her death will serve as a reminder that I will not tolerate disloyalty."

Gemma flushed and fought to hold back the wall of tears building in her eyes as Draven flashed a smile at the pain he caused. She offered only, "Yes, sir," before turning her back and walking out of Draven's office. Gemma prayed to be an eyewitness when Pontiff Conti's scheme assassinated this evil man.

❧

Draven entered the UE command center, greeted by a white-hot, glowing object. He stopped as a swarm of whispers and voices overtook his thoughts. The presence of the Prince of This World overtook him, leaving him a prisoner to his dark master. The voices in unison chanted, "*Your time is short. Do something.*"

"What do you want!" Draven screamed.

The steady din of chaos suddenly stopped at Draven's outburst. He tried to compose himself as Evan made his way to him.

Draven felt command of his mind return, as Evan asked, "Are you okay, sir?"

"I am fine. Tell me this disaster is under control."

"Sir, Dr. Jacobsen advises we do not launch a nuclear weapon at the comet. He believes there—"

Draven interrupted him. "I don't want to hear excuses for inaction. I should kill the good Dr. Jacobsen where he stands for not offering a solution to stop the last asteroid. Launch the nuclear weapon now!"

Draven watched Evan turn and walk toward General Quan while gesturing with his hands to get rolling, which prompted the general to begin a tense phone conversation, with whom Draven assumed were those in charge of launching missiles. He accepted compliance with his orders by adjusting his hair and tie before briefing the world of his success.

Gemma approached Draven. "Sir, the command center media room is ready for you."

"Excellent. It's time for the world to appreciate my efforts and realize it's me and not the two fools in Jerusalem and their God who rule this world."

Draven strode with Gemma in tow to a lectern offset from a large video monitor that displayed a giant comet.

"My fellow global citizens. I address you this afternoon, not from a state of panic over the prognostications of two insane and evil men in Jerusalem. Tonight's message is one of hope and action. I ordered moments ago a prepared weapon to neutralize the comet threat. In a few moments, the missile will destroy the comet outside the Earth's atmosphere. I conclude my remarks today, believing our best days lie ahead. May peace reign on Earth."

When the camera in front of Draven went black, his attention turned to the media on the television monitor like millions worldwide. ANN provided split views between the glowing apocalypse named Wormwood by the Two Witnesses and a nuclear missile racing to intercept. The disaster, now brighter than a hundred full moons, overshadowed the flames of the missile that merged into view of the comet, creating a bright blob across televisions around the world.

Draven flashed a broad smile as a countdown appeared on the monitor in the last minute before impact. The energy released at 2000 km above the Earth, when the unstoppable force racing toward the planet met the immovable hope launched by Draven, caused a white-out of the video feed.

Draven turned to Gemma. "We got it. Tell Evan to confirm my success."

Before Gemma could leave the media room, Evan burst in. "There's a problem. The comet split into two halves and vaporized above the northern and southern hemispheres."

Draven swore. He kicked over the lectern where he claimed success over the God of the Bible minutes ago. "How could you idiots fail so epically? Are large fragments raining down?"

Evan responded, "No, sir. There are countless small fragments according to radar. It's like a mist raining across the planet. I think we succeeded."

"If you're wrong… I'm heading back to my office to watch Gabriella's execution. It's one thing I've been excited for all day." Draven's hands quivered as he pushed past Evan and out of the command center.

꒰

CHAPTER 22

When Nkoie, Christopher, and Jackson pulled into a small boat pier at Little Bay Beach, the background noise of Jackson describing the rapture and tribulation to Nkoie failed to register. Christopher's focus was not on Jackson's description of the third trumpet judgment during the drive to the pier. His thoughts centered on rescuing Gabriella.

Christopher stared out of the truck as two tall, scrawny resistance fighters prepped a twenty-foot dark blue boat for launch. The men's effort to get ready for the mission made him anxious.

"Alright, Jackson, it's time to get to work."

"One second, college boy. Nkoie, are you a believer?" Jackson challenged.

Christopher turned to look at Nkoie. His face drained of color, and he gripped the truck's steering wheel, causing veins to raise in his hands.

"Is it true, Jackson?" Nkoie asked.

"What?"

"The disappearances and disasters are at the command of a real God? I thought my sister was crazy. I thought she turned her back on the beliefs of our ancestors, but... now."

After Nkoie put his head on the steering wheel, Christopher placed a hand on his back. "I know it's a lot to understand. But everything Jackson said is true. Nkoie, you need to decide right now if you want peace of mind. Accept Jesus as your Lord and savior."

Nkoie's two resistance fighters approached the truck with wide eyes. Christopher held up his hand to stop them. He turned his attention back to Nkoie.

"Do you want peace like Amahle? That no matter what happens tonight or in the future, you'll live forever?"

Christopher saw fear in Nkoie's tear-filled eyes as his head nodded. Jackson and his eyes met, appreciating the moment they'd both experienced before Christopher told Nkoie to repeat after him.

"God, I am afraid and don't know You. I know You are real and that I need You in my life to find peace and redemption. I have led my life without You, but I don't want to live another second without You. I accept Jesus Christ's offer of dying on the cross for my sins and believe Jesus sits next to You after rising from the dead after three days."

After he repeated the last words, Nkoie rubbed the tears from his eyes. "Thank you. I don't know how to explain—"

Christopher cut him off. "Freedom. For the first time in your life, you're free. That's what you're feeling."

"Yes."

Christopher watched as Nkoie's resistance fighters refused to be separated from him and began shouting in what he assumed was Zulu. He turned to the tearful face of Nkoie. "It's time to go, brother."

"Yes, let us save your friend."

Christopher and Jackson followed Nkoie and his confused men to the boat. One fighter extended a callous marked hand to help Christopher and Jackson aboard.

The man's long gaunt frame hid his strength as he squeezed Christopher's hand. "I will be captain of this boat. My name is Mpilo."

Jackson jumped into the conversation before Christopher could respond. "Mpilo, my friend, as long as you don't put us in the drink tonight, you're okay with me."

Christopher wanted to laugh as Mpilo's dark eyes followed Jackson as he sat his gear on a bench seat. "Don't worry about the old guy, Mpilo. The way he talks confuses everyone. Let's get going."

Mpilo nodded and started the boat's engines.

Christopher leaned over the side as Nkoie shouted, "You have a good sign with you. Mpilo's name means 'life.'"

Christopher waved to Nkoie as the boat began moving out to sea. The sky filled with clouds in shades of purple and rose as the sea consumed the sun. The cold air pushed his senses to full alert. He prayed for God's favor and mercy in the hours ahead as the distant lights of the Robben Island UE Prison illuminated the horizon.

≈

Gemma's stomach swirled as Draven and Evan played hosts to a macabre party in Draven's office for the UE HQ staffers. General Ahuja was the next highest senior official to Draven and Evan in the room, but true to his nature sat uninterested watching the setup of Gabriella's gallows.

Where are Christopher and his team? Gemma thought as Draven's clink of his wine glass caused her hands to tremble and the room to go quiet.

The enthusiasm in Draven's voice made Gemma rub her temples. "Ladies and gentlemen, I celebrate this event as vindication for the vision that all of you work so hard to bring about for this world. The vision of peace and equality for all humanity. Gabriella betrayed the UE's purpose and all of you, and the justice she will receive is a warning for any that seek to stop the UE from accomplishing its mission."

Gemma felt the judgment and stares of the group as applause to Draven's declaration echoed through his large workspace. She resigned herself to the potential of watching her beloved friend die.

The shattering of a wine glass, and a torrent of cursing flowing from Draven caused Gemma's eyes to widen and fixate on the massive monitor behind Draven's desk. The screen glowed orange-white and the indistinguishable crack of an explosion followed as a fireball consumed the gallows. Before Draven could say it, Gemma knew Omega's rescue was underway. She silently cheered listening to Draven order General Ahuja to get reinforcements to Robben Island.

While the sound of gunfire began to come across the screen, Gemma prayed, *God, please watch over my friends.*

⋰

Gilana awoke to an explosion and a bright orange fireball illuminating the distant Robben Island dock. She kicked Kerim. "Why didn't you wake me?"

"Nothing was happening until now," Kerim responded.

Gilana grabbed the binoculars scanning the dark horizon near the explosion. She picked up the movement of two operatives, whom she assumed were Christopher and Jackson moving toward the prison's central area where Gabriella was located.

"The fuel tank. Shoot it now!" Gilana shouted, aiming at the fuel tank outside a building where UE soldiers poured out. A wave of heat and sound blew through the hedgerow. Gilana stood grabbing extra ammo magazines near her, shouting to Kerim. "Let's go, we need to reposition to support Christopher and Jackson."

The shrill of UE bullets filled the night as the wails and moans of the UE's wounded faded away. As Gilana and Kerim took cover behind a supply container, the crackle of a radio message from Christopher interrupted chaos by searching for them.

"Gilana, what's your location?"

"We moved from our overwatch. There's UE heading toward you. We're taking cover behind the rear of a supply container."

"I see the supply container across the courtyard. We're approaching from docks to your twelve." Gilana listened to Christopher reply while peering around the container hoping to spot her teammates. Her moment of distraction allowed a UE soldier to take aim at Kerim and her.

"Kerim!" Gilana's warning came too late as an RPG exploded near the container, bouncing Kerim against the side of the container and sending Gilana sliding into the courtyard.

Before the world faded away, she keyed the radio. "We're down."

✥

Christopher said nothing after Gilana's radio message came through. Instead, he tried to keep up with the sprinting Jackson as they approached the prison courtyard from the Robben Island beach.

"Jackson, hold on."

"We need to get to them now," Jackson said.

"I agree, but remember, the enemy could be anywhere."

Jackson leaned against the main prison wall as he switched radio channels to reach Nkoie.

"Nkoie, I need your teams to come ashore. We've got two down!"

"I'm coming."

Christopher heard more explosions and gunfire coming from the boat dock a few seconds later. He switched back to the Omega internal radio channel. "Okay, now we go. Nkoie bought us a few moments."

Christopher followed Jackson as they entered the courtyard, scanning for threats that thankfully moved on as they approached Gilana. The greenish glow of his night-vision goggles couldn't hide Gilana's injuries. She was bleeding from the side of her face, evidenced by a dark pool of liquid building around her. Gilana's right arm contorted in an unnatural position. He feared the worst.

"Is she dead, Jackson?"

"No, but we have little time to save her?"

Christopher didn't respond as Jackson bandaged Gilana's wounds. He walked over to what he thought was Kerim. Christopher's stomach dropped at the sight of Kerim's shredded body. "Kerim's gone."

Christopher heard distant gunfire and watched Jackson turn toward him before both men reacted to the sounds of boots. They instinctively sought protection behind the damaged shipping container. The smell of Kerim's singed flesh caused Christopher to lose the battle over his emotions as tears streamed down his face.

"Christopher and Jackson, don't shoot. It's Nkoie."

"Nkoie, Gilana needs hospital care," Christopher said.

"I know a place that will help. Where is Kerim?"

Christopher shook his head at Nkoie's question as a cold rain started, bringing an uncomfortable stillness that fell across Robben Island. As the group looked on, Jackson grabbed a tarpaulin from the ground near the container to cover Kerim's body. Christopher gave the stoic Jackson a pat on the back as he walked toward the wall that stood between them and Gabriella.

"Nkoie, what about the UE soldiers? It's too quiet," Christopher said.

"We took care of the few moving toward the docks from here. A credit to your training us, but I am sure more will come from Cape Town soon," Nkoie said.

"Okay. I need you take Gilana. I will stay with Jackson to rescue Gabriella. Leave one crew here for support. We're not done with this mission yet."

Nkoie and his men departed for the boat dock with Gilana on a makeshift gurney of branches and tarps. Jackson prepped to breach the prison wall to free Gabriella, and Kerim's body lay motionless in the rain-soaked courtyard. It was a scene for Christopher that spawned doubt in God's plan. Doubting God was easy for him to do, but as Christopher reached Jackson, he decided to trust God no matter what came next.

⤨

CHAPTER 23

GEMMA STOOD AT a distance observing the meltdown Omega had created within UE HQ, with Evan and her being the only staff that remain with Draven. The moments prior to the explosion at the Robben Island docks were filled with laughter surrounding the anticipated death of Gabriella. Now, Draven seemed a second away from a nervous breakdown. The same crazed look filled his eyes that she saw in the limo in Naples.

Gemma sensed the presence that was always with Draven increase, adding an uncomfortable weight to the room. Draven must have felt the same as he turned his wrath from cursing at the monitor and the destruction at Robben Island to Evan. She felt sorry for Evan who was screaming on the phone, while being berated by Draven.

Draven swore, then demanded, "Evan, tell me that the reinforcements are nearing Robben Island. I don't want Gabriella escaping."

Evan responded, "The additional units from Cape Town are meeting fierce resistance."

Gemma wanted to run from the office as Draven's voice carried a tone of darkness. "I want whatever resources we have available to find Gabriella and Omega. I want them to suffer. Both of you get out of my office now!"

Gemma walked back to her desk and prayed that God would not allow Draven's evil for her friends to come to pass.

⤝

After endless explosions and gunfire, Gabriella huddled in the corner of her cell physically and mentally broken. The fighting inside the prison sounded as intense as what she imagined Christopher and the others faced trying to reach her. Amahle had told her to stay in the corner she curled into and not to leave until Christopher or her came. She squeezed her frail legs for comfort, praying her friends were okay.

Amahle's last words to her before she moved back toward the guard's post were, "I won't let anyone hurt you."

Gabriella prayed like she never had during the fierce firefight, while screams of pain echoed through the prison raising Gabriella's concerns. Her helplessness at the situation pressed her. Doubts and worry crowded the cell, making the space feel tight.

The noises of the gunfire and shrieks of people dying grew closer to Gabriella. She screamed as Amahle's large frame fell against the metal bars of her cell. Gabriella jumped from the corner. "Are you okay!" she yelled.

Amahle held a hand up toward Gabriella. "They're coming for you."

The tackle of a guard cut Amahle off, and Gabriella looked on in horror as the two wrestled on the ground. The report of two gunshots ended the struggle as Amahle lay motionless atop the guard who tackled her. The man who gunned down Amahle shamelessly pushed her body off the first guard. Now the two-armed men turned their attention to Gabriella.

"God, help me please!" Gabriella yelled.

An explosion of rock and light flooded the far end of her cell, slamming Gabriella to the ground. A cold salt-laden wind rushed through the void, stealing her breath. Gabriella grabbed her ears as they rang from the explosion and the dull thuds of gunshots. She feared the worst as smoke and dust filled the cell. But it was the smooth, familiar cadence of a voice from within the chaos that made her heart skip a beat.

"Gabriella, you alright?"

"Christopher?"

Gabriella felt the strong embrace of her friend, but quickly pulled away from him to find Amahle. The explosion had knocked the lights out across her cell block but Gabriella crawled over rubble and the UE guards' bodies until Christopher shone his white light on her.

"We need to go. Can you walk?" Christopher pleaded.

"I need to find Amahle!"

Gabriella heard Jackson, say what she already knew, "Gabriella, Amahle's gone."

The dazzling white light from Jackson and Christopher's rifles found Amahle lying in a pool of blood with her eyes open but unfocused. Gabriella began to wail and continued crawling on her hands and knees to her friend. Gabriella rolled Amahle into her arms. She wiped the blood from Amahle's face and closed her eyes while hot tears fell on her friend's delicate face.

Gabriella didn't care to live. God felt distant and cold in the moment as guilt poured over her, while her cries of pain echoed off the walls. She barely noticed Jackson move past her toward the guard's post.

Gabriella sat rocking Amahle like a mother with a newborn. It was Christopher's voice that broke through her sorrow. "Gabriella, I know you're hurting, but we need to get you to safety."

"I will not leave here without Amahle! Please?" Gabriella replied.

The fresh crack of distant gunfire signaled the UE's resolve and the lack of time facing the rescue mission. Gabriella felt Christopher grab her right arm attempting to pull her to her feet. But she jerked away from him.

"What are you doing? The UE is closing in," Christopher said.

"And I told you, I am not leaving here without Amahle," Gabriella said.

Gabriella and Christopher's eyes met and she could see the desperation on Christopher's face as he called for Jackson.

Gabriella continued to squeeze Amahle as Christopher turned back to her. "Please listen. I promise we won't leave Amahle behind, but we can't fight the UE here. If we do, we all will die. Do you understand me, Gabriella?"

Jackson added, "I promise we will not leave her. But we need to go."

Gabriella trembled as her tears intermixed with Amahle's blood soaking her prison uniform top. She relented to her friends as the guilt of one death crushed her soul. The thought of others dying because of her pushed Gabriella to her feet.

Gabriella grew numb as Christopher handed her his 45-pistol. "You might need this."

She nodded and tried to hide the struggle caused by the weight of the pistol. Months of atrophy ruled her muscles after rotting in a prison cell and countless hours of torture. The pistol felt like a lead weight.

Gabriella moved between Christopher and Jackson as Christopher directed the group. "We're taking a detour. We will exit the front of the prison and flank the UE."

Gabriella peered around Christopher as Jackson moved in front of a large steel door that teetered off its hinges in such a way that made pulling it open time consuming. She guessed the explosion jarred the door that separated her cell block and main part of the prison out of position as Jackson set a C4 and detonator charge. Gabriella then moved back around the hallway corner with Christopher and Jackson pressing against the wall as Jackson shouted, "Fire in the hole!"

Gabriella was unsure if her hearing would ever return to normal when the explosion created a large clang as the steel door slammed to the ground clearing their path.

Gabriella met Christopher's eyes again as he told her, "Stay behind Jackson and me. Jackson, IR lights on."

Gabriella followed Christopher and Jackson out of the cellblock and to the right, guided by their shadowy silhouettes. Gabriella read an emergency-light illuminated sign that read "Guard Station, Visitor Lobby" in the direction they were moving. The trio turned a tight left corner to find the floor covered with ammo casings. Christopher pulled Gabriella closer to him. The group slowly made their way to a large circular room with destroyed and bullet-riddled CCTV monitors observing the cells.

Gabriella looked at the guard station, and the story became clear that it served as a trap for the UE guards and a desperate stand for a lone person, Amahle. As Jackson and Christopher went to white light, the enhanced visuals of the room completed the tale of what happened before Amahle died.

Gabriella looked at the two dead UE guards in the command station and the desk and chairs piled next to the main prison section door appreciating Amahle's sacrifice. Amahle had used the guard post to keep at least ten UE guards from advancing to kill her. Amahle had given Christopher and Jackson the time to save her from the guards. The lone working monitor rolled through various scenes throughout the prison, depicting the intended fate of Gabriella. The other prison cells contained dead inmates. Gabriella's heart broke thinking of Amahle standing with courage between the enemy and herself.

Christopher brought conclusion to Gabriella's piecing together Amahle's final moments. "Jackson, we need to go." Christopher pointed to the working monitor that showed three UE soldiers entering the front of the prison.

Gabriella watched Jackson move out into the prison visitor center as Christopher spoke to her. "Amahle was brave, and now she is with Jesus. Stay here while Jackson and I deal with these guys," Christopher said, wiping the matted hair from Gabriella's face.

Gabriella grew scared with the thought of being alone and clung to Christopher's hand. She struggled against him when he pried his hand away.

"We will be right here in the lobby. Stay low and quiet."

Gabriella's curiosity would not allow her to stay low. She peered through the broken guard post front window watching Jackson and Christopher exit the guard station, stepping over two UE guards' bodies.

Gabriella overheard Christopher directing the ambush on the advancing prison guards. "Jackson, look." Christopher pointed to a narrow hallway leading to the front of the prison, split into two separate corridors that lead to opposite sides of the prison.

"I want you to set up behind the reception desk, and I will be in the hallway to your right. When the UE enters this foyer, we will ambush them."

"Good idea, college boy."

"Just go," Christopher said.

Christopher barely made it to the hallway Gabriella noticed before the UE timidly entered the foyer. Gabriella could imagine, surprise, then death overtaking the faces of the first two guards in the lobby as Jackson's shots from the left side of the lobby echoed. Christopher sent the third man to his eternal destiny, ending the immediate threat. Gunfire continued to call out from the boat dock, signaling the fight ahead.

Christopher called her, "Gabriella, let's go so we can help Nkoie's men."

Gabriella moved again between Christopher behind her and Jackson out front in an overwatch position as the men switched to white light combing the shadows of the prison entrance. Tears fell in waves as Gabriella tried to shake the feeling that more people she cared about might die tonight saving her.

∽

CHAPTER 24

THE COLD AIR of the South African winter night hit Christopher's sweaty skin like a slap in the face. He shivered for a few seconds and pushed his mind to focus on the threat instead of his discomfort. While he could see the gunfight between Nkoie's men and the UE, he struggled to see a way to approach. It was likely that Nkoie's team would open fire on them as they attempted to flank the UE.

Christopher hesitated causing Gabriella to bump into him when Jackson held his right hand up like a fist and took a knee at the infamous Robben Island Prison gateway. Christopher and Gabriella moved up to him.

Christopher kneeled asking Jackson, "What's wrong?"

"If we go traipsing up there without a plan, there's no telling which group will shoot at us first."

Christopher asked, "You've got any 203-rounds?"

"I've got one," Jackson said.

Christopher stood up. "Well, make it count. I think everyone will know we're good guys. That's if you don't miss."

"Miss? Watch this," Jackson said.

Christopher along with the frazzled Gabriella looked on as Jackson steadied himself on his left knee raising the "leaf sight" on his rifle, aiming at the UE soldiers firing at Nkoie's men. The signature "low thump" of a 203-grenade taking flight brought a smile to Jackson's face. A few moments later, an explosion of wooden crates and screams filled the air, followed by silence, ending the UE presence on Robben Island.

A few moments later Nkoie's team approach Christopher's group from their previously pinned down positions. Christopher assumed Nkoie's team would be amped up after the firefight, and he didn't want to startle them. When the group of fighters came within visual recognition range, Christopher shouted out, "Don't shoot. It's Jackson and Christopher."

The familiar voice of Nkoie pierced the night confirming Christopher's ally survived as the two groups met near the warehouse where Nkoie's team fought. "Brothers, thank you. The UE will need at least a day to conduct another attack."

"I thought you took Gilana to the hospital?" Jackson questioned asking the same thing on Christopher's mind.

"Solomon and Mpilo took her. But where is Amahle?" Nkoie asked.

Jackson hesitated as his voice cracked. "Christopher, please tell him?"

Christopher paused from telling Nkoie the truth of his sister. He looked on with the others while Jackson walked alone toward the boat dock, being consumed by the night and likely his thoughts. An eerie sense of déjà vu came over Christopher as Jackson walked away, a flashback to Rev's death in Iraq.

Nkoie's hand on his right shoulder signaled to Christopher the inevitable could wait no longer. "Please, tell me what's come of Amahle?"

"There is no easy way to say this. Amahle is dead." Christopher embraced a man that had become dear to him over the past month.

"It was my fault. I'm so sorry, Nkoie." Gabriella blurted as a painful moan engulfed her.

Nkoie turned to Gabriella. "Amahle loved you. She spoke of you often. If she died defending you, then know it was without hesitation and filled with love."

Christopher couldn't stop the tears flowing as he watched Nkoie embrace Gabriella.

"Where is Amahle's body?" Nkoie asked.

"I will take you," Gabriella responded.

"I'm going to check on Jackson. Meet us at the dock."

A sense of gratitude rose in Christopher for the people around him during this trying time as Gabriella, Nkoie, and his team disappeared into the Robben Island prison void to retrieve the bodies of Kerim and Amahle. While the pain of this day would linger, Christopher was glad he was not alone.

Christopher found Jackson sitting at the edge of a boat ramp, staring at the distant lights of Cape Town. He didn't want to say anything, just make his presence known for his friend. Since the immediate threat of the UE was over, Christopher pulled his ballistic helmet off and stretched his bruised frame in the cold sea breeze. Nkoie's forces rose to the challenge, a miracle from God based on what he'd witnessed in training the past two weeks.

Jackson broke the silence. "This reminds me of the night Rev died; the same twinges of pain and anger are gnawing at me. The only difference now is I know God exists," Jackson said.

Christopher sat next to his friend. "Yeah, a lot has changed over the past two and half years. I would be a fool to deny God isn't real. My question is, are you okay?"

Jackson sighed. "I'll be fine. Knowing we lost two good people tonight hurts, but I'm glad they're both in Heaven. How's Gabriella?"

"It's hard to say. I think the shock of the rescue hasn't worn off yet."

Before Jackson could respond to Christopher, Gabriella and Nkoie returned with their teammates, carrying two stretchers, one with a tarpaulin draped over it.

Christopher walked over to Gabriella, who watched the men load Amahle and Kerim's bodies onto a nearby boat, one of the few boats in the dock, not on fire or sunk. Her bright green jumpsuit carried a dark red smear across the front. The last working dock light magnified the contrast between the blood and jumpsuit.

Christopher asked Gabriella, "How are you holding up?"

"Chris, I… "

Gabriella couldn't seem to finish what she was going to say. Instead, she walked away from Christopher and sat in the boat next to Amahle's and Kerim's bodies.

He wanted to say it wasn't her fault. That everything would be okay. But Christopher knew Gabriella's heart was not ready to listen. The sorrows they all faced would end in one of two ways: the return of Christ or going to Heaven as Amahle and Kerim did tonight. Christopher prayed they all would make it to see Jesus when Jackson and Nkoie approached him.

"We should go. The UE is wounded but remains dangerous," Nkoie said.

"I am with Nkoie. We've done our duty and need to check on Gilana," Jackson said.

Christopher nodded and boarded the boat with Gabriella. As the darkness of the night overtook them, leaving the dock, he watched as Gabriella sobbed, leaning her head on Amahle's now blanket-draped body. He prayed, *God, bring Gabriella peace and all of us mercy.*

CHAPTER 25

GEMMA FOUND SLEEP difficult after Christopher's phone call confirmed Gabriella's rescue. The elation of Gabriella's freedom mixed with the sorrow of losing Amahle and Kerim led to an endless night. Now, as she walked into UE Command Suite, the world felt small and she felt isolated.

"Gemma, thank goodness you're not late today. We need to prepare the Secretary-General's response to the crisis," Evan said.

Gemma's first thought focused on Evan's slight regarding her punctuality. She was never late. The more important thing Evan said was there was a fresh crisis. She hoped the problem was Gabriella's rescue.

"Let's go, sir."

Gemma followed Evan into Draven's office. However, Draven pointed back toward the door as he marched past Evan and herself. She watched as Evan scrambled to keep up with the Secretary-General, knowing blame would follow him for whatever issue plagued Draven.

"Sir, could you tell Gemma and me where you're going?" Evan inquired.

"To see the problem firsthand."

Two men from Draven's security detail joined Gemma and Evan. One of the security agents was Demir Ersoy. *God, I hope today is the day of Draven's demise.* Gemma's face flushed at her desire for Draven's death as the group made their way off the command suite elevators.

"Gemma, you look faint. Show some poise in front of the Secretary-General," Evan mumbled to her.

Evan's acknowledgment of the internal turmoil Gemma wrestled with caused her to focus on the moment. She needed no further attention from Draven or Evan. "I'm fine, sir."

Evan studied her face before nodding acceptance of Gemma's answer as Draven halted at a UE garden overlook of the Tiber River.

Draven swore. "Evan, now do you understand the problem. Gabriella and Omega destroy a UE prison and escape. The crying from the Headquarters staff over water echoes the minds of others worldwide. By this time tomorrow, I'll lose credibility with millions. From their pedestal in Jerusalem, those two fools will claim their God is punishing me with this disaster. So, what is the response?"

Gemma was at a loss. *There was a problem with the water?* The water she used for her morning cup of Earl Gray tea was okay. The truth came to mind as she saw Draven's face turn red, as he cursed at Evan. God had decreed the next event in the Tribulation timeline. The previous steel blue Tiber River now was brown. Dead fish and waterfowl floated in the tepid river. The color of the Tiber reminded Gemma of the hot cocoa her mother made on cold English nights. Breaking an awkward silence by the group overlooking the effects of God's third trumpet judgment, Draven closed the question he asked.

"The answer I will give the world is that the phenomena directly correlate to the prior red tide caused by the Mediterranean meteorite strike. I am leaving for Jerusalem to establish my presence in direct contrast to the Two Witnesses. The world needs to see that I am not afraid of these men and their God. Do I make myself clear?"

Gemma and Evan nodded.

"I need some water," Draven demanded.

Demir Ersoy produced a water bottle dripping with condensation and handed the clear liquid to Draven.

I hope it's poisoned, Gemma thought.

Draven took a deep drink, swore once more, and threw the empty bottle back to Demir.

"I need everyone to get tougher on the zealots influenced by the Two Witnesses. I want these Omega terrorists dead. Ensure I am en route to Jerusalem within the hour, with you two accompanying."

Draven hesitated as he walked back to headquarters. He glared at Gemma before speaking to Evan. "One last thing. Place a 100 million UE dollar bounty on the heads of Gabriella and the Omega thugs. Ensure every available resource is given to John Barnes to hunt them down. Kill them and anyone helping them on sight."

Gemma clasped her hands as they trembled at the words and maniacal smile of Draven. As she ambled behind the evil world leader and his lieutenant, Gemma knew time was not on her side.

⌇

Nkoie, yet again, impressed Christopher with his operational security and ingenuity. The new safe house, a former Stellenbosch wine estate, was remote and well supplied. There was enough food and sleeping quarters to last 30 people a couple of months. According to Jackson, the bonus was a modest medical clinic, Nkoie's men established.

The previous night's stormy winter weather gave way to what appeared to be a better day. As the sun rose over False Bay, southeast of Cape Town, flanked by the eastern slope of Table Mountain, Christopher rubbed the rough stubble emerging on his face. He soaked in the inspiring view, nursing a cup of black coffee. The thought of how many sunrises he'd witnessed after a dangerous all-night mission brought endless memories to mind. Specifically, a night three years ago when Rev died, days before the Rapture. *How much longer can we go on like this?* Christopher fought to suppress his long-held habit of doubting God. Instead, he tried to determine what his broken and hunted team would do next.

Swallowing the last bit of the coffee, Christopher made his way from the cliff side toward a large stone building at the heart of the winery. In the previous history of the winery, Christopher envisioned the building as an event hall. Today, the space would host a memorial for Amahle and Kerim. He hoped to spend a few moments alone processing the feelings of losing more people close to him and contemplating ways to slow Draven's diabolical plans.

When Christopher pushed two ten-foot-tall ornate mahogany doors open, the sight of Nkoie sitting in front of the caskets of Amahle and Kerim caused him to pause.

"I wondered when someone would join me. It's been a long night, my friend," Nkoie said.

Christopher moved closer to Nkoie. "It's hard to forget nights like we've had for sure."

"I made myself busy. I got the caskets, notified family, checked security. Anything to keep my mind off Amahle. She acted more like my mother."

Christopher half-smiled at Nkoie's reference to his sister. He tried to match the expression of the man who had lost so much in the past month.

"You know I have the peace you described before the rescue. I know Amahle would be happy."

"I'm glad you found some peace in this situation."

Nkoie turned to face Christopher with tear-stained eyes. "Have you found any peace? You were out on the cliff most of the night. I thought you might jump."

Christopher sat back in his chair. "I am trying to find peace. In the short time I've been a Christian, I've learned that the more I hold on to things, the less peace I have. You're newer to trusting Jesus. My best advice, give God your pain. Cry your eyes, yell out if you need. Don't hold on to the pain, or it will lead to anger and you turning from God."

As Christopher rose from his chair, Nkoie embraced him with a reprimand. "If I may return some advice to you. Get some rest. Your team needs you. To ease your troubled mind, know that Gilana is resting and protected by Solomon and a few other men. After the funeral tonight, I will take your team to see her. Now go and sleep."

"Thank you, Nkoie. For everything," Christopher said.

Walking from the building, Christopher prayed God would grant him peace and mercy in the days ahead.

~§

Jackson glanced away from his plate of what he believed was beef and chewy noodles as he watched Christopher walk toward the sleeping quarters. He knew his leader and friend had slept little last night and prayed Christopher was not placing the deaths of Amahle and Kerim on his shoulders. Jackson was in no place to console anyone. While a part of him understood and accepted that death and heartache were a part of these last days, it never took the sting away from losing good people.

Anger and depression were constant companions with Jackson. The thoughts of not being with his wife Sarah and their two girls in the last moments of their lives haunted him with each death of someone he knew. If it weren't for the grace of God he found each day in studying Rev's Bible that he left behind… Jackson shook his head, trying to free his mind of thoughts that he'd considered harming himself.

The light shuffle of feet and the rattle of the ladle caused Jackson to look up from his "food" to see Gabriella join him in the empty dining room.

He returned to eating as she asked, "You mind if I sit with you?"

"It's a free… " Jackson stopped his snarky reply. "Some company would be nice."

"Is the food not good? It looks like you're staring more than eating."

"It will keep you alive if that's how you define good. I'm forcing myself to eat over continuing to lie in bed thinking about stuff I can't control."

After sprinkling salt on her food, Gabriella added, "Well, misery loves company because as much as I would like to sleep forever, I've spent more time staring at the ceiling. Have you seen Chris?"

"Chris-e-poo, walked by here recently. Heading for a bed is my guess."

"Really, Jackson. You will never let me live down calling Christopher, Chris instead, huh?"

"Ahh, it wouldn't be the same if I didn't keep you riled up. So, what's on your mind?"

"I'm not sure I know where to start. You go first."

Gabriella was devouring her food. Jackson knew that the behavior she displayed stemmed from being starved in prison. He'd seen rescued hostages behave the same way. The thought of his past missions caused him to unload his mind.

Jackson rubbed his beard. "I'm thinking the next three and half years are going to be rough. I miss my wife. I long to hold my girls. I wish I could have done more to protect General Havid, Gilana, Jimbo, Rev, Amahle, Charlie, and Kerim. That's what I am thinking."

"That's a lot. I know you've done everything possible to protect those you care about. You're a good and loving man, horrible with English, but a great man," Gabriella said taking another bite.

"Watch it. I speak as good as any of you college folks."

"Jackson, you went to college. I'm sure you slept through English 101, but you're college-educated like us."

"Well, I went to a small school in Alabama; you and 'Chris' went to fancy colleges."

Gabriella licked her fork clean as she walked toward the pot of beef and noodles. "How's Gilana?"

"According to Nkoie, she is stable, but will need to recover for several weeks. I'm not sure when or where we're going next, but I'm sure Gilana will be in South Africa for a while."

Gabriella's right hand tremble as she dropped the ladle against the stainless-steel pot. "Gilana, Amahle, and Kerim are my fault, Jackson. You guys should have let me die."

Jackson moved toward Gabriella, who now faced away from him as her shoulders heaved and sobs arose. "Listen. There is no way that either Christopher or I would let you rot in some prison. Now come and sit down. My back really hurts, so if I keep standing here and holding you, either my back or you are going to be in trouble."

A brief smile crested the scarred face of Gabriella as Jackson walked her back to the table before continuing to encourage her. "Gabriella, you can't go down the road of blaming yourself. You and Christopher at least have that in common. You are so quick to blame yourselves for everything. In case you've missed the destruction and crazy stuff happening with nature, we're living in the Tribulation. These are the last days of human history. Every day is a scrap for survival. Kerim is in Heaven, along with Amahle. Like all of us, the choices they made led to them suffering through the Tribulation until their deaths. Take comfort in the fact they knew the Lord."

Gabriella sniffled. "I betrayed you guys. During waterboarding, I told the UE that Omega was in Australia."

Jackson took a bite of the lukewarm beef and noodles, causing him to scowl. "You didn't betray us. It was Draven, through his errand-boy John Barnes, that sold us all up the river. Plus, I remember being waterboarded during SERE school, and I would have sold my mama for a nickel to have them stop. My experience was in a controlled environment, not being tortured by the enemy. Ease up on yourself, little sister."

Gabriella folded her arms. "It doesn't feel that way. I agree Draven caused the losses I've experienced in the last three years. I want Draven to feel some pain, to suffer."

"That makes two of us. That son of the devil deserves a slow, painful death. However, the Bible tells us we will have to wait for a while to see that day."

"Jackson, I'm going to make him pay."

"Who?" Christopher's voice caused Jackson and Gabriella to look over to the food pot as Christopher swirled the ladle while scrunching his face.

"You're sneaking around now? And shouldn't you be sleeping?" Jackson asked.

"I could ask you two the same thing. I think we're all facing some demons, but it sounds like you two are plotting trouble," Christopher said, flipping a chair around to join Jackson and Gabriella.

"I'm trying to keep Ms. Trouble here away from her crazy thoughts," Jackson said.

Gabriella stood. "I spent two months in that living hell. Neither of you will lecture me. Draven will suffer at my hands, or I will die trying."

"What do you think all of us focused on the last two months? Let me help you with the answer; it was trying to save you! Kerim and Amahle are dead trying to save you. And Gilana, well, let's hope for the best." Christopher challenged.

"Chris, how could… ?" Gabriella walked out of the dining room sobbing.

Jackson stood up leaning forward on the table to stare Christopher in the face. "What is your deal? That woman has suffered in ways I don't want to think about, and you pull the 'tough love' routine. You were wrong there, brother."

"I'm not sure I want to keep fighting, Draven. I think you would agree the cost has been steep. Let's not forget the UE locked General Havid up," Christopher said.

Jackson straightened, staring at Christopher with his arms folded. "I never thought I'd see the day Christopher Barrett lost his nerve. Since you brought up the general, what do you think he would tell you?"

When Christopher started to reply, Jackson cut him off. "He would tell you to stop feeling sorry for yourself. Stop doubting what you can't control, which is the future. God has a plan for all of us. We won't live one second longer than God's plan. So, I won't hide and hope I live to see Jesus in three and half years. No, sir. I'm taking the fight to Draven every day."

Jackson slapped the table and walked out, hoping to leave Christopher with some motivation.

∽

CHAPTER 26

GEMMA'S STOMACH KNOTTED up with thoughts about the days ahead during the UE One captain's one-hour from arrival announcement for Ben Gurion Airport. Draven and Evan hid the entire flight in the Secretary-General's suite, adding to her anxiety.

Who knows what evil they're plotting? I need to know. Gemma went to the galley, poured two tonic water drinks with a dash of lime, and took them to the command suite.

Gemma knocked on the command suite door before barging into the room.

"What do you want, Gemma?" Draven demanded.

"I thought you could you a refreshment."

"Excellent. Running the world is tough work," Evan said.

Draven snidely remarked, "Yes, especially when you're doing it on your own. Leave the drinks and get out."

Gemma nodded to Draven while studying a whiteboard with the word *Eliminate.* She memorized the names written on the board while slowly placing Draven's drink on a coaster on his desk.

"Will there be anything else, sir, before we land?"

"No, get out."

Gemma walked out of the command suite, bound for her laptop. Christopher and Omega needed to know what Draven planned.

❦

Christopher sat sulking, debating if it was worth the pain to continue eating what he found in the pot or facing Jackson and Gabriella, who were mad at him. Thankfully, as he got up to see Jackson and Gabriella, Nkoie burst into the dining hall.

"Why are you not watching the news?" Nkoie asked.

"I'm not interested in hearing lies about how great Draven Cross is today. What's up?"

Nkoie moved past Christopher to turn on a television mounted above a nearby food service counter. Nkoie turned up the volume before returning to sit next to him.

An anchor in the studio was first on the screen. "Good afternoon, I'm Stewart Davis here in the ANN Global Studios in Rome. If you're just joining us, we're following the emerging disaster plaguing the world's water supplies. I am joined in studio by Dr. Jacobsen, the UE Chief Scientist, and from Jerusalem Sam Morrow, ANN's lead for covering the Two Witnesses. Sam, I want to start with you. Can you provide any insight into the proclamations of the Two Witnesses and issues with the water?"

"Well, I would point everyone back to what Reuel and Eliyahu said a little over twenty-four hours ago. 'God's judgments should soften your hearts and lead you to seek Heaven's mercy and offer of salvation.' The Witnesses have made clear God orchestrated this latest crisis."

The EU scientist interrupted the reporter. "Steward, Dr. Jacobsen here, if I may interrupt. I disagree with referencing any statements of these witnesses and a mythical god they purportedly represent. Those two fools in Jerusalem are merely stating the obvious after the fact. When the Secretary-General launched the nuclear weapon at the asteroid yesterday, destroying the threat, the remnants of the asteroid intermixed with nuclear debris and filtered down into many of Earth's water systems. The problem will clear up in a matter of days."

Nkoie shut off the television, opening his arms wide while grinning at Christopher.

"What am I missing, Nkoie? I realize this was God's third trumpet judgment, but we knew that yesterday."

Nkoie laughed. "I am a newborn in God's family and can see the truth. God spared us."

Christopher didn't have time to process what Nkoie told him before being dragged to the open space between the dining facility and event hall where Kerim and Amahle's bodies were. The fifteen remaining members of Nkoie's resistance, including Solomon, were awaiting him with cups or buckets or anything they could find filled with water.

"Nkoie, I don't understand," Christopher said.

"Please pray with them, as Jackson did with me."

Christopher was exhausted and in the moment God seemed distant. The "miracle" inspiring Nkoie and his team was not evident. He hoped he was not about to make another friend mad. "Who's protecting Gilana, if Solomon is here?"

"She is fine. Mpilo is with her."

As one of Nkoie's warriors laughed and tossed a cup of water into the air allowing it to splash on his head, the reason for their rejoicing became clear. God opened Christopher's eyes in that moment. The water at the safe house had been spared from judgment. Nkoie and his team had served God in the rescue of Gabriella and now the Lord gave them the chance to receive his gift of salvation.

Christopher fought to compose himself. How foolish and selfish he had been earlier, doubting God's faithfulness even as God continued to provide for everyone he cared about.

Christopher nodded before saying, "Everyone—"

Nkoie tapped him on the shoulder. "They all have seen the truth that the God of the Bible lives and all want to know Jesus. I will translate. Everyone cannot speak English."

Christopher cleared his throat before he began his prayer. Nkoie's baritone voice added a dramatic flair to the moment as he translated Christopher's words.

"Everyone, please bow your heads and close your eyes. God, thank you for watching over me, even as a sinner at war with You. Thank you for loving me for who I am at this moment with all my flaws. Father, I believe You sent Your only son, Jesus Christ, to die on the cross for my sins. I believe Jesus rose again on the third day and lives, sitting next to You in Heaven. Forgive me of my sins and guide my life as my Lord from this day until You call me to You in Heaven. Amen."

Nkoie and his team let out a whoop that boomed across the winery. "Thank you, my brother. We are all now family."

"Yes, we are, Nkoie," Christopher said.

⋘

Jackson found Gabriella sitting on a bench that overlooked the barren, black-earth rows, where in years past vines would droop with plump grapes. A cool breeze and the fading sun behind Stellenbosch Mountain at the far end of the rows made an idyllic setting. Gabriella's sobs and shoulder heaves, however, painted a different picture.

Gabriella turned to Jackson as he sat next to her. "Do you ever think about how much suffering the jobs we chose caused in the world?"

Jackson ran his hands through his hair. "I like to think that I've eased more suffering than I've caused. Maybe it's the lie I tell myself, so I sleep at night."

"Jackson, Chris was right. So many people died because of me, including Kerim and Amahle. I spent my career at the CIA tracking down the 'bad guys' to pass the information off to the likes of you. How many innocent people died at my hands while evil men like Draven escaped?"

"The college boy was wrong for what he said, but he didn't blame you for Kerim and Amahle's death. They believed in the same God you do, a God who said, 'Greater love has no one than this: to lay down one's life for one's friends.' As far as your time in the Agency, you were protecting millions who never knew they were in danger. The world is not a fairy tale; there is evil out there that needs to be put down."

"Exactly. Draven must die!"

More than the twilight and stiff breeze caused a chill to run over Jackson. Gabriella was bent on trying to kill Draven. *How do I help her, Lord?*

As Jackson prepared to respond, he heard a shout coming from the central area of the winery. Gabriella began making her way toward the noise before Jackson could stand up. "Gabriella, wait up. It could be trouble."

"I am not afraid of dying, Jackson. Our time is short."

Jackson shook his head as he caught up to Gabriella, pulling his pistol from the holster and racking a round into the chamber as they neared the dining facility.

✍

Jackson pushed Gabriella against a wall with his left arm, causing a loud sigh from her as he peered around a corner to determine the threat.

"What's going on, Jackson?" Gabriella asked.

Jackson smiled as Nkoie and Christopher approached. "Come on, it's okay."

"Our night of mourning has turned into a day of celebration," Nkoie said.

Christopher smiled as he watched a traditional Zulu celebratory dance.

"Have you guys found some wine around here?" Jackson questioned.

"I was going to ask the same thing," Gabriella added.

"Christopher led my men to Christ. God's protection of our water inspired them to believe," Nkoie said.

Gabriella smirked. "Water?"

"ANN is reporting that water sources worldwide are killing people," Christopher said.

Nkoie added, "Yet, we have clean water to drink. Amahle would be singing and dancing right now."

Nkoie and the other Zulu tribesmen chanted and danced toward the event space as Jackson and the other two members of Omega prepared for the farewell of two great people.

Jackson prayed, *God, let this be the last memorial I attend before your return.*

∽

Gemma took notice of a distraction during the ride to the UE Middle East Regional headquarters. There was a growing crowd along the Jerusalem streets approaching the headquarters. Along the road, the people's faces carried scowls. Gemma imagined the Hebrew picket signs dozens held had similar messages to those written in English. The posters in English stated, "Draven is the Beast, Water is a right, and Pontiff Conti gives us hope."

Gemma knew that the last message would send Draven into an emotional meltdown.

Streams of profanity flowing from the global leader confirmed her assumption. "I hate these people and this country. I should unleash the UE military on this hovel of a nation and wipe them from the face of the Earth," Draven said.

A cheeky remark stirred within Gemma. She fought the urge to say, *It didn't work out seven years ago when the Russian-Iranian coalition attacked Israel.*

"Gemma, where is that peacock Conti? He should have removed this mob before my arrival," Draven asked.

Before Gemma could respond, Evan provided the answer, "Conti is in Prague. He's leading an Interfaith aide rally at Old Town Square."

Gemma was grateful Draven's wrath turned to Evan. "How long have you known about this rally?"

"I only learned of Conti's efforts moments ago as I began preparing for our arrival after landing."

As the motorcade entered the Middle East regional headquarters, Gemma watched as Draven took a moment to adjust his appearance after his meltdown. "Evan, ensure the rabble that welcomed me to this worthless nation has an encounter with the UE security forces.

167

Gemma, have John Barnes at this office within the hour. I expect a press statement to be released in the next thirty minutes stating I dispatched Conti to provide aid around the world."

Gemma nodded as Draven exited the car to the flashes of cameras and applause from the Middle East regional staff. However, the cheers competed with heckling from the "rabble," which caused Draven's smile to fade. Gemma hoped Christopher received her message highlighting Draven's elimination plot. She had yet to get a response from him. Gemma prayed Omega could save the general and her before it was too late.

Christopher walked behind Jackson and Gabriella as the procession of dancing and chanting Zulu warriors took the bodies of Amahle and Kerim to their temporary resting place. He shook his head; three years ago, he would have never thought of bodies being buried as a short-term thing. The reality facing Christopher and everyone in the tribulation was the uncertainty of life. The last year proved that even believers escaping death's reach was not guaranteed in the final years of human history.

The funeral of Amahle and Kerim was a touching tribute to the Christians they'd become, and the efforts of Christopher's team to thwart God's enemies personified in Draven Cross. However, the emotional high of watching 15 new souls join God's Kingdom faded. The funeral of dear friends and the troubles to come caused doubt to creep back into his mind. Christopher wondered if he had the ability or desire to continue such a one-sided fight. The cost had been steep since the Rapture for his team, while Satan's henchmen Draven prospered.

Now, Christopher sat for the second time in 24-hours on the cliff overlooking False Bay. The setting sun behind him turned the South Atlantic Ocean a dark purple color. The rustling of rocks announced the footsteps he assumed were Jackson or Gabriella looking for him. But the voice caused Christopher to whirl and gasp.

"I'm not sure why you struggle with trusting God. How many times has God allowed you to live in the past three years? How many deployments did you complete?"

"Who are you?" Christopher asked.

"God assigned me to you before your birth, as he knit you in your mother's womb. As the Lord Jesus declared in Matthew 18:10, *'See that you do not despise one of these little ones. For I tell you that their angels in heaven always see the face of my Father in heaven.'* I am your guardian angel. I've been a stranger that gave you an encouraging word after your mother's funeral. I've given you a push at the right moment, so you fell behind that tree in Afghanistan moments before the ambush tore through your platoon. Christopher, my name is of little importance, but who I represent and His care for you means the world. But because I know you so well, let me ease your fears with my name; I am Caleb."

Christopher stood and scrambled a few feet away from the impressive "man" standing over him. The angel was at least six foot three and appeared carved from solid muscle. His smooth, dark skin reminded Christopher of Amahle. However, Caleb's most striking feature was his piercing gray eyes, which brought an intensity that made it hard to look him in the face.

Christopher felt as if Caleb could see through him. "How? I mean, I have so many questions."

Caleb laughed. "You've always been curious. One of my favorite memories is when you wanted to know what the inside of a hornet's nest looked like. The look on your face as you jumped into your grandmother's pond was priceless."

"I remember. I was eight years old."

"I know you're shocked, as I've never conversed with you in this manner. I can't answer all the questions you have. God did not send me here for that purpose today. Christopher, trust that God loves you. He's always loved you, even through the most painful days you've faced. You must continue to lead your team. Christopher, you can save many believers before this season of tribulation is complete. As the Great Tribulation draws near, survival will be your hope each day. Stop doubting God and start living with his power. While the choices you made caused you to live through this period, God has worked all things in your life toward good because He loves you."

Christopher teared up at the words of Caleb. He turned from his guardian angel as he heard the churning of rocks as someone else approached the cliffside.

"Caleb, I want to tell you thanks… ?"

Christopher's words faded away as Caleb had done, leaving Nkoie and Jackson standing in front of him.

"We must go. Gilana is in danger," Nkoie said.

"Are you okay? You look like you've seen a ghost," Jackson added.

Christopher knew Caleb was real but remained shaken from the experience. "I'm fine. Let's get going. You can fill me in on the details as we go."

The beep of an incoming text message caused Christopher to stop running after Nkoie and Jackson.

Gemma's message read: *Draven is planning on executing General Havid publicly at the UE peace treaty celebration next month. His plan for extermination also extended to Omega, and 'every Christian' before or soon after the celebration of signing the UE peace treaty with Israel in a month. There is a 100 million UE dollar bounty on your heads. I don't know what to do, besides trying to get you here. I am sending a UE transport to pick you up and bring you to Israel. By the time you arrive in Israel, I'll have a safe house for you. More to follow. God bless.*

Jackson turned back to Christopher as he finished reading the message. "What happened?"

"There's a $100 million bounty out for us, and Gemma is sending a transport. We need to get Gabriella and get to Gilana. We're leaving South Africa for Israel tomorrow."

Following after Jackson and his pursuit of Gabriella, Christopher prayed, *God protect us.*

❧

CHAPTER 27

THE CROWD'S ROAR echoed through Old Town Square in Prague. Each Interfaith rally across Europe was larger than the last. Pontiff Conti felt waves of electric energy flowing over him and within the air. The Prince of This World, the spirit he believed was the true god of the universe, spoke in his dreams last night. *"Your efforts support my plans."*

Standing behind a curtain that wafted in a warm summer breeze, Conti knew this was his moment. The sight of dirty, sunken faces awaiting his remarks brought a smile to his face. He realized his power as millions depended upon him for food and water. *Draven is not the most powerful man in the world; I am.* Conti relished his thoughts as a thunderous shout welcomed him to the main stage.

"I am here with you tonight to bring you comfort in your time of suffering. It is horrid that some leaders have been slow to act while you've starved. How can we trust a leader that watched your fields and crops burn and now allows you to witness loved ones die of bitter waters?"

Conti soaked in the applause from the young and the old who expected the free food, water, and clothing that his Interfaith rallies provided.

"Let me end tonight with this. The world will soon have a choice for leadership. You can have a loving leader or those that care for themselves over the people. May peace reign on Earth and the light shine within you."

The Pontiff felt the firm grasp of his aide Giuseppe on his shoulder as he waved and smiled to the ANN cameras and the world. He turned and followed Giuseppe, returning behind the curtain as music played during the food distributions.

"*Troppo mia eminenza.*"

"You believe I say too much, Giuseppe. I've said too little. That monster in Rome benefits from serving only himself. Draven is a dictator with new clothes. There is no comparing my influence on the world versus his. I have drawn the people's hearts toward a peaceful future he's only promised. So, I will not be silent any longer."

Giuseppe's phone rang and his face flushed. "Ayatollah al-Farshid. Do you want me to answer?"

Conti took the phone from Giuseppe. "Ayatollah. What a pleasant surprise."

"Pontiff Conti. My patience is growing thin. The *Hashishin* I've provided is precious, and you've wasted his skills. Instead of touring the world for your own benefit, perhaps you should remember the oath you've made. You have one month to rid the world of the Beast, or I will rid the world of both of you." Al-Farshid hung up.

Conti handed the phone back to Giuseppe. "We have a problem. Al-Farshid wants Draven dead now and threatens to kill me if Demir doesn't complete his mission within a month. What my narrow-minded accomplice is missing is the timing for the assassination has to be perfect to deflect away from me. I have to wait for the ceremony."

Giuseppe ran his calloused hands through his black hair. "*Che macello!* You should tell the Ayatollah the reason for delay. We don't want to make an enemy like him."

Pontiff Conti paced. "This is a mess. However, you don't see the opportunity before us. At next month's Israel-UE treaty ceremony, we will kill Draven and blame the event on Al-Farshid. The UE will remove the Ayatollah, and Draven will be dead. Giuseppe, everything is falling into place for my ascension. Now, let's get to the airport and on to Oslo; the people need their benevolent leader."

෴

Christopher had more worries than assurance as he, along with Jackson and Gabriella, sped toward Gilana's hospital in Nkoie's truck. Two additional trucks carrying Nkoie's fighters followed them as the sunset behind the Stellenbosch mountains.

"So let me get this straight. There's a bounty for us and we're heading back to Israel, where Draven has issued a kill on sight order for us," Jackson said.

Christopher replied, "You got it."

"Your plan sounds rushed," Nkoie said, turning his focus from the winding mountain road. "I think you should stay here."

"We can't stay here, Nkoie. A man who risked his life for us has an execution date, and we need to stop it. Plus, with the bounty, if anyone identifies us with you, we are putting you and your team at risk. Now tell me, what's waiting for us at the hospital?"

Nkoie said, "Mpilo identified a large group coming to the hospital. If what Gemma has told us about the bounty is true. We cannot leave Gilana there. She will need to come to the safe house."

When the trucks crested the last hill before reaching Gilana, the "threat" became apparent to Christopher. There was no military presence, only suffering people heading toward the clinic. Exhausted faces carrying dead and dying loved ones walked beside a line of stagnant vehicles filled with people seeking help. Those that continue to reject Jesus Christ faced the effect of the third trumpet judgment. The mass of humanity covered at least a half-mile and was growing.

Christopher stared at several sick people in the back of a truck. "Nkoie, do you have any ideas on how we can get past these people and Gilana out of the hospital?"

Nkoie answered Christopher by weaving the truck through a gaggle of people who looked like zombies focused on only moving forward. Nkoie brought the truck to rest under a buffalo thorn tree before calling Mpilo. Christopher listened as the men had a conversation in Zulu.

Nkoie said, "I told Mpilo to load Gilana into the Mfezi and bring her to us."

"Let me ask what's on everyone's mind here. What in the world is a Mfezi? Is that some sort of animal?" Jackson questioned.

Christopher shook his head as Nkoie laughed so hard tears ran down his cheeks. "Mfezi, my friend, is what we called the ambulance in the South African military. Mpilo will get through the crowd in the ambulance. It will take him a few minutes to get here."

Christopher had spent enough time in South Africa and around Nkoie to know if he said something would only take a few minutes, it could be hours. He took the inevitable delay as an opportunity to mend his relationship with Gabriella. The fading light cast a shadow over part of Gabriella's face in the rear of Nkoie's truck. He found the light and dark shadows battling over Gabriella's face, symbolic of the war raging within her.

"Gabriella, can I talk with you outside for a second?"

Gabriella let out a sigh and rolled her eyes hard at Christopher. "Sure."

Christopher felt less confident Gabriella wanted to talk with him based on her body language, but he got reassuring nods from Jackson and Nkoie.

Like a teenage boy asking a girl to the prom, Christopher blurted as soon as he was out of the vehicle. "Gabriella, I am sorry for how I spoke to you earlier. I wasn't trying to blame you for Amahle or Kerim's deaths."

Gabriella spoke with folded arms. "Thanks for saying that, Chris. Your bluntness hurt, but I understood what you were trying to say. I know all of you were trying to help me."

"I can't imagine, and I am afraid to know what you've been through the last few months. But a suicide mission against Draven won't fill the hole in your heart."

Gabriella moved her hands to her jean pockets and kicked the dirt. "Chris, I don't intend to sit around and wait for Draven to kill me. I believe God has a purpose for me in these final years before his return. I want to make an impact."

Christopher walked in front of Gabriella. "Do you want to make an impact for yourself or for God?"

"Why do I have to choose? If screwing up every plan Draven has fits God's needs, all the better. I believe my goals and God's align."

"Bold statement, Gabriella. Look"—Christopher paused as the cartoonish whirl of a siren drew near—"I will support you with my life, but I will not stand by while you're being foolish. I care about… "

Gabriella put a finger to Christopher's lips, stopping him from completing his thought. "Chris, this is not the time or place to share personal feelings. Let's get Gilana and get after Draven."

Gabriella left Christopher and walked toward the ambulance and the others. He wanted to say more, but like the moment years ago in Damascus when they first worked together, Gabriella saw his heart and silenced him. Christopher resigned himself to keep his feelings for Gabriella buried, as she wanted.

Christopher approached the ambulance—which was nothing more than a large box van—and found the team hovering and talking all at once. The gaggle stood in front of the two back panel doors like moths attracted to light.

"How's Gilana?" Christopher asked.

"Well, ask her yourself," Jackson said.

The team parted as Christopher stepped up on the first step into the van's rear to find Gabriella seated next to Gilana's gurney. He knew it was Gilana only because he knew the plan that led him to this moment. Gilana's wounds caused severe swelling in her face, with the right side bandaged. IV bags dangled from a support that dripped pain medication into Gilana's veins.

"Christopher is here," Gabriella said.

Gilana opened her bloodshot and blackened left eye. She struggled to force her dry, cracked lips to part. "I am alive."

Christopher ducked his head into the ambulance. "Yes, you are my friend. We won't keep you long, but we're heading back to Israel to gear up for the fight ahead. Nkoie and his people will care for you until you can rejoin us. We can't take you with us nor leave you at the hospital. Draven is looking for us."

A tear fell from Gilana's eye, while she nodded.

"We love you and will avenge Kerim, Amahle, and you," Gabriella said.

Christopher worried about the cost it would take to make Gabriella's statement true as she moved past him and into the darkness with Jackson and the others. As he prepared to close the ambulance panel doors, Gilana waved him toward her.

Christopher kneeled beside her in the cramped space as she said, "Trust no one in the IDF. Remember what they did to the general."

"We will not forget. You have my word, Gilana. Christopher squeezed Gilana's hand before leaving and closing the panel doors to the ambulance. He found Jackson, Gabriella, and Mpilo huddled near Nkoie's vehicle.

Nkoie spoke to the group. "We will care for Gilana with our lives. Let's pray that God heals her in a way that she can make our enemies pay for her suffering."

Christopher's thoughts were interrupted by Jackson. "That woman is tougher than a piece of beef jerky left in the Alabama summer sun. She will be with us in no time."

Jackson's moment of levity eased the transition Christopher knew needed to happen for the ragtag group of operatives.

"We need to get to the airport and wait for our ride to Israel to prevent compromising your team. Thank you, Nkoie, for all you're doing for us and the Kingdom of God," Christopher said.

"Fewer worries, my friend. Let's get your team to the airport. Mpilo and Solomon will take Gilana back to our safe house."

Christopher loaded up into Nkoie's truck as he followed the ambulance through the mass of humanity that wandered to a Zulu-run clinic managed by members of Nkoie's tribe. He prayed to himself as Nkoie's truck turned toward the airport while the ambulance circled back into the mountains. *God, give us the mercy we don't deserve and the grace we need.*

⤚

Gemma sat at her desk frantically typing a text message to Christopher to update him on the transport to Israel, highlighting the pilot's name and estimated arrival early tomorrow morning. She'd used the UE Logistics Division director Hank Mankenson's name in vain. Given the deceit she'd been engaged in, the sound of a gruff voice startled her.

"I didn't mean to scare you, but you're a sight any condemned man would request. What I'm trying to say is, I am always happy to see you, Gemma," John Barnes said.

"John, I wish I could return the sentiment. Yet, every time we meet, it turns into more work for me. What do you want this time?"

Veins emerged in Barnes's temples, and his fist became tight. "Gemma, one of these days, you will learn your place, and I will be your teacher! Do your job and tell the boss I am here to see him!"

Gemma noticed Draven exit his office and move behind Barnes. "There will be no need to tell me anything, John. You're late."

Barnes nearly fell on the ground, trying to give himself space from the piercing glare of Draven, causing Gemma to resist a chuckle. "I am sorry, sir. I was here, but Gemma... "

Draven ignored John's excuse. "Gemma will provide you a contact I sent to her via email from the IDF. This contact will ensure you accomplish the mission that thus eludes you, ferreting out the Christian insurgents supporting the two fools at the temple."

Draven drew near John Barnes, silencing the man as Evan joined the group around her desk. "As you told Gemma, let me reiterate to you; do your job, John, or I will ensure your demise comes sooner than expected. Are we clear?"

"Yes, Secretary-General. I won't fail you." -

"Fatal last words."

Draven and Evan entered the command suite elevators as John Barnes attempted to regain his composure. Gemma handed him a note that read, "Noam Cohen, IDF Major, will be wearing a red jacket, Mamilla Mall, Old City Entrance in one hour."

"What's this?" John asked.

"I suggest your attention to detail improves quickly based on what the Secretary-General threatened. This is the contact he wants you to meet."

John snatched the piece of paper from Gemma and cursed under his breath.

"Until we meet again, Mr. Barnes," Gemma said.

Barnes used a derogatory hand gesture toward Gemma as the elevator doors closed. She laughed off the slight, trying to prepare mentally for the burden heading her way. Omega's arrival in Israel meant the dawning of a new, dangerous era for Gemma in service to Draven Cross.

≪⊰

The UE-owned luxury penthouse purchased for Draven was the jewel in an exclusive central Jerusalem neighborhood. Draven assuaged his ego and the lack of media fawning on the never-ending series of crises befalling the world. A broad smile rose across his face with all the attention his motorcade garnered as a nest of white camera flashes erupted, breaking the dark void along the street.

Draven's limo door opened at the entrance of his new home, but the world leader lingered. He waved the guard away before speaking with Evan.

"We are a month away from celebrating my crowning moment, ensuring a lasting peace between Israel and the world. The Prince of This World has assured me I will be regarded as the greatest leader in human history. Yet, three things mar my story, the Two Witnesses, the Christian terrorists, and the Interfaith religion."

Draven reacted to Evan. "Spare me your shock over Interfaith, challenging my power. Was it not you, Evan, that warned me mere months ago of Conti's ambition?"

"I did, sir, but… will you destroy the religion because of a poor leader?"

"I never share my power with anyone. Not my father, not you, or your fairy-tale religion. I have found my Judas within the Christian network. That jackal John Barnes is meeting with him now. I expect Conti, the Witnesses, Interfaith, and every rebelling Christian to be dead in a month. I am all the world needs."

Draven exited his limo, slamming the door on Evan and any doubts his deputy had toward the challengers to his rule overtaking him.

❦

John Barnes could feel the stare of Noem Cohen, if that was his real name, as he walked toward a coffee shop. The scenario he found himself within brought his thoughts back to the human intelligence operations course of his early special forces career. The course instructors hid in crowds, judging candidates' abilities to pass and receive sensitive intelligence. John's veins engorged in his forehead as he thought about someone playing a game with him.

This guy should come to me. He should seek my help. John sat down and ordered a cup of coffee. He tried to keep his emotions and thoughts under control.

The waiter returned his coffee, and Noem had yet to join him. John sipped the coffee, scanning the thin crowd of people in the shopping mall. As he finished the small espresso and stood to leave, he heard footsteps approaching from the opposite direction.

John identified the tall slender younger man wearing a tailored red blazer and black slacks approaching him as Noem Cohen.

"Mr. Barnes, are you nervous? You know looking around when in a crowd draws attention," Noem said.

"Where do you get off judging me? Is this a game for you? We're supposed to be working for the same people."

"Mr. Barnes—"

John cut him off. "Call me John, and you're Noem, right?"

"Yes, I am Noem. This environment will challenge you from everything I've seen of you tonight."

John stepped toward the man, who had at least two inches over his six-foot frame.

Noem held his hands up. "Excuse my harsh tone. If you want to find the Christian zealots, you need to operate like the enemy is watching. The Christians survive using methods that seem less like a religion and more like your CIA from the old world. So, let's go."

"Go where? I don't know you," John protested.

"Trust and getting to know others are not always an option for men like us. We are going to a Bible meeting. Now follow me. There are men more dangerous than me watching, so it's to your health not to make a scene. Your choice, John."

John looked around, only seeing shop owners closing as he walked behind Noem into the parking lot. Noem disappeared as a canvas bag thrust John's head back, blinding him to the world. He felt the strength of at least two men as they slammed him to the ground and zip-tied his hands. His lips quivered as thoughts of the unknown filled his mind. John wondered if the screech of tires, a whiff of burned rubber, and rushed Hebrew voices would be his last memories as he landed on his side in the back of a vehicle.

John tried to remember his survival and evasion training as the vehicle made several turns. *I was walking toward the west when someone grabbed me.* He screamed as he couldn't remember how many turns the van made. John concluded he would die tonight. His stomach churned, and he started sweating, hearing voices outside the van's doors.

Suddenly, the doors burst open.

What John thought was the voice of Noem whispered, "Listen carefully. Act like a 'seeker,' a person wanting to know Jesus, or you will die. Nod your head if you understand."

John nodded, and seconds later, he was being pulled from the van and onto his feet. An unfamiliar male voice shouted, "Walk!"

The faceless men pulled John down a set of stairs and into a bright room, where he heard the whispers of others before they snatched the canvas bag from his head.

"Why did you meet our brother Noem?" an onion breathed middle-aged man asked.

John winced from the man's breath and the sharp light flooding his eyes. "I am here seeking Jesus."

A murmur grew from the shadows. The foul-breathed man disappeared from in front of John. Moments later, he smelled the man behind him breaking the zip-ties binding his hands.

"Your search has led to the right place. Welcome, brother. I am Ori."

John rubbed his wrist and his eyes as the spotlight turned off. He sat in the middle of a large classroom. There were dozens of people sitting in chairs around him.

He glanced at the scarred and careworn faces staring at him. "This is not the type of welcome I would expect from Christians."

John met Noem's eyes, where disapproval radiated after his sarcasm.

Ori stepped in front of John. "My apologies again, John, but these are standard practices when an unknown seeker contacts a group member. The Beast wants to kill all who desire the truth found in Jesus Christ. Jesus told his disciples in Matthew 10:16-17, *I am sending you out like sheep among wolves. Therefore be as shrewd as snakes and as innocent as doves. Be on your guard; you will be handed over to the local councils and be flogged in the synagogues.'* The words of our Savior ring true in these trying times, our methods keep the doves alive. Noem told us you sought him out, so we sent a security team to follow. You will hear a message from our leader, but you will leave here the same way you arrived."

Before John could respond, a broadcasted voice echoed through the conference room.

"Ori, your security precautions have helped us, but remember, Jesus said the way we love each other is how the world would know us. John, welcome. Please take a seat so we can begin. There is much to discuss. God's Witnesses continue to provide truth. We will prepare for more souls to search for us in the days ahead. The Witnesses' messages and the truth they represent will cause more seekers to appear. The sad news is God's Witnesses have little time remaining for their purpose. The end of the Witnesses will bring about the darkest days yet.

"In the next two weeks, the new members amongst you will sit for the 'Assigning' where you'll receive your role within the church. You will join our brothers and sisters, preparing safe havens for all who choose Jesus over the Beast. Prepare your hearts now, as judgments of God will intensify, and the cruelty of the Beast will burn to destroy God's beloved. Remember the Lord will not leave or forsake us, even in these trying times. Jesus's death on the cross for all our sins and our hope in Him ensures that even death will not take us from His love."

John touched the side of his temple, checking to see if there was a crack in his head where waves of shooting pain coursed across his face. He knew the discomfort came partly from his treatment getting here. Wherever here was. However, a sense of guilt rose within him, hearing the speaker's words and the sincerity of the people in the room. He didn't believe in God. Still, he felt something, as he looked at the scared and gaunt faces around him. An acute sense of conviction arose within him to learn about Jesus. It felt like a presence surrounding him, pushing him to reflect on the wrongs in his life, urging him to change.

John wondered how hard he'd hit his head in the van. These feelings were wholly out of character for him. "When will we move? When will we be safe?" a man near John blurted.

John was happy the man broke the "spell" he felt in the room as he rubbed his temple.

The voice said, "The details of our plans will be forthcoming. I will leave you with a point of encouragement. I have word that a group of believers will arrive in Israel soon to ensure we reach our stronghold and free those dear to us held captive. Until we meet again, stay vigilant and continue to seek God's guidance."

John turned to Noem, but the canvas bag was back on his head and his hands tied before he spoke. As the Christians eased John into a van seat, this ride carried more dignity. After several minutes and turns, the vehicle stopped, and they let John out. He heard the van drive away before someone removed the canvas bag. Noem was the only person standing with him.

The two men stood alone at the Mamilla Mall entrance, where John had begun his search for Noem hours ago.

"I told you the Christians were cautious. I've never seen their leader or received his name. It's always the same, only a voice. What do you think?" Noem asked.

John was conflicted to say the least. The terrorists, as Draven labeled the Christians, were made of up of women, the elderly, and desperate people, not a credible threat to his power. The message from the voice stirred in John a feeling that he lacked the ability to describe. He shook his head regaining focus on the task Draven had for him. "The Christians are crafty, but there was one thing from tonight we can exploit. The voice mentioned help was coming to free those held captive. The Omega group may be the help they're expecting. General Havid is the top prisoner every Christian in Israel wants to see free. I will bring a device to pinpoint the voice's location at the next meeting. We need to take down this network with a single attack, and if I get Omega, all the better. When do they meet again?"

Noem said, "They will let me know. There is never a schedule. Only last-minute meetings. Their technique is wise but hard to anticipate. I expect the next meeting will center on the Omega terrorist if your assumption about them is correct,"

John shivered in the chilly night, folding his arms as he studied Noem. "What's your story?

"You passed the test tonight, and that is all that matters. I will call you when I have something. Assume you're being watched at all times," Noem said, walking toward the parking lot where the van abducted John.

John shouted after Noem, "How do you know I passed the test?"

"You're alive."

∽

CHAPTER 28

CHRISTOPHER AWOKE IN a cold sweat. It was four in the morning in Jerusalem, and for the past two weeks, the same nightmare plagued his mind. Jackson died in front of him, and Gabriella struggled in danger beyond his help. He sat on the edge of the bed in a safe house; Omega had yet to venture beyond since their arrival in Jerusalem two weeks ago. Christopher pulled his phone from the charger, reviewing Gemma's text from yesterday.

It read: *Tomorrow, I expect fireworks as Draven plans to interrupt the morning message of the Two Witnesses. I know you all are eager to free, General Havid, but the timing must center on the treaty celebration, when his public execution is planned. John Barnes has been unusually low key, communicating with Evan or Draven via email only. Still, I know he is searching for the Christian resistance here, and likely Omega. Please be careful and let me know what you need as you complete the plan for the General's rescue.*

Christopher wished God would tell him what it all meant.

While Christopher didn't get an answer to the troubles surrounding him, he had the pieces in place to complete the plan to rescue General Havid. Ori, the man who had brought them to the safe house, provided ambush points on multiple routes leading to the

Wailing Wall Plaza and had fighters ready when the time came to rescue the general.

Christopher walked into his room's bathroom and finished preparing for the day, before gathering his planning notes for General Havid's rescue. Christopher made his way downstairs within the two-story townhome with plans in his hands and sleep still clouding his eyes.

The intense, flowery-and-sweet smell of the brewing Arabica beans met him at the bottom of the stairs, along with a bright light drawing him toward the kitchen. Christopher found Gabriella sitting at the kitchen bar, nursing a cup of coffee.

"I see you gave up on staring at the ceiling, too," Christopher said.

"It's strange that laying in silence in a nice bed is more uncomfortable for me than the screams and smells of that prison."

"Gabriella, give yourself time to heal. Peace will come."

She'd hear none of it. "I will find peace when Draven is dead."

Christopher prayed to find the right words. He stalled, waiting for Heaven's answer. "You mind pouring me a cup of coffee?" He watched Gabriella walk to a cabinet and grab a mug, filling it with the liquid courage Christopher needed.

When she handed him the cup, Christopher found the words he wanted. "Do you want to get rid of the anger and pain?"

Christopher sipped the black coffee, enjoying the warm sensation flowing down his throat and across his chest as he awaited Gabriella's answer. He watched Gabriella sit atop the kitchen bar, twirling a finger around the rim of her coffee mug. She kept her eyes fixed on the edge of her coffee cup.

"No!"

"How can you say no?" Christopher challenged.

"Easy. Amahle and Kerim died trying to save me. I betrayed Omega, and Gilana's wounds will scar her for life. If I pray it all away, I get a pass to start over, but they don't."

Christopher moved beside Gabriella, embracing her as she sobbed against his chest. "Kerim and Amahle cared for you. They would never blame you for their deaths. I hate that you feel you played a part in their deaths."

"It's sort of your fault; remember what you told me in South Africa?" Gabriella said.

Christopher pushed Gabriella back from him to look at a devious smile rising on her tear-soaked face. "Yeah, I was a jerk for making it seem like we were taking an unnecessary risk to rescue you. We all wanted you free more than anything. We love you."

Gabriella pushed Christopher away and hopped off the kitchen counter, staring at him as the magnitude of his statement settled into the room. Christopher and Gabriella held hands as an uncomfortable silence fell over them.

Christopher felt warm and sweaty as the quiet echoed his heartbeat in his ears, amplifying his perceived poor choice of words in his thoughts. Why had he said love? He should have said care.

"I mean, you're a sister in Christ, so of course, we love you."

Christopher's muscles tensed as Gabriella moved closer to him, gazing into his eyes. She hugged him tightly. "I know, Chris, and I love all of you."

⁓

The energizing smell of caffeine pulled Jackson from a fitful sleep. In his dreams, he'd been pushing his two girls, Katie and Sadie, in park swings. He sat on the edge of his bed, massaging battered and scarred limbs into a willingness to work. The clock read 5:30 a.m. but he felt like it was much earlier.

After Jackson dressed, he followed his nose to the door of his room. He was unsurprised by the flood of light coming from downstairs. The light at this early hour pointed to the tortured souls he shared the safe house with, as peaceful sleep was a luxury that no one he knew enjoyed. If someone told him this safe house served as a lab for psychology students, it would make sense considering the mental health of the "roommates" and him. Ghosts of the past sat with Christopher, Gabriella, and him twenty-four hours a day. The strain of moving from crisis to crisis the past three and half years left Jackson on the verge of insanity every day, or so it felt.

He instinctively paused at the bottom of the stairs. The lack of sounds and years of instruction forged into him the habit of "clearing corners," making him peek to find Christopher and Gabriella.

What Jackson saw was a sight that brought memories of his wife, Sarah, and the way she would squeeze him after his return from a deployment. Christopher and Gabriella were in a deep, eyes closed embrace. While neither Christopher nor Gabriella would admit their feelings for each other, Jackson knew where there was smoke, there was a fire.

"Well-well. This is what's happens in the safe house after dark? Late-night rendezvous between Chris and little Ms. Trouble."

Jackson laughed, watching Christopher and Gabriella jump back from their embrace at the sound of his voice.

"Jackson, you always think the worst!" Gabriella shouted.

Gabriella punched Jackson in his arm before turning toward the stairs.

"Gabriella, where are you going?" Christopher asked.

"I'm heading to bed. Wake me up when something interesting happens."

Jackson rubbed his arm. "Like Jesus coming back?"

"That would be something, but even I know we have three more years for that moment. Good night, boys," Gabriella said.

Jackson walked over to the coffeepot, pouring a cup as he returned the stare of Christopher. "What's on your mind, Chrisssssss?"

Christopher laughed. "You missed your calling in life. Stand-up comedy is where you could've left a mark on this world."

"My mama always said I could make a Baptist preacher laugh on Sunday. But here we are, two unemployed special forces soldiers. What's important is the happenings down here between Gabriella and you."

Jackson sipped the strong coffee as Christopher unrolled the blueprints to the *Hekal Emah* prison.

"I was finalizing the plan to rescue the general when I found Gabriella. Nothing else to say, Jackson," Christopher said.

"There is a lot to say, but I get it. Besides, sleeping is a scary place for all of us right now. Well, let's finish up the plan. Ori said we're two weeks away from the peace treaty ceremony, our one window to free General Havid."

Christopher pulled a legal pad from under the blueprints and laid it on the kitchen counter between Jackson and himself. "There is no way to get to the general before they transport him and live. *Hekal Emah* makes Robben Island's security look like a convenience store. We're going to need to ambush the convoy and take the general, before they get to the Wailing Wall Plaza."

Jackson took a sip of coffee. "You've got my attention. Go on."

"The plan is pretty straightforward. The first problem is identifying when and in what type of vehicle the UE will transport the general. I want to ask Ori if he has any sources at the prison that could give us insight into the UE's transport plans, maybe we could have one of Ori's guys be the driver for the general's vehicle."

Jackson chimed in, "I agree with you on not trying a second prison break. The key to pulling off this ambush is finding the right spot."

Christopher pulled out a tourist city map of Jerusalem. "I am well ahead of you, my friend. There is a tight y-intersection here." Christopher pointed to the intersection of *Gey Ben Hinom* and *Ma'a lot Ir David* streets. "This intersection is flanked on two-sides by terraced shrubbery hedgerows. The best part about this spot is the vehicles will be almost at a standstill as they make their way north to the Old City due to the gradient."

Jackson rubbed his beard and finished his coffee. "Solid plan, brother, and textbook location for the ambush."

"I hear a 'but' in your statement," Christopher said.

"But, if we don't have an inside driver, how do we stop the vehicles, neutralize the UE, and not get the general killed by the UE or us?"

Christopher pushed the maps and his notes away rubbing his

right hand over his face. "That's the tough part. We're going to need to assume some risk to pull this off."

"You mean risk to the general's life?" Jackson asked.

Christopher sighed. "Yes."

"How 'bout this. We place an IED that blows up when the lead vehicle's front axle hits our designated mark. Let's pray that they're in a three-vehicle-convoy configuration and the general's in the second car. In that scenario, the post-explosion should cause the second vehicle to swerve off the street. Based on what you've shown me on the map—we need to confirm in person, of course—that second vehicle will slam into one of the terraces. If we're lucky, the general will be in the car that runs off the road where my group will neutralize any UE and grab the general for extract to a vehicle driven by Gabriella. Meanwhile, your group ensures the third UE vehicle is a non-factor."

Jackson rummaged through the sparse cupboards and refrigerator as Christopher thought over the proposal.

Christopher tapped on the tourist map. "Great idea, but we need spotters with radios to help with timing. There are so many unknowns with this. I've never been in an ambush where we were not trying to kill everybody; this is tough. Thankfully, we have the resources to pull our plan off, based on Ori. Your idea is our most likely and most dangerous course of action. The best case is we keep the parts of killing the lead and trail UE vehicles, but at a designated point, our inside driver pulls out of the convoy and back to the safe house."

"I think our best case is wishful thinking, brother, but we'll see. All we can do is ask Ori if he has that kind of placement and access at the prison. If not, let God's will be done. Speaking of Ori, are we sure he will come through for us?" Jackson said.

Christopher pushed backed. "I understand your concern, but we're short-handed. We've been here two weeks with a $100 million bounty out for us; yet, here we are still alive. That's got to count for something in terms of trusting Ori. The bottom line is we don't have the luxury of not taking the risk of using Ori's fighters."

Christopher's point landed with Jackson, despite reservations lingering surrounding Ori and his fighters. A quiet tension filled the room as both men contemplated the depth of the days ahead. It was terrifying to consider living the next three years missing another member of Omega, but the odds were not in their favor and more risk would be required to live until the glorious appearance of Jesus Christ.

Jackson broke the silence throwing his hands up. "Okay let's move forward, but we need to push Ori to place his best people, including Ori himself, in harm's way. I want them to have some skin in this fight. Call Ori and have him come over. We need to make sure he understands his role."

Christopher took his phone out and called Ori, likely waking the man, considering it was 6:30 in the morning.

Jackson prayed Ori and his fighters would be up to the task, or these would be Omega's last days on Earth.

As the sunlight of a new day filled the safe house in a west Jerusalem neighborhood, Christopher snacked the meager rations they'd been provided, which at this point in the Tribulation consisted of stale protein bars, as the group awaited Ori. On cue, a few minutes later, a loud rap on the door and a booming voice announced Ori.

Jackson opened the door while fending off a bear hug. Ori's love of onions made this invasive and often smelly encounter tough on all his male friends each time they met.

"Good morning, warriors of God! I am ready to make the Devil suffer today. How about you?" Ori shouted. He moved past Jackson and toward Christopher, his next hugging victim.

Ori picked up Christopher and squeezed, causing him to wince not only from the pressure on his ribs but also from Ori's aroma.

"Ori, did you eat onions before coming over here?" Christopher asked.

Jackson added, "You should take your love of onions in moderation, my friend."

Ori slapped the kitchen table, laughing before sitting. "Onions keep me alive. They give me strength."

"We've finished the plan to rescue the general and want to go over it with you," Christopher said, joining Ori at the table.

Before Christopher started talking about the plan, Ori held one of his large hands up. "Where is Gabriella?"

"I'm right here."

Gabriella's voice caused all three men to look toward the stairs.

"How could I sleep when Ori comes over?" Gabriella said.

The group laughed, and Ori stood as Gabriella approached the table. Christopher watched the tough middle-aged man become a charming gentleman as he took Gabriella's right hand, pulling her seat at the kitchen table out for her.

"You've never been that nice to me," Jackson said.

Christopher pushed the conversation along. "Let's focus on the plan."

He felt the stares of the others as he pulled out his legal pad and the tourist map of Jerusalem.

Christopher refused to apologize for being serious about this mission given the risk to the general's life.

The awkward silence in the kitchen told Christopher his point of concentrating on the task at hand stuck. Whether he'd offended his friends yet again was another matter he'd likely hear about later. Christopher relayed the mission requirements for Ori and Gabriella.

"So, Ori do you have someone on the inside of *Hekal Emah* prison that can serve as the driver and do you have the fighters for the ambush?" Gabriella asked.

Christopher half-smiled at the boldness of Gabriella.

Ori sat back with his arms folded. "I don't have that kind of person inside the prison, but I do have people that will support the ambush, including spotters. I will have the spotters as street vendors, reducing their signature. I can also get the explosives we will need. The location you've picked is perfect for an ambush. We can go there tonight so you can designate the spots for the IED and I can make a few recommendations on the spotter locations and hide sites in the terraces.

"The only trouble I see is identifying which vehicle the general will travel in to the ceremony. I can place a few men to watch the prison the day of the ceremony, maybe we get lucky and see the UE loading the general into a certain vehicle. Otherwise, I pray God watches over the general and guides our hands not to harm him," Ori said.

"Let's pray we get a break and know where the general is in the convoy," Christopher said.

Distant sirens drew the group's attention from planning. Ori stood and moved toward the door.

"Where are you going, Ori? Are you good with the plan?" Christopher asked.

"I'm sorry, my friends, but sirens mean people seeking refuge. I need to return to prepare for tonight's meeting. The persecution by the UE has pushed more and more to seek our Savior, Jesus. Three years of no rain has made finding clean water difficult across Israel. Now the judgment on freshwater has pushed many over the edge. However, I will return for you tonight to scout the ambush site."

Gabriella chased Ori with a question that caused him to stop. "Ori, what brought you to accept Jesus as the Messiah?"

A smile rose on the middle-aged man's face. "For you my lovely friend, I will spare a few moments to tell tale."

Christopher laughed as he was sure Ori never missed a chance to tell a story, especially about himself.

Ori began in dramatic fashion returning to sit on the careworn sofa as Christopher, Gabriella, and Jackson gathered with him. "My story is as old as Israel. I went to synagogue every week, listened to my parents, and rebelled against God every chance I got. When the disappearances happened in the chaos, I lost several of my extended and immediate family, including my father and brother. Like many Israelis we took no notice of what this event meant for our nation and us as a people, so I focused on my job as a director in internal police service. Right after the peace treaty with the UE, one of my cousins,

Yacov, began talking about Jesus all the time. How Jesus was the Messiah. How the Two Witnesses were God's ambassadors. Yacov, pulled me to the side before he began his calling, as he described the urge to leave and talk to the world about Jesus. He told me that God wanted to use me to help our people. I cried like a baby and Yacov led me to accept Jesus as my Lord."

Jackson said, "So, Yacov was a part of 144,000."

Ori stood moving toward the door. "Yes, he is a part of great army of witnesses. What an honor. Yacov will live to see the return of Jesus; I hope for the same. Goodbye, my friends. Expect my return late tonight. The misery surrounding our daily lives and the small comfort that turning to Jesus in these dark days offers leads many to the resistance's doorstep each day. While Jesus is the 'well that never runs dry,' his servants must prepare to serve the thirsty. Stay out of sight. The Beast has people hunting for you. So don't give him the chance to kill you."

Ori's words hung in Christopher's mind. It had only been a few short weeks ago in South Africa where he wrestled with wanting to stop fighting Draven. Now, he was coming to accept that fighting Draven was his best hope of survival and finding purpose in the Tribulation.

As Christopher dialed Nkoie to check on Gilana, he knew Ori's words, to remain safe and out of sight were wistful. If Omega would survive the next three and half years, taking chances was the only way they would make it.

≈

CHAPTER 29

GEMMA SAT, WRINGING her hands and praying her stomach would settle as Draven, Evan, and herself via a limo made their way toward the Temple Mount. She knew Draven's aim was confronting Eliyahu and Reuel, God's chosen ambassadors, to the Tribulation world. The one-sided confrontation was a sad attempt to reclaim the world's attention from a rival, or so Gemma thought. In the 'public opinion polls,' Draven believed he trailed both the Witnesses and Conti for approval. The fact public disapproval mattered little in Draven's one-world government escaped him as the desire to kill Conti and the Witnesses grew daily.

As the UE Secretary-General's motorcade entered the old city, Gemma marveled at Draven expressing and acting on his fears. For the ten years she had known him, fearful never crossed her mind when describing the attributes of Draven. Perhaps it was the pressure his dark master, who Gemma sensed was Satan, was applying to Draven that caused his polished veneer to crack. Or maybe the stress of running the world, after years of pursuing the dream of world domination, caused him to worry. Whatever the cause for Draven's fear, it made him seem less like an Antichrist and more like so many other dictators before him. While she believed Draven was the Biblical

Antichrist, his present manic state challenged the notion he thought that's who he was in the present.

Before Draven exited the limo, Gemma watched a worried Evan plead his case for not confronting Eliyahu and Reuel.

"Sir, I think it would be wise if you found another way of engaging these men."

Draven flashed a snow-white smile at Gemma and Evan. "Sentiments like that, Evan, are the reason I rule the world and you serve me. The Prince of This World has guided me to this moment. I will humiliate these men before they're delivered into my hands within the month. One final thought, Gemma, are the reporters and podium in place?"

Gemma imagined the ominous spirit that surrounded Draven was the opposite of the Holy Spirit within her. The picture of her as a young girl playing with two ends of magnets repelling each became vivid in her mind. The resistance to the evil guiding Draven, she knew, was God's Holy Spirit protecting her. The battle of the ages was being played out in the Antichrist's limo. Gemma grew calm, knowing God watched her even as she worked within the enemy camp.

"Gemma, have you gone mad? What is the answer to my question?" Draven shouted.

The cold splash of a liquid in her face snapped Gemma from her thoughts. Evan had thrown water at her.

"That was uncalled for, sir. I was collecting my thoughts!" Gemma shouted.

Evan laughed. "You would be wise to lower your tone with me. You should be grateful I didn't slap you. Now answer the Secretary-General's question about the reporters and podium."

Gemma tasted bile as she humbly replied to Evan's demand and a laughing Draven.

"Sir, the podium and reporters are in place, awaiting your arrival."

Draven laughed in Gemma's face as she followed Evan and him out of the limo, flanked by a crowd of supporters and armed soldiers holding back a mob of those that hated him.

God, let today be the day you take this evil man's life, Gemma thought.

༜

Veins in Draven's temples rose as he walked through a mixed crowd of his supporters and those less enamored by him. He wanted to order the UE soldiers to execute anyone daring to defile his name. However, the Prince of This World told him to focus on the Two Witnesses; Draven's spirit guide repeated the message that soon the two men would fall into his hands.

He stepped behind a podium, hoping to interrupt the morning message of the Two Witnesses. Draven, however, tried to find comfort in the promise of the Prince of This World as the piercing stare of Eliyahu and Reuel met him. The men had apparently stopped speaking as he arrived at the Temple Mount.

Draven willed himself to flash a smile, as the media cameras clicked and his enemies stared him down. "Well, I am glad to hear silence in this hallowed spot over the usual hate that spews from your mouths. Your days of promoting fear are ending. I've tried to be reasonable and take a peaceful approach to your followers and you, but you pushed my hand away."

A strong wind arose, causing Draven to cower behind the podium as thoughts of being rushed to the hospital after the Two Witnesses silenced him rushed to his mind. He watched his adversaries prepare to respond via a large video screen.

Reuel stood before the gathering crowd of thousands and the countless watching on TV to answer the world's chosen leader. The man of God stood defiant, adorned in his sackcloth robe, with shimmering white hair blowing in a steady breeze. It seemed to Draven that Reuel's brown eyes flashed before his thunderous voice, rattling the stones in the Wailing Wall Plaza.

"Israel! The Father of Lies has sent his son to come before you, mocking not us but the God of Abraham, Isaac, and Jacob. Did God not send Pharaoh the same message ten times before his hardened heart submitted to God's request? Your generation, like your ancestors, demands a sign before yielding your life to God. But, Israel, you've missed your Messiah, the Lord Jesus. Yet, you honor the 'man of sin.' You've failed to hear the living words we've spoken before you these three and a half years. The Beast and his False Prophet will make you suffer in the days ahead. Know that this false king's regime and all who follow him will fall. Jesus Christ, the true King of Israel, will return for you as your cries reach Heaven, lest all flesh on this Earth perish."

Draven felt the Prince of This World urging him to stand and confront his enemies. He mustered the strength to move back to his feet, but as Eliyahu glared toward Draven, he stood helpless as the second Witness looked through him. The shorter man's snow-white hair and beard seemed to radiate, causing Draven to squint to see the man. Eliyahu's intense brown eyes carried the same flash of power found in Reuel as he started speaking. Draven gripped the podium tight as a tremble began in his hands at Eliyahu's voice echoed in his soul. He saw the audience covering their ears and faces. The scene spoke to the power

Eliyahu's voice carried a sound of rushing water. "Israel! What more will you require from God before you accept His son Jesus Christ as your rightful king? Why do you pursue Satan and death when the living God of Heaven offers life? For three and a half years, you've seen signs and wonders from Heaven. Since we asked the sky to close through God's power, has it not ceased to rain? The opening of the seals of judgment has not softened your hearts. The first three trumpet judgments have not brought you to a place of repentance."

Eliyahu pointed at Draven before continuing his message to the nation of Israel, "The Beast will cause you to run into the arms of God at the cost of your life. This false king signed the treaty for peace and security between the world and you with your own blood. For a month, you have desired freshwater, as God turned the waters bitter throughout the promised land. Hear our last words before the Great Tribulation, as our time before you ends."

Draven's smile at hearing the confirmation of the Prince of This

World's message signaling the demise of his foes turned to concern as the bright mid-morning day faded. As Reuel joined Eliyahu, he looked on as a chill raced down his spine.

The Two Witnesses proclaimed the subsequent judgment of God on Israel and the world, *"The fourth angel sounded his trumpet, and a third of the sun was struck, a third of the moon, and a third of the stars, so that a third of them turned dark. A third of the day was without light, and also a third of the night."*

With shrieks of horror filling the Wailing Wall Plaza, Draven knew he had lost the battle between the Two Witnesses and himself. The day had become night instantly. As chaos erupted around him and the pleas of his security detail rang in his ears, Draven tried to match the icy stares of Eliyahu and Reuel. However, a powerful sense of shame welled up within him. He was grateful that his security team pulled him away from the stares of the Two Witnesses.

Draven entered his limo, with Evan and Gemma trailing behind him. He squeezed his right hand, trying to stop a tremble. Though Draven would never express it in any audible manner, confronting the Two Witnesses exposed for the first time the Prince of This World's inability to control a situation. Draven felt weaker and in need of something every time he confronted the Two Witnesses, despite having anything his heart desired in this world. The men's power and confidence in their God, Draven knew he didn't have in his spiritual guide.

He ran his hands over his face as the limo pulled away from his latest defeat with two men who claim to represent the living God. If he couldn't win the battle, he would win the war. Draven thought he needed to rely on himself more. *Why shouldn't I trust myself and no one else? It has been my talents that have propelled me to rule the world.* As thoughts of his accomplishment rose in his mind, so did Draven's pride. He turned his attention to his underlings to carry out his plans.

"Evan, I won't have Conti benefiting from this latest disaster those two madmen claim is a judgment of their God. You will release a press statement within the hour saying the UE determined the present astrological occurrence is a rare coincidence. The event is a condition of the ongoing healing of the planet's atmosphere from the asteroid strike."

Draven snapped his fingers at Gemma. His long-time aide provided him a chilled glass filled with a swirling concoction of Pimm's No. 1 and a generous helping of mint sprigs, cucumber, orange slices, and strawberries.

After savoring the first cooling sip of his favorite cocktail, Draven gave more orders to Gemma. "Have John Barnes provide an update on where he stands with Noem Cohen in eliminating the Christian resistance network. I also want you to pass along the message that Conti's presence at the Peace Treaty celebration next week is unwelcomed."

Draven settled into his seat as his motorcade wound through the streets of Jerusalem, back to the regional offices of the UE. The once bright late summer day had faded into an uncertain night at the command of his enemies. While he had confidently given orders combating the threats to his reign, the haunting words of the Prince of This World, that time was short, unnerved him. Draven needed a break, and he'd hoped next week would change his fate.

CHAPTER 30

DAYS AWAY FROM what Pontiff Conti believed was his date with destiny, the global leader sat with Giuseppe on the rooftop terrace of the Grand Hotel in Oslo. Despite the UE's counter, the Two Witnesses' proclamation of their God striking the sun and stars remained unnerving. For Oslo, summer usually brought white nights where the sun's light lingered well into the evening hours. The Oslo Conti observed was pitch black by three in the afternoon.

Despite the panic the latest calamity generated, the Pontiff admired the still sizeable crowd lingering in the nearby City Hall Square. The people of Oslo enjoyed the break from suffering he provided after his mid-day Interfaith rally. The spectacular views of Oslo Fjord dominated the distant horizon as the Norwegian capital's natural beauty masked the scars of three years of horrors following the disappearances.

To his delight during the rally, the people chanted Conti and merciful Pontiff. Conti felt assured his efforts to overtake Draven as ruler of the world were all but guaranteed. The encouragement he'd experienced over the past year of elevating the Interfaith religion globally seemed a sure sign they welcomed his leadership. The world's adoration for him validated his worth and belief that he was now serving the real god of the universe, after the shame of being the most senior Cardinal remaining after the disappearances.

Yet his inadequacies as a leader would remain in the people's eyes, Conti believed, if Draven Cross was alive. Draven's shadow covered the future the Prince of This World promised Conti for leading the Interfaith religion. Conti knew that Demir Ersoy's killing of Draven later in the week at the Israel-UE Peace Treaty ceremony must be flawless. Any errors in the assassination plot would complicate a successful transition to power. Draven's warning, via Gemma Sutherland, not to attend the ceremony would be the last offense from a man Conti hated, he hoped.

"Giuseppe, are you sure that Demir is ready to execute Draven? Demir is the vital element in elevating me to world leader."

"Pontiff, the assassin's abilities are not a concern. I am worried about Evan and his reaction to the Beast's death. He will not allow you to take power over the UE and the world without a fight."

"The moment that I put Draven's dog, Evan, in his place is a thought that often brings a smile to my face. When I bring together every tribe and nation on the planet in the wake of Draven's death, do you think Evan would dare challenge me? Draven's death will be the end of Evan. You will ensure Evan meets the fate he deserves."

"Pontiff, I promised Maria. You've already made me go back on my sacred word by killing Draven's bodyguard. *Non lo farò*."

Conti watched Giuseppe leave the terrace. His aide flopped into a plush recliner in the penthouse suite, holding his face in his hands. Manipulation had always come naturally to Conti. He could play off the emotions of others to get what he wanted most. His skill ensured he rose through the ranks of the former Vatican.

"Giuseppe, *mio figlio*, do you remember your words when you found me suicidal in the papal office after discovering the church leaders had disappeared?"

Conti waited for Giuseppe to lift his head. As his aide's eyes met his, he kneeled down.

"I said you must be strong, Excellence. You represent the hope found in the church."

"That's right, Giuseppe. It is the same now. I carry this great responsibility to lead those suffering in this world. Interfaith is the new church, and Draven and Evan are men who would put all of us in chains. You must help free us from the tyrant."

The Pontiff looked on as Giuseppe stood and then embraced him.

"I understand what I must do when the time comes."

"Excellent! Ensure you have a safe house located for us. The immediate days after the assassination will be dangerous. In fact… " Conti stopped speaking as a thought to distance himself from the pending assassination came to mind. He grabbed his cell phone from Giuseppe.

Pontiff Conti began a text to the Ayatollah-Al Farshid: *Dear, Ayatollah Al-Farshid. I want to invite you to the peace ceremony. I know the event is something you would love to see in person.*

Conti allowed Giuseppe to read the message.

"Excellence! Why did you tell Al-Farshid you would be in Jerusalem? That was a mistake. Al-Farshid will question your absence."

"You assume he will speak with Draven or Evan and if he does, it will be too late. It will be fine, Giuseppe. When Draven dies with Al-Farshid, a man who has openly spewed hate toward the Secretary-General, in attendance, why would anyone at the UE suspect a beloved religious figure, not present at Draven's order. Now make the arraignments."

On a warm evening with the peace treaty celebration in three days, John Barnes wrestled with what came next. In an old truck, he sat in the dark along an empty dirt road in the Negev Desert next to an unlikely ally, Noem Cohen. The men were waiting for the Christian resistance leader—a man who he only knew as Ori—to provide them instructions for their role to save General Havid. John was assigned to security working with Ori and Noem after his acceptance into the resistance church two weeks ago.

John had integrated fully into the resistance over the past two weeks, providing only one proof of life message back to Evan during this time highlighting his confidence that he could end the Omega threat and dismantle the Christian resistance network. The latter strangely mattered less after spending time with the Christians. The daily messages about Jesus and the evil of Draven pushed John to reflect on his life in ways that made him uncomfortable. He was no closer to determining if Omega was coming for the general or understanding the plan for his rescue, which bothered him less than expected.

What John knew for sure was he hated Draven. The man feasted on the pain of others, as he had learned firsthand. John wanted to get away from Draven, the Christians, everyone, and make his own mark in this new chaotic world. His service to the UE was ending. He had no country, but it mattered little as nations existed only in name in Draven's world. John understood his future was murky, but his gut said he couldn't continue working for the UE and live. His only desire beyond leaving the UE was knowing Omega was destroyed.

Over the past two weeks, his efforts centered on keeping himself alive until he could determine his next move. The only mistake the protective Ori made was after the Assigning meeting in the underground Christian church, he divulged the identity of the 'voice' leading the church. The voice was the former aide of General Havid, a man named Jonathan, who took orders from the general during visits to his prison.

What Ori withheld was if Omega would be a part of the rescue attempt. John looked around the inky horizons of the desert surrounding him with a sense that Christopher and Jackson could be surveilling Ori, and by association himself. It was a thought that caused the hairs on his neck to rise and his fist to tighten. All John could do was hope he had the element of surprise over the Omega operatives, if they did make an appearance. He needed to send a message to Evan to place extra security at the *Hekal Emah* prison and ceremony site.

However, for all the sureness John felt in exacting revenge against Omega, he couldn't shake a sense of doubt that he was missing something in his life that continuing to work for the UE would not supply.

"John, you're quiet this evening. Do you have a long-term plan that doesn't involve the UE? I think it's only a matter of time before they come after men like us," Noem said.

Noem's question caused John to focus on the other car occupant. He perked up as the question struck at thoughts racing through his mind. "What do you mean, men like us?"

Noem flicked a cigarette out the passenger window. "We are skilled operatives. In a dictatorship, guys like us disappear all the time. A man like Draven will always look at you and me as threats."

The words seemed to penetrate deep in John's mind. "I have given my future some thought lately. A lot of my future over the past three years has centered on getting revenge against my old unit, Omega. I've been consumed with anger for so long, I've forgotten other things. Ori is still not here. You want to give me your story?"

Noem sighed. "It's a long story. My father went crazy after losing his brother in a poorly planned Israeli government operation against the Islamic terrorists. He hated God, my mom, and me when he came home. The only thing he loved was drinking. The first chance I got I left home, abandoning my mom to deal with the abuse and rejection my father practiced. I first joined the Army trying to find a purpose. After three years, I was accepted into Mossad and worked with an amazing group of operatives. My commander went rogue, disappearing about two years ago, after a failed mission in Iraq. I found out with the announcement of General Havid's betrayal that my commander was working with the general and Omega. I lost everyone I considered family with that announcement. No one trusted my unit, and we were disbanded. I fell into my work, hunting whoever the state called our enemy, trying to prove my loyalty. To find a family again. So, here I am sitting with you waiting for the orders to dismantle the Christian network."

John opened the door on his side of the truck lighting a cigarette. "So, your old commander was Gilana Edri?"

"Yes."

"She was with Omega when they attacked my team in Jakarta, Indonesia, last year." John said.

A flash of white light flooded the truck announcing Ori's arrival. John exited the truck along with Noem to greet Ori. "Don't say a word about Gilana to Ori," John ordered.

"What a night. God's power is shining, or I should say not shining here in the desert. Look"—Ori pointed to a void above them—"stars are missing, and the moon seems dimmer to me. The fourth trumpet judgment is something to see, right, guys?"

"Yes, God is something. You want to tell us why we're in the middle of the desert," John said.

"Forgive me taking so long to get here, but the numbers of seekers are growing so fast each day. I want you both to serve as observers on the day we rescue the general. *Hekal Emah* is over the ridge two kilometers down this road. This road ends at an overlook that will provide you sightlines of the front and rear entrances of the prison. You will call me when the UE load the general into a vehicle to take him to the ceremony at the Wailing Wall Plaza. Your role will ensure our friends can save him at the plaza." Ori said.

John asked, "Who are our friends? Are they already in Israel?"

"What I know is in three days, the general will be free thanks to this group's support. We must focus on our roles. I will leave you until the night of the attack. Stay hidden when back in the city and come back here at night. Draven"—Ori spat on the ground—"has his agents hunting for us, so do nothing to draw attention to yourself before the rescue."

John and Noem watched Ori depart back into the night.

Noem said, "I think Omega are the friends Ori won't name. They will attempt to rescue the general at the ceremony. We need to warn the UE."

John climbed back into the truck. "I agree Omega will attempt a rescue of the general at the ceremony. We will be ready, and they all will die."

⌘

CHAPTER 31

EVEN THOUGH HE sat near two of the people that mattered most to him, loneliness crawled all over Christopher. He was struggling with the sense Omega was ill-prepared for the fight with the UE fast approaching. The plan in place and the forces available forced Christopher into the uncomfortable space of trusting others, specifically God. Yes, he told himself he was at peace and trusted God. Still, the willingness didn't remove the crushing pressure he felt when thoughts of others doing their jobs to ensure Omega's success came to mind. Trust was a daily struggle for Christopher, amplified by the ever-present reminder that time was not an ally.

The TV replayed the Two Witnesses' announcement of the fourth trumpet judgment, now with added ANN commentary downplaying the events that followed. The days were shorter and the nights darker, another sign for Christopher that there was little time to make a difference in the war between God and Satan's kingdoms.

Daily calls with Gilana over the past week were a welcomed change to the monotony of "surviving." While her strength was returning quickly, Christopher would not have Gilana on the team in a few days for General Havid's rescue. Nkoie had told him the truth surrounding Gilana's health that her pride was blind to. Gilana needed the one thing they didn't have, more time. Christopher appeased her powerful will by bringing her into the post-rescue reconsolidation plan, where Gilana made a solid recommendation for a location of a new safe house.

"Hey, college boy, did you hear what I said?" Jackson's teasing brought Christopher from his thoughts.

"I'm sorry. What did you say?"

"What time is Ori dropping off the vehicle we will use to get to the ambush site? But, never mind that right now. The lost in my thoughts routine you're pulling has me worried about you. What's on your mind?"

Gabriella further pressed Christopher. "Let me guess. You're struggling with trusting something about this mission?"

Christopher stood up and ran his hands over his head as he walked over to the large living room window.

Jackson pressed, "Well, what's the deal?"

Christopher sighed. "I'm afraid that one of you will not make it back from this mission. I've seen so many friends get hurt or die over the last three years that I'm scared."

"At least you told half of the truth," Jackson said.

"What do you mean I told half of the truth?" Christopher asked.

"You're scared; that's a fact. This conversation, your mannerism the last week, everything about you, Christopher, tells me you're full of fear. I hope that means you're ready for this fight. You haven't gotten so holy that living doesn't matter. But you're lying. Gabriella hit the nail on the head when she said the root of the problem is you lack trust. That's what's scaring you. You're scared God will not answer the prayer that all of us live through the rescue. Tell me I'm wrong, and I'll shut up."

Christopher smirked. "You're wrong, so please shut up."

Jackson waved a playful fist at Christopher. "Why, you little—"

Gabriella interrupted Jackson. "In my short time believing in God, I've learned that it's okay to be afraid, but it's wrong not to trust him. I understand now that my wanting to save everyone to do things my way came at a high cost. I landed in prison, faced torture, and provided the situation that took Kerim and Amahle's lives. I've been arrogant and rash and not submitted to God's will. Bottom line, I've been you, Chris, never trusting others, especially not God."

Christopher moved back to the recliner, where he tried to make sense of the added context of his friends' thoughts.

Before Christopher could reply, Jackson piled on. "Look. There is nothing certain for us as believers beyond going to Heaven if we die in three days during the mission. I have been angry and depressed, sometimes all at once and often for days. I've prayed to die. Don't look shocked; I believe my girls Katie and Sadie are in Heaven. I have thoughts almost everyday where I believe the sooner, I die, the quicker I get to see their faces. But, guys, when I'm thinking like that, in my selfish motives, I could have gotten one of you killed. I haven't been trusting God to sustain me through the pain to give me the peace I preach y'all need. Forgive me. Thanks for listening."

Gabriella erupted into a guttural laugh. "I'm sorry, Jackson. It's not what you said, but how. Why did you feel the need to wrap up your thoughts like you were at a group counseling session?"

"Excuse me, Ms. Perfect. I thought we were clearing the air in case we died. I mean, you and *Chris* did it."

Christopher chuckled. "You two keep me laughing. You're right, both of you. I'm afraid that God won't protect us. I've tried to control things that belong to God. I don't know what the rescue will hold for us, but I feel better about trusting God with the outcome. So, thanks for caring and sharing."

"Now that we've all had our free counseling session and your head is free to think like a special ops operative again, what are we going to do about Gemma? She wants to leave her current employer the Beast," Jackson said.

"Simple, she will need to come to us once the dust settles after the rescue," Christopher said.

Gabriella nodded. "I agree. It's too dangerous to link up with Gemma and rescue the general all at once."

Christopher said, "Hopefully, by the time we're ready to plan something for Gemma, Gilana will be back with us. Ori will be here shortly with our vehicle, so finish preparing your assault packs in case we need to leave quickly."

As Jackson and Gabriella moved to their rooms to finish preparing, Christopher prayed, *God, Your will be done in our lives.*

⋘

Gemma drifted into daydreaming sitting at her desk in the UE's Middle East office. Tomorrow would be a day of days that stirred many feelings for Gemma. Knowing that her efforts would lead to Draven's assassination caused guilt. It didn't help that Draven was making her open the ceremony with a speech of loyalty. She understood why the Two Witnesses called Draven the Beast, the Biblical Antichrist, but was he beyond redeeming? Draven had given so much to charities. Gemma even held hopes at one point her boss would marry her. Would the world be worse if he ruled? Three years ago, she never dreamed of pursuing anything but Draven's goals. These traitorous thoughts never would have entered her mind.

A calming voice filled Gemma's mind, easing her thought storm. What she knew now as the Holy Spirit reminded her that Draven's path was of his making, like her choice to serve God. It was a self-delusion, believing Draven was anything less than a monster, the Antichrist. He had tortured Gabriella and her. Draven killed millions in a global war and enjoyed every decision along the way. It was hard now to stomach any more than a few minutes in Draven's presence because the spirit guiding her differed from Draven's.

"Gemma, stop being lazy and follow me. We need to do our part to ensure the Secretary-General's moment tomorrow is a resounding success," Evan snapped.

Gemma had grown so sick of Evan and the degrading way he treated her and other women. Nevertheless, her mission wasn't complete and she couldn't walk away yet. She followed Evan into Draven's office, where General Vivaan Ahuja and Draven waited.

Draven stood as Gemma and Evan sat around his office conference table.

"I have little time or patience for failure tomorrow, so let's get down to business. Evan, do you have confirmation that all the regional ambassadors are arriving here today?"

"I do, sir, minus Pontiff Conti."

Draven paced the room. "Yes, I'm glad Evan brought you to this meeting, General Ahuja. John Barnes indicates there could be a rescue attempt by Omega at the ceremony tomorrow. I want the intelligence services to confirm. If these savages try anything, I want you to eliminate them."

"Understood, sir, I will ensure we have a large contingency force around the plaza. I have also commanded the Israeli military garrison near the prison to a full readiness level starting today through tomorrow evening," General Ahuja said.

Gemma thought of Gabriella now, because she always described General Ahuja as a robot disguised as a man. The general's stoic style never displayed emotion as she listened to his response.

"All fine, General. Ayatollah Al-Farshid has coordinated with our protocol office as VIP attendee. This is a curious matter. As I remember, he is not a fan of mine nor the Israelis, so I want someone to watch him. If one rock lands near me, I want you to eliminate him and anyone with him and then level his home in Qom. Evan, you're finally meeting my expectations. Let's hope you've accomplished similar results with the rest of my agenda."

Gemma began praying to herself that the meeting would end soon. She needed to get this information to Christopher. *God, give me a chance to help my friends.*

As Draven stood behind his desk, she hoped he provided his final guidance. To Gemma's relief, Draven waved Evan, General Ahuja, and her out of his office without saying a word. The slight mattered little to her. What was important was speaking with Christopher.

Gemma grabbed her phone from her desk and moved toward the building smoker station. She saw it as a poor replacement for covert calls compared to the UE Gardens, but the space met the task. Hopefully, the information she had did the same for Omega.

⏵

It was near six in the morning. As Christopher and four of Ori's trusted fighters sat in a hedgerow terrace 50 meters above the Gey Ben Hinom overlooking a pile of rubbish on the adjacent Ma' a lot Ir David street curb which hid an improvised explosive device. From this vantage he could see Gabriella parked along Gey Ben Hinom in the exfil vehicle. While he couldn't see Jackson and four other members of Ori's team, he knew they were ready. He awaited word from Ori on which vehicle carried the general.

General Havid was a man that served as mentor and spiritual guide for Christopher during storms of the past few years. Christopher reflected on his earlier conversations with Gemma and Ori. He thought about how everyone on his team arrived at this moment. Christopher sensed Ori had a hidden pressure on his shoulders but couldn't get him to discuss the problem.

Ori didn't take Christopher's warning based on Gemma's intel that Draven sensed an attack and increased security well. He responded with ominous words, "I will take care of it. We will succeed."

With Gemma, Christopher had reassured her several times during their discussion that the details she provided saved their lives. Now he waited and trusted that things would go the way he prayed.

⏵

Ori found Noem alone at the remote overlook of *Hekal Emah* as he had instructed John Barnes and him a few days ago. Christopher's message from Gemma confirmed what he suspected of Noem months ago, he was a fraud. Noem had always shown little interest in the Bible teachings; he was too eager to learn names and other safe house locations. That's why after Noem's church Assigning, he placed him on the security team so Ori could keep an eye on him. He'd hoped to prevent the disaster that now was unfolding, betrayal.

212

Ori stared at Noem, who was lying in a prone position looking through a pair of high-power binoculars. He shuffled to his feet upon Ori's approach.

"You scared me, Ori. I didn't even hear you walking up. I see you remember your military training," Noem said.

"Yes, some things you never forget. Have the UE started any movements yet?" Ori asked.

"Three black SUVs were brought to the front of the prison about a half-an hour ago and the general was loaded into the last vehicle. They should depart soon. I think they want to get ahead of any surprises considering the ceremony starts at 10."

Ori sent a text message to Christopher with the general's location in the convoy and types of vehicles as Noem turned his back and crouched observing the prison.

"Where's John?" Ori asked stuffing his cell phone back into his pants pocket.

Still looking at the distant prison instead of Ori, Noem replied, "John fell ill yesterday evening and couldn't support the mission. This is a one-man job."

Ori knew John Barnes and Noem had lied to him, confirmed by Noem saying John was sick. He burned with anger. The two men were agents of the Devil, and he had brought them into his home. Thoughts of guilt swirled in his mind as he believed it would be his fault for the mission failing. Omega and the general's blood would be on his hands.

"I've been a fool, and it will cost many lives tonight, I fear," Ori said.

An awkward silence grew between the men as Ori moved toward Noem who moved to his feet. Ori quickly drew a combat knife he'd used as an Israeli soldier years ago holding the blade to Noem's throat.

"What are you doing?" Noem shouted.

"Shut up! You and Barnes work for the UE. The Beast"—Ori spat in Noem's face—"suspected an attack at the ceremony. How could you sell out your country, Noem?"

"I don't have a country. Everything I do is for myself. You're the traitor working with Omega."

A single gunshot brought the argument to a close. Ori felt a sting deep in his stomach. His anger faded into resolve as he ran his knife across Noem's neck when the man attempted to push him away. As Ori curled over with his blood pooling around him, he watched Noem stagger a few meters, holding his throat before he collapsed.

Ori said, "Forgive me, Lord," before the world faded away.

CHAPTER 32

THE VIBRATION OF his phone brought a flood of adrenaline into Christopher's veins. Ori's text read as a blessing and curse. He knew what vehicle the general was in, but discovered it was the last vehicle. Christopher keyed his hand-held radio passing the message to Jackson, Gabriella, and the spotters. Now came the worst part of every mission, waiting. Did they pick the correct spot for the ambush? What if the UE didn't take the most direct route? What if the general gets hurt or worse? *Stop?*

Christopher forced himself to exhale. *I need to trust God. That's all that can be done now.* From the prison to ambush site was only a twenty-minute drive but seemed as if Christopher had more time than he wanted. He grew anxious waiting for the moment to save the general. Christopher glanced at his watch. *Let us succeed, God,* Christopher prayed softly as the first spotter, a little over a mile away, announced the convoy moving toward the ambush site.

The sun, now over the Judean hills flooded the route with light at the worst possible angle as Christopher was blinded from seeing the marker to initiate the explosive for the ambush.

The second spotter who sat at the bottom of the hill 500 meters from the ambush site reported the convoy made its final turn toward Christopher and Jackson's teams.

"Jackson, I can't see the marker. The sun is blinding me."

"Hit the trigger when I tell you. Get ready, now!" Jackson said.

Christopher squeezed the radio detonator causing a flash of light to mix with the sounds of metal twisting and glass shattering, as the lead UE SUV flipped end over end blocking the UE's desired route toward the Old City.

Before Jackson's team could shoot and neutralize the second SUV threat, the driver of the vehicle helped the Omega plan. The SUV was following to close to the lead vehicle and was sprayed by fragments from the explosion. The driver swerved and struck the lead vehicle causing it to overturn coming to rest on the driver side.

Christopher while on the move toward the third SUV glanced at Jackson and his team mopping up any lingering threats from the second vehicle. Time was not on their side. The explosion and probable call from the UE guards in the third SUV to their superiors would bring reinforcements soon. General Havid's SUV made a desperate attempt to back up, as Christopher's team made their approach, causing smoke to pour from the tires.

"Aim for their tires!" Christopher shouted to Ori's fighters with him as he threw two hand grenades at the SUV.

The first-hand grenade detonated mid-air in front of the vehicle's windshield, while the second one exploded below the undercarriage, which blew out the back passenger side tire making the SUV jerk to a stop.

When the driver and two UE guards emerged bloody, quick spurts of semi-automatic rifle fire ended the men's lives. Christopher grew sick as he heard the 'pop' of a pistol and then a thud of someone hitting the ground. Soon after the concerning pistol shot, another UE guard then ran away from the ambush. Still, Ori's fighters caught him and gunned the man down.

There is a silence that is deep and penetrating that follows an extremely violent event that only those that have experienced such moments understand. Christopher was in yet another moment in time where the world stood still after violence. He hated that he knew this feeling so well. This brief pause in the chaos filled quickly with sirens and panic. Christopher cleared the general's SUV working around to the passenger side where he heard the thud after the pistol shot. His worst fears were confirmed. The UE guard shot the general before trying to escape.

Christopher screamed in his radio, "Gabriella bring the SUV down the hill now!" He bent down trying to apply pressure to the building crimson pool emerging on the general's bright orange prison uniform. General Havid looked like a shell of the mythical special operations warrior he first met almost six years ago after the Russian-led invasion of Israel. It was evident that the UE had tortured him.

When Christopher applied pressure on a strip of cloth he used as gauze, General Havid cried out in pain.

Through labored breathing, the general tried to speak to him. "It's good to see you."

Christopher didn't fight the tears back as he heard the approach of the small SUV Ori had provided the team for the mission. "I am sorry, sir."

"Not now, son, you must be strong. I have served God," General Havid mumbled.

Jackson swore as he caught up to the scene. "We need to get him out of here."

"Gabriella, hold the cloth in place. Jackson, grab his upper body and I'll grab his legs. You two"—Christopher pointed to two of Ori's fighters—"open the back of the SUV and then leave. Everyone else remember the plan; get back to your safe houses and await instructions from Ori. Now move!"

The group acted on Christopher's commands. Jackson and himself moved the fading general into the back of the SUV. After getting the general in, Gabriella climbed in the back seat with Christopher to support the general, while Jackson drove.

After the core of Omega made their escape from the ambush, the screech of police sirens and movement of common citizens, traveled opposite to where Christopher and Omega were heading physically or mentally. The ambush at y-intersection had served as the liberation point for General Havid and for Omega. It was a transition point that the fight for souls and survival entered a new and riskier phase, sadly Christopher realized it was not meant for the general to lead them through it. The general would always draw a lot of attention; it would've been untenable to count on his support and be effective for the Kingdom. Christopher would need to lead and find new allies against Draven; that is how he would honor General Havid and God.

Like in a big budget Hollywood movie, Christopher fantasized as the "good guys" escaped that the general would say something deep and personal to each Omega team member before he passed away. What Jackson, Gabriella, and he got was nothing from their mentor. He died, and they were left with the hollow victory that Draven didn't get the opportunity to humiliate their beloved mentor.

Gabriella cried as did Jackson, and Christopher knew that more tears would come from him in the days ahead reflecting on the loss of the general. For now, however, Christopher was numb thinking about the impact this great man of God had on him and God's plans. As Omega made its way back to the safe house, Christopher cradled the general's body. They would bury him late tonight at his residence were his beloved wife Abagail was interned. It was what he would have wanted, Christopher was sure.

General Havid had been more than a mentor to him the past three years; he was a friend and a father-figure. Tears flowed again breaking through the shock and dullness that engulfed Christopher when he thought about wanting more time with the general. He would resist focusing on the pain of the situation or his anger toward Draven and the UE. Instead, Christopher choose to focus on General Havid's last words.

"I have served God."

What a statement. A declaration Christopher hoped to live up too during this transition to the Tribulation to come.

❧

John Barnes reacted differently from those gathered at the large platform in the Wailing Wall Plaza at the sound of explosion somewhere close. He knew it was Omega. They had beat him yet again to the X, this time stealing General Havid during transport. *I should have been in that convoy.* He thought for once he would be a step ahead, awaiting Omega to make a move at the ceremony. Self-flagellation would have to wait, because Evan approached, his eyes dancing with energy.

"Do you have an answer of why I am hearing explosions across Jerusalem!" Evan shouted.

"Sir, I think General Ahuja sits in a better position to answer that question. My guess is Omega took the Secretary-General's prize away," John said.

Evan drew closer to John. "Are you being smug? You dare tell me the group, you've been tasked to eliminate multiple times is in Israel. You shouldn't utter the name Omega without wanting to hang yourself. Your consistent failure to eliminate these terrorists is disgraceful. It makes me wonder. Are you working with them?"

John shot back, "I am not working with Omega. I hate them."

Evan laughed. "For hating them so much, you think it would drive you to succeed, to achieve excellence; however, they always outwit you. It's not hard to outsmart someone as stupid as you. I don't have the time to deal with you now, but you should hope that I don't discover that for the second time in three months, Omega has rescued enemies of the Secretary-General. Now find out exactly what happened and be prepared to dazzle me with an answer after the ceremony or you can expect to never see another day."

John didn't say anything. He silently stared through Evan as Draven's deputy turned his back on him and walked away. John wanted to stomp Evan's delicate face into the ground as he'd done to the UE soldier laughing at him when he first arrived in Israel. After the ceremony, the answer would be it was not Omega no matter what he discovered. Evan's threats were becoming a problem and it was only a matter of time before he was killed. John knew he needed to leave the services of the UE, but the pull to exploit Draven's resources to punish and destroy Christopher Barrett was strong.

John's phone rang displaying the name Colonel Ohayon, the *Hekal Emah* Prison Superintendent. "You're late in telling me your guards failed and General Havid escaped."

Colonel Ohayon responded, "Yes, but how did you know all of this?"

"All that matters, Colonel is the fact that your team let the number one prisoner in all of Israel miss his execution appointment. You should be worried about the response from the Secretary-General in the wake of your failure."

John hung up the phone. He knew the fall out would end Colonel Ohayon's life and buy him time to save his own. John needed to make it hard for Draven and Evan to kill him, until he could escape their grip. He departed the Wailing Wall to discover the truth he knew; Omega was behind the general's escape and his life depending on stopping them in the future.

∽

CHAPTER 33

DRAVEN AWOKE ON a vast plain surrounded by a darkness that seemed to live. He had a similar experience when the Prince of This World brought him to this place. Snarls and screams poured from the surrounding void as a single point of light flickered in the distance. It scared Draven to stand, sensing that something stood near him, wanting to harm him. Instead, he crawled toward the faint light, slowly coming near the spot.

When Draven came within a few feet of the light source, it became so bright that he could no longer see. As the light receded, he found himself on a marble-floored, open-air rotunda instead of the dirt he crawled through moments ago. In an instant, soft piano music replaced the nightmarish sounds. UE ceremonial guards stood next to a silver casket with a glass lid. Draven hesitated before walking over to the coffin. He screamed and fell to the floor as he was the person in the casket.

"Where are you? You're supposed to be my spirit guide, my protector, Prince of This World. How could you let this happen to me?"

Draven felt a gush of wind and then footsteps behind him. He whirled around to find a mirror image of himself standing above him.

The Prince of This World spoke in Draven's own voice. "You're a petulant child far beneath me. I've given you so much in life, and what have you done with my gifts, Draven? Do you think you're the first man in history I've bestowed such power? You're nothing without me. I was known for eons as Lucifer, the anointed cherub of God. I stood up for myself and lost my title and name because of God's love for His precious humans. For what? To give you the power to rule this world and glorify me for my gifts only to watch you squander every opportunity to succeed? You've proven without question that humanity shouldn't exist, but I will have my vengeance when all the children of Adam serve me. I have grown tired of you allowing my enemy to reign blow after blow to my kingdom, without consequence."

Draven quibbled as he coward on the floor. "My lord, I have done everything you've asked. It's not my fault."

"Silence. I will not tolerate your stupidity any longer. Your leniency of my enemies sealed your fate. I will accomplish my purpose. Time is short," the Prince of This World said.

"What does that mean, master?" Draven cried.

"Your life belongs to me."

Draven awoke in his Jerusalem penthouse with Lucifer's last words ringing in the room as if just spoken. He was sweating and shaking. The sun of a new day rose over the distant Judean hills, but Draven felt his sovereignty faced its final hours. Now his hidden protector, Lucifer, another name he knew associated with his spirit guide, the Prince of This World, seemed to have abandoned him.

Draven's jaw clenched as he swore and smoldered with resentment over the experience he had with Lucifer.

"Why do I need him? I am already ruling the world. I can finish my vision on my strength and intelligence alone."

After boosting his confidence with a rant against his hidden master, Draven prepared for the celebration of his crowning achievement, peace in the Middle East, ready to face the future without Lucifer.

❧

Gemma sat starring out into the sky from the balcony of her apartment awaiting Draven's limo to pick her up for the ceremony. While it was mid-day, the reduced light gave a feel of the time being much later to Gemma. There was a crisp bite to early fall air, and the sky reflected a stunning late afternoon bluish hue that masked the challenges to come. She had been up for almost 24 hours, unable to focus until Omega checked into the temporary safe house. Christopher's message that the rescue failed and General Havid died stung. It was hard to lose followers of Jesus to followers of Satan.

As she glanced at her watch, Gemma reflected on the early morning conversation where Omega accepted her recommendation to leave Israel for South Africa. Gemma knew the hunt for her friends would intensify after today's events. Draven's fury would erupt once he learned that General Havid had been freed. Gemma coordinated directly for a flight back to Cape Town with the emerging ally Captain Liu, who quickly agreed to take Omega back to the relative safety of South Africa.

Gemma began to cry as a sense of isolation rolled over her. An hour from now she would be humiliated, forced to remind the world of her loyalty to Draven ahead of the peace ceremony. Why was there no escape for her? She wanted to accept the pleas of Gabriella to leave, but the Holy Spirit echoed in her mind countless times in the past month that her service next to Draven was needed. She cried out in her mind, *God, why me? I want to give up.* Sobs flowed from deep within Gemma as she closed her eyes and squeezed her curled legs.

It took her a moment to realize someone had moved onto the balcony with her. She looked up to see an onyx-haired woman clothed in a dress that seemed to shimmer despite no evidence of sequins or metallic material on the dress. While startled, Gemma found comfort in the woman's presence as her jade green eyes somehow eased her fears.

"Gemma, I am sorry I scared you, but there is little time to have a conversation. I am your guardian angel and God has sent me to comfort you in this trying moment," the angel said.

"I didn't know I had a guardian angel," Gemma said sitting up.

"Yes, all humans are given this gift at birth, though all lose their guardian when they reject Jesus Christ as their Savior. I stood over-watching you from the front yard of the 144,000 members, Jacob and Michael in Jakarta. I stopped that car from hitting you when you were seven after you ran ahead of your mom leaving the supermarket. I was the kind old woman outside The Bodleian Library, encouraging you not to quit after your first semester at Oxford. God stood by you all those years, knowing you would accept His offer of redemption through His son Jesus. Gemma, you're not alone, but you have a great purpose for the Kingdom of God, that will cause you to suffer. The Great Tribulation is coming and you will be a light in the darkness to come here at the UE. I must go, but never doubt God's care for you even as you work next to Satan."

"Thank you for everything. What's your name?" Gemma asked.

"You need not thank me, but know God loves and cares for us all. My name in this form is Anna. Remember you're not alone, and you have a purpose with the UE."

Before Gemma could beg the angel to stay longer, the doorbell rang. "One second, Anna, my ride to the peace ceremony is here." Gemma watched Anna nod before she walked toward the door.

Gemma asked Draven's driver for five minutes hoping to gain more insight and comfort from her unseen guardian. However, when she closed her apartment door and turned back to the balcony, Anna was gone. God's messenger departed as mysteriously as she entered. Gemma fixed her makeup and grabbed the prepared remarks from her coffee table. She fought to contain her emotion to prevent smearing her makeup again, as the limo made its way to pick up Draven. Considering all that had happened over the last day, it honored Gemma to serve God's kingdom and his warriors in Omega. While worries over the future remained, God had given her the confidence to face the uncertainty and gratitude filled her heart.

❧

Draven looked aged and stressed to Gemma as he entered the limo. He had not been the same since the Naples incident. Now, the time had come for Draven to meet his destiny. Draven's look and demeanor almost convinced her she was not the only one that knew today marked his last day on Earth. Gemma wondered if Draven knew his life belonged to Satan. The Draven she knew, as evil of a man he was, compared little to the monster he'd served in Satan.

"Gemma, today is a big moment for me. It's validation that I am the greatest leader in human history. Can you believe I achieved unity over all governments? No one helped me," Draven said.

Gemma was unsure if Draven's comments were to her or himself. "Sir, you have many accomplishments that are worthy of adulation." Her pulse quickened, thinking about the moments ahead. Hundreds of pre-screened supporters filled the Wailing Wall Plaza, with ample barricades emplaced to create distance between the crowd and the Two Witnesses. Gemma felt the same calm Anna exuded as she looked at Reuel and Eliyahu, standing with an unflinching stare at the podium that Draven would soon stand behind.

Evan waved his hands toward a band who began playing ceremonial music flourishes, during Draven's walk along the UE blue carpet to the dais. Gemma, who had walked behind the man of the hour countless time, noted how Draven seemed to linger amongst his supporters longer than usual as the UE soldiers strained to keep the crowd at bay.

No sooner than Gemma was atop the stage, than Evan hurried to her. "You will be the first speaker I announce. Stick to your script and make sure you look happy. This is your redemption hour."

Gemma looked around at the various dignitaries that included the ten UE regional ambassadors and strangely Ayatollah Al-Farshid. Who she didn't see among the UE Secretary-General security detail was Demir Ersoy, the man who would cause the Biblically described "mortal wound" to the Beast.

Evan moved to the lectern, his porcelain veneered smile glistening. Since her torture and humiliation at Draven's order, Gemma had prayed to witness this moment for months. She had studied the passages in Revelation 13:3, but here she was living a moment of history foretold thousands of years before and Gemma wanted to be a million miles from the platform filled with global dignitaries. Her seat grew harder and more uncomfortable by the minute, causing Gemma to shift back and forth.

What if people know I planted Demir Ersoy's file to help the assassination? Gemma's thoughts ran wild before she grabbed her trembling hands. She told herself, *Get it together, Gemma, or you're going to draw suspicion.*

Evan called her name, and it felt as if she moved in slow motion. She looked at Draven who gave her a fake smile and nod of approval. The crowd seemed small and distant. As she gathered her speech, she made eye contact with Reuel and Eliyahu. The typical steel-eyed men's stare fell on her, but she didn't sense judgment only love and support. She had never been so close to the Witnesses, and the love that God was providing her today made her smile as she began to speak.

"Good morning, my fellow global citizens. I have had the privilege for the past decade to serve the Secretary-General. I want to say to the world that I wish… "

Gemma stumbled in reading the next lines as they cut to her soul. After what seemed like an eternity, she continued, "I wish I could have identified the treachery of Dr. Gabriella Costa aimed against the Secretary-General and his vision of global peace. Perhaps many lives could have been spared. However, my failings and redemption at the hands of Secretary-General Cross highlight this great day and his leadership. I thank you, sir, for your leadership, mentorship, and for being a friend to all humanity. May peace reign on Earth."

Gemma nearly fainted as she moved away from the podium. She didn't try to fight the tears from saying such lies. The moment grew worse when Draven embraced her as she returned to her seat.

She watched Evan step to the podium. The Deputy UE Secretary-General beamed as he gave a glowing false narrative of the UE's success over the past three years under Draven's leadership. Gemma glanced at the Two Witnesses, who remained stoic as Draven's puppet supported his master's vision. The crowd of sycophants erupted as Evan introduced Draven Cross. Gemma's stomach rolled as Draven took a moment to smile and shake hands with the various global and Israeli dignitaries, including ironically Ayatollah Al-Farshid, the mastermind of his pending death. Every movement and action Draven took felt like it could be his last to Gemma.

During Draven's speech, Gemma scanned the platform again for Demir Ersoy, but couldn't find him. *When will it happen? How will Demir do it?* Gemma thought. After her latest attempt to spot Demir, she became acutely aware that her seat was behind Draven. *God, I hope he doesn't fall into my lap.*

Draven paused for the audience's applause as he called the Israeli Prime Minister to stand next to him. Cameras flashed as the two leaders prepared to sign a new 100-year symbolic peace treaty between the UE and Israel.

Did Demir back out? When is he going to kill him. How is going to do it? she thought. Gemma rocked back and forth in her seat anticipating Draven's death. She glanced at the Ayatollah as the cheers rose in the seconds after Draven signed the document. She noticed the Ayatollah was tapping his wrist, and he wasn't wearing a watch.

Gemma reeled as a loud crack echoed across the platform. She watched the Israeli Prime Minister tumble off the stage. Shrieks rose from the crowd. Draven stumbled back as blood spewed from his head like a geyser. He landed near Gemma's feet and she watched as his eyes rolled back into his head and a pool of blood formed around her shoes, soaking Draven's once-charcoal gray suit.

It seemed like a lot of time had passed as Gemma tried to wrap her mind on what was happening, but seconds later a subsequent shot forced Gemma toward the rear of the stage seeking safety. She stumbled over her chair but caught herself before landing in Draven's blood that now flowed off the back of the stage. It was clear by the crumpled position of Ayatollah Al-Farshid on the ground he had been the target of the second loud gunshot.

Pandemonium filled the Wailing Wall Plaza as more gunshots rang out from UE security guards near the platform. Evan shouted for medical personnel, and UE soldiers pushed and beat the crowd away from the plaza. Gemma trembled at the sight of a lifeless Draven dragged in an undignified manner to a stretcher and toward the center of the plaza. The demise of a man who decried himself the greatest leader of all time ended like so many dictators before him, in gory death. Sirens blared and screams echoed off the Temple Mount as a medical evacuation helicopter began its descent to pick up the fallen leader.

"Ma'am, we need to get you back to the headquarters!" a UE bodyguard screamed, ending the nightmare Gemma had lived through.

As Gemma rode alone back to the UE regional headquarters, barefoot and hands covered in the blood, warm tears flowed across her flushed cheeks. *"Why am I crying? An evil man is dead,* she thought.

The realization of her sorrow hit her as the sun was consumed early as a new post-fourth trumpet judgment night began. Draven's death signaled the beginning of woes.

Jackson and Gabriella sat watching the drama of Draven's assassination unfold on a small television without speaking in a small office at Ben Gurion International Airport. Christopher forced himself to blink as he watched the foretold death of the Antichrist, Draven Cross. Christopher's thoughts went to Gemma. She had lived through the event in a way that made him shutter. First, she had to speak utter lies about the now-dead Draven. If that was not enough, as the ANN report showed, Draven nearly fell on her after he was shot. Gemma was seen screaming and scrambling to get away from her dead tormentor and boss.

Christopher understood that the death of Draven meant something different for each member of his team and himself. Gabriella had been on his staff and believed in the man before coming to accept Jesus and facing torture at Draven's orders.

Like him, Gabriella's first thought was to reach out to Gabriella. "She needs to hear from us."

Jackson long foretold that Saint Nick was the Devil in disguise. Jackson, however, didn't celebrate Draven's death the way Christopher imagined. Instead, Jackson had grown quiet and distant. "It's hard to imagine that today we're transitioning to something worse."

Christopher savored the moment, winning a battle in the war against Satan. Draven had cost Christopher some of the dearest friends he had ever made. While the future was uncertain, he knew Draven suffered. Though he tried to be a good Christian, for today, the day he lost General Havid, Christopher would enjoy the thought of Draven's suffering.

As sirens wailed across Israel, Captain Liu ran into the office, announcing the obvious to Omega. "Time's up."

Christopher watched his core team and cherished loved ones walk out onto the tarmac to board a flight back to South Africa. While the Great Tribulation stood between Omega and Jesus's return, Christopher vowed to fight every day of the next three and a half years until his dying breath or the Glorious Appearance of Jesus Christ.

⌘

The aftermath of Draven's death was predictable, or so Christopher thought. He sat in the dining room of the winery safe house reminiscing and watching television with Nkoie, Gilana, and Jackson. ANN provided 24-hour coverage of world leaders, celebrities, and the public, filing through the Jewish temple's marble-floored visitor rotunda for the past three days. Reuel and Eliyahu, true to their word, had not spoken since their confrontation with Draven days ago. The two men of God sat with their backs to the Temple Mount, where the body of God's enemy desecrated the holy ground laying in state outside the Holy of Holies.

It had taken Gemma three days after Draven's death to get a chance to securely communicate with Omega. Gemma warned the group, which include a rehabilitated Gilana, that the UE was conducting a manhunt in Norway for Pontiff Conti. Evidence found in the missile-destroyed home of Al-Farshid implemented the Pontiff in the assassination of Draven. She rejoiced to God that her name was on no document tied to the event. Draven's assassin was killed the same night of the assassination at a border crossing into Jordan by UE forces.

Gemma also gave insight into the fallout from the investigation with General Havid's rescue. The prison superintendent of *Hekal Emah* prison was executed and blamed for the general's escape. The UE remain unsure of the general's whereabouts, but Christopher explained to Gemma that the team buried him before leaving Jerusalem. John Barnes claimed Omega was working with the prison superintendent and vowed to root out and destroy the terrorist group.

The hardest thing Christopher and Gilana discovered from Gemma's update was the Israeli army found Ori and Noem Cohen dead at an overlook near *Hekal Emah*. Gilana said that Noem was a good soldier that always saw their team as a family. True to her nature, Gilana told the group nothing more, keeping her emotions on the subject close to her. The loss of Ori was unfortunate. Ori had proven to be a faithful man of God until the end as his sacrifice ensured Omega had the opportunity to try and save the general. Christopher looked forward to seeing Ori in Heaven along with so many other great warriors that had died in the last three years.

Back in South Africa, a UE outpost where the world's most infamous "terrorist group" found refuge, Christopher felt grateful for God's timeline. A revelation that took him over a year to process and appreciate.

"Look, something's happening with Draven!" Jackson shouted.

While Jackson turned the television up, Nkoie called in Solomon, Mpilo, and a few other fighters to gather around the television in the safe house dining room. ANN reporter, Sam Morrow, spoke of a strong wind blowing through Jerusalem. Lightning filled the suddenly darkened skies over the eternal city as people ran from the temple visitor rotunda, screaming into ANN cameras, "He's alive!"

The lightning began striking people who ran from the Temple Mount, causing more chaos as people trampled each other trying to escape. Before an ANN camera was destroyed, two final images were broadcast that sent a chill down Christopher's spine. The first was of a man's dark silhouette standing near Draven's coffin. The other image was the Two Witnesses facing the Temple of God.

Christopher said the first thing that came to mind, "God, help us. The Great Tribulation has begun."

≈ঙ

I hope you enjoyed Wrath of The Lamb. Christopher Barrett will return in the next book in the Rapture series, Shadows of Eternity, 2023.

However, before you go, I want to ask you to help this writing ministry. Please take a few moments to follow the below link or scan the QR Code, which will take you to Wrath of The Lamb's Amazon page. Provide a review. Open and honest reviews are tough to come by, but they definitely help more people discover the message about Jesus Christ. Thank you.
Jocolby Phillips

Wrath of The Lamb Amazon link:
https://www.amazon.com/dp/B09PGQV63C

Wrath of The Lamb QR Code: